Now that the sensual nuance was gone from his voice and the look of desire seemed to have cooled, Lesley tensed, wondering what Darren had in mind to discuss. She paced back and forth before the floor-to-ceiling window in the living room, waiting for him to come back.

Darren entered the room and just stood watching Lesley for a few moments.

"Relax and stop acting like Daniel awaiting his final appointment in the lion's den."

"Are you the lion lying in wait to—?"

"Devour you? No," he said advancing closer.

Lesley took a step back. "Revenge, then?"

BOUND BY LOVE

BEVERLY CLARK

Genesis Press, Inc.

Indigo Love Stories

An imprint of Genesis Press, Inc.
Publishing Company

Genesis Press, Inc.
P.O. Box 101
Columbus, MS 39703

All characters in this book have no existence outside the imagination of the author and have no relation whatsoever to anyone bearing the same name or names. They are not even distantly inspired by any individual known or unknown to the author and all incidents are pure invention.

ISBN: 1-58571-232-9
Manufactured in the United States of America

First Edition 2000
Second Edition 2007

Visit us at www.genesis-press.com or call at 1-888-Indigo-1

PROLOGUE

Darren Taylor removed his coat and tie, tossing them onto the back of a chair. Then after slipping the top two buttons on his shirt free, he walked over to the hotel's well-stocked bar to pour himself a brandy. Seconds later, he sank down on the plush, green velvet sofa. And although the urgent need to relax pulled at him after the long flight from Philadelphia to Los Angeles, it was not to be. Unbidden, his thoughts strayed back to the day he'd gotten a call from Arthur Rainville.

Rainville was anxious to sell his fashion business to Darren's company. Taylor's hadn't been actively considering any such ventures on the West Coast, but after hanging up with the man, Darren had his friend and investigator, Ashton Price, run a check on Rainville's company, Rainville's Raiments. The next evening, Ash reported back to him.

"This could be a wild card, but we may just have bagged two birds with one shot."

"Cut to the chase, Ash."

"Raiments has a good reputation and the company is solid, probably a good investment. But get this, Rainville has a woman named Lesley Evans working for him as his lead designer."

"And?"

"Remember you've had me actively looking for Lesley Wells? Hello?"

"You think this Lesley Evans is—because the first names are the same? Lesley isn't so uncommon a name, you know."

Think about it. The woman's name is Lesley, she's a designer, and started working for Raiments a little over five years ago."

"You think it's too much of a coincidence, huh?"

"Don't you? Look, I can have someone snap a picture of this woman and—"

"No. Don't do that. I have a gut feeling you're right And since I'll be in L.A. for Clam Benson's party, and to take care of a few other business matters, I'll follow through on this personally."

Darren had phoned Arthur Rainville back to set up a time and place to meet.

Darren pushed up from the sofa and strode over to the huge plate glass window of his twenty-fifth floor hotel suite and watched the sun set over the palm-tree silhouetted skyline of Los Angeles. Was this where Lesley had run off to? Could this really be where she'd kept herself hidden from him all this time? His fingers tightened around the bowl of his brandy glass. His instincts convinced him it was.

A muscle worked in his jaw as a mental image of the warm, vulnerable young girl of six years ago, who had worn her coal black hair in a short sassy style like that of the singer Toni Braxton, floated before his mind's eye.

Anger raged to life inside him. Had she really thought to completely escape his wrath? He had to grudgingly admit that, if this woman proved to be Lesley Wells, she'd almost succeeded.

Though Darren felt an unwanted excitement at the thought of seeing her again, he thrust these strangely disturbing feelings from his mind and set his glass down. It was time to get dressed for tonight's party.

Tomorrow was soon enough to deal with his coming meeting with Rainville and this Lesley Evans. Although he had no need to buy Raiments, it would be worth every penny to have Lesley Wells where he wanted her. He intended to see that this destroyer of dreams paid the full price for the damage she'd done to him and his family.

ONE

Lesley wasn't looking forward to going to the Benson party. She usually skipped these affairs. This time she had practically begged her boss to let her off the hook. And he had decided to, but then at the last minute he called to say that he wouldn't be able to make it because his wife wasn't feeling well.

There was probably nothing wrong with Lola, other than that she wanted Arthur all to herself, as usual. Lesley gazed at her friend and escort Greg Saxon as he guided his gold Lexus into the valet parking area of the Bonaventure Hotel. A few minutes later they were heading for the elevators. Greg let Lesley walk a few steps ahead of him and gave her a low whistle.

"Umph, Umph, Umph." He smiled appreciatively. "On you that dress is definitely the bomb. You're going to have Clare Benson's tongue hanging out, and more determined than ever to spirit you away from Raiments."

Arthur had insisted that Lesley wear one of the evening gown originals that she had designed to the party. She had to admit it was one of her best creations, a long, flowing, figure-hugging, royal blue satin evening gown with a single strap made of delicate ivory-silk orchids draping the left shoulder while the right shoulder was left bare. A pattern of the same orchids printed onto the blue satin spilled down the left front of the dress to its hem.

"I'd never leave Raiments."

The elevator doors opened onto the ballroom floor and Greg guided her down the hall to the party.

"Would you stay on at Raiments if Arthur sells the company?"

"Sells the company!" She frowned. "Where did you hear that? You know something I don't?"

"Only rumor. But would you? Stay, I mean?"

"I don't know," she said thoughtfully. "I'll worry about it if and when it happens."

Lesley and Greg entered the ballroom, to oohs and ahs of appreciation, along with jealous catty whispers from people who stared at Lesley's dress. Pride in her work put a smile on her face. Clare Benson walked up to welcome them.

"Lesley, dear, you look fabulous in that dress. Arthur is a lucky man to have you designing for him. You are Raiments," Clare complimented her. "You sure you won't reconsider my offer to come and work for Benson's?"

"Yes, very sure," Lesley answered confidently.

Greg whispered. "Am I good or what?"

"If you ever change your mind…" She smiled, angling her head for them to follow her across the room. "We have a special guest with us tonight. You just have to meet him."

Lesley glanced askance at Greg. He hunched his shoulders as they hurried to catch up with their hostess.

"Darren darling!" Clare exclaimed.

Lesley's stomach jerked, knotting tight with tension.

A look of surprised shock splashed her face while bitter anguish scored her mind like nails scraped across a blackboard.

"Darren Taylor, Lesley Evans, Rainville's Raiments talented head designer." Clare smiled and looked at Lesley's companion. "And her escort, Greg Saxon, merchandising manager for Cheerful Children's Wear."

Darren took Lesley's hand in his and gazed deeply into her eyes. "Ms. Evans." Then as an afterthought, he sliced a glance Greg's way. "Saxon," he said curtly.

"You and Lesley an item these days, Greg?" Clare asked.

"Let's just say we enjoy each other's company," Greg replied smoothly, drawing Lesley closer to his side, smiling into her eyes. "Right, love?"

Lesley returned his smile and answered, "Right."

"Darren, I see Gazja and Bijon from Exclusive Elegance. I want you to meet them." Clare slipped her arm around his. "If you two will excuse us," she said to Lesley and Greg, then led Darren away.

A sigh of relief blew from Lesley's lips.

Greg frowned in concern. "You all right, baby? You look like you've just seen a ghost."

"Not a ghost, exactly."

"You know Taylor. I'd say very well if your reaction is anything to go by."

"You'd be right on the money. I did know him years ago."

Greg quirked his lips. "I'll bet there's a fascinating story behind that look you gave the brother. But you don't want to talk about it. Right?"

"No, I don't." Dammit! Why did she have to see Darren Taylor tonight after six years of expecting it to happen? Dreading it would happen?

"Care to dance?"

"What I'd really like to do is go home."

"Can't do that. We just got here. You don't want Taylor to think he's scared you off, do you?"

"I know you're right. And I don't, but..."

"Hey, it's a big party. I know you can manage to duck him until a time when we can discreetly make our escape. Come on, dance with me, woman," he said, and not waiting for her to answer, guided her out onto the dance floor.

As they danced, Lesley felt eyes riveted on her back and knew to whom they belonged. When the music ended and she and Greg were heading for the buffet table, she saw Darren watching her and she stumbled.

"Careful, baby," Greg whispered. "Taylor must have really meant something to you," he remarked, switching his gaze from Lesley to Darren then back to Lesley.

"He did once, but that was a long time ago."

"From the vibes I'm getting, evidently not long enough."

"Oh, Greg."

He took her hand and urged her on to the buffet spread.

Darren glowered at the one woman he had every reason to hate, only to find that wasn't the emotion he was feeling. Just for a moment he hadn't been sure how he felt about her. He waited until her friend headed for the punch bowl before approaching her.

"It's been a long time, hasn't it, sweetheart?"

Lesley made to walk away from him, but Darren grasped her wrist.

"I think we're overdue in the serious discussion department, don't you?"

"I don't agree."

"You don't have to."

"As long as you have things your way, that's all that counts. Right?"

Ignoring her remark, Darren quickly ushered Lesley through a nearby terrace door, leading her to a deserted spot near a spiral fountain.

"Darren, I—"

"Forget it. We're going to talk, Lesley."

She saw the determined look on his face, but she wasn't ready to talk to this man. She didn't know if she ever would be.

"I have nothing to say."

"Oh, I think you do."

"The last time I tried, you didn't want to hear it."

"All you had to do was tell me the truth."

"I did."

"We both know you didn't, so don't even…" Darren scowled at her, wondering why she persisted in lying to him. He drew her into his arms. When he looked into her eyes, some emotion he couldn't read flashed in her eyes. Was it pain? Or fear? Surely it couldn't be fear of him. He'd never physically touched her, or any other woman, in anger. He tamped down his indignation. Maybe she did have reason to fear him in other areas, because he intended to see that she paid some serious dues. And payback was a mother.

Lesley sought to evade Darren's scrutiny by lowering her lashes. Darren Taylor had been very special to her six years ago, but not anymore, and not ever again.

As Darren continued to study Lesley, he saw another emotion flare in her eyes before she could hide it. He recognized it as one of desire. In that instant any thought of talking left him. And with a feral groan, he lowered his lips to hers, unable to hold himself back from kissing her. The taste of her aroused the long dormant feelings he'd locked away after he'd found her out. A surge of raw anger gave him the strength to finally push her away from him.

Lesley was trembling by the time he released her mouth.

"Why did you do it, Lesley? Why did you run away? Unless you were guilty."

Lesley gritted her teeth; nothing had changed, he still didn't believe her, wouldn't even give her the benefit of the doubt. "Does any of it matter now?" she answered coolly.

"Yes, it damn well matters. I loved you, woman."

"Did you? If you had, you would have believed in me, trusted me, but you didn't. You believed I could betray you, betray the love we felt for each other. That, I can never forgive you for."

"You can never forgive me when it was you who—"

Lesley threw up her hands. "Whatever, Darren. Believe whatever in the hell you want to believe. I don't give a damn. Go back to Philadelphia and forget you ever saw me." Before he could stop her, she marched back into the ballroom.

Lesley found Greg. "Please, take me home." When he didn't respond right away, she realized he was looking past her to the doorway she'd just come through, staring at Darren, who was standing just inside the ballroom glaring daggers at them both.

"All right, baby," Greg answered finally.

Lesley was contemplative during the ride to her house, surprised she could even function, considering the shock she'd suffered at seeing Darren at the party. She had known there was the possibility that she would one day run into Darren Taylor since they worked in the same profession. That was the reason she avoided most of the fashion galas or their after parties. She thought when she finally did see him it wouldn't hurt like this. But she was wrong. It hurt like hell.

After Greg parked his car in front of Lesley's house, he glanced over at her. "Are you sure you're all right, Lesley?"

She smiled at Greg. "I'll live. I'd invite you in, but I have some last minute things to work on before Raiments' showing tomorrow."

"You sure I can't help?"

Greg Saxon was fine with those sexy, smoke-dark eyes and almond-brown skin, but he was not for her. "You're sweet, Greg, but…"

"I get the message. Never let it be said that Greg Saxon was too thick to take a hint." He grinned rakishly. "If you change your mind—"

"I don't think I will."

"Think, huh? That means I still have a chance."

"Greg…"

"Don't sweat it, baby. See you 'round."

Lesley smiled, shaking her head, then got out of his car and watched as he drove away, then unlocked her door and let herself inside the house.

As Lesley walked in, Millie James flicked the TV off and asked, "How was the party?"

Lesley avoided looking directly at her and answered, "The usual." She flopped down on the couch and kicked off her shoes, wiggling her toes.

"From the look on your face you didn't enjoy it very much."

"You don't miss a beat, do you, Millie?"

"No, not when it comes to you. Want to talk about what's bothering you?"

"Dara's father was at the party."

Millie arched a surprised brow. "I thought he lived in Philadelphia."

"He does. Since I chose to stay in the same profession as Darren, I knew it was just a matter of time before we ran into each other."

"And did you tell him he has a daughter?"

"No. His attitude toward me hasn't changed; he still hates me for what he thinks I did to him. There was just no way I could tell him."

"You're going to have to sooner or later, Lesley. Dara is at a point where a father is important to a child, especially a little girl child."

"I know all that, Millie." She sighed. "I'm afraid of what he might do once he does find out."

"Maybe if you talked to him and the two of you——"

"You wouldn't say that if you knew Darren Taylor. Trust me, he would be anything but reasonable, Millie."

"Men, God love 'em. You can't live with 'em or without 'em."

"Believe me, l can live quite nicely without them, thank you."

Millie shot Lesley a sidelong glance, then eased off the couch. "I'd better get some sleep. I have to deal with your very active little daughter tomorrow." She laughed.

"Dara isn't too much for you, is she, Millie?"

"No. She's just a perceptive—and very determined—person for her age, that's all."

"She's a lot like her father. I wish—never mind. What I wanted he couldn't give me, still can't give me." She said the last in a pain-filled voice. "Look, I have to get to Raiments early to set up for the showing, and I still have some last minute things to do before I go to sleep tonight."

"You work too hard." Millie raised her hand. "All right, I won't nag. Good night."

As Lesley watched her live-in housekeeper/ nanny/friend head down the hall to her room, her conscience began to plague her about Darren. Should she have told him about Dara?

Lesley walked into her daughter's room to check on her. She smiled. Dara was so like her father in temperament, as well as looks.

Darren would probably be on his way back to Philadelphia tomorrow, and she would in all likelihood not see him again, unless she decided to get in touch with him there. When she thought about her daughter, a deep sadness filled her. Her child deserved to know her father. *Damn you, Darren Taylor. Damn you for putting me in this position.*

TWO

Lesley glanced at her watch for the sixth time in as many minutes as she moved around the dressing room. Where was Arthur? It wasn't like him to be late for one of Raiments' fashion shows. She walked over to one of the models.

"Margo, the scarf is worn draped over the shoulder." She indicated where before transferring it there from around the model's throat. "Like so."

The voices of renowned entrepreneurs, foreign as well as local buyers, and world famous designers filtered through the partially opened door of the dressing room.

Lesley caught a glimpse of fashion photographers busily flashing pictures, and media people with video cameras taping the pre-show opening unfolding on the huge run way showroom of L.A.'s fashion industry center, the California Mart.

Lesley smiled. The thrill of accomplishment always gave her an instant head rush before a showing of her work. She glanced back at the models. They were ready to parade down the runway beneath the flickering strobe lights, accompanied by the blare of steady streams of popular music and the whistles and catcalls of enthusiastic admirers.

"All right, girls, let's do it." She added a thumbs up along with her words.

Equipped with pad and pencil, and ready to jot down notes as she did at every showing, Lesley stationed herself in a seat midway to the back of the showroom. She raised her eyes from the pad just as Arthur entered from a side door across the room. Her smile widened, but it disappeared almost immediately. Her insides froze in shock when she saw the face of the man who had followed him inside.

"No! It can't be!" she said in whispered shout. She'd thought that seeing him at the Benson party was just a fluke, a twist of fate. Had Darren come to L.A. for a reason other than to attend the party? She didn't want to venture a guess as to what that reason might be! He was supposed to be on a plane headed for Philadelphia. Sheer panic threatened to escape her throat in the form of a screech.

Deep in a discussion with Arthur, Darren hadn't seen her yet. It was pure agony watching them slowly work their way farther into the room, closer to her.

Instinct, self-preservation, Lesley didn't know which, screamed at her to get the hell out of there. My God, hadn't seeing Darren last night been punishment enough? He was the only man she had ever loved, who had six years before judged and condemned her for a crime she'd never committed. Last night he had mentioned her betrayal when his was the one that had charred her heart and gutted her soul.

In a few seconds he would look up and see her. She couldn't go through what she had last night. She'd barely survived the experience. As she'd barely endured losing his love all those years ago. She had to get out of here! Eyeing the exit, she hurriedly threaded her way through the throng to reach it.

"Lesley," Arthur called to her.

Although the din of noise in the room was deafening, Lesley heard him. Her hand was on the door handle. She had to make a spit-second decision to stay or to dash through the exit. The urge to run was great, but to do so would be cowardly. And she refused to show Darren her fear. She'd run away from him once—make it twice if you counted last night. No. She sighed heavily; she'd wait to see things through this time.

Lesley straightened her shoulders, gathering her composure, then turned to face her fate.

When Darren's glittering, dark brown eyes met hers, she saw triumph spread over his face. What did that look mean?

"Where were you on your way?" Arthur asked when she reached them. "Your designs have just begun to appear on the runway."

"I just wanted to grab a quick breath of fresh air. It is close in here." She eyed Darren sharply, daring him to contradict her explanation.

"You're right, it is," Arthur agreed, then returning his attention to his companion, cleared his throat. "I'd like you to meet someone. Lesley Evans, Darren Taylor from Taylor-Made Creations."

Darren's brows arched over a narrow-eyed gaze, and with a slight twist of his lips he said, "We met at the party last night."

"Oh, did you?" Arthur cast him an apologetic smile. "I'm sorry I couldn't make it, Darren. My wife wasn't feeling well."

The noise in the room suddenly quieted, and the people around them cast irritated glances their way that demanded they shut up and take their seats.

"I think we'd better find our places before we're ostracized," Arthur suggested. "We'll have plenty of time afterward to get better acquainted in the private conference room Raiments reserves for times when we give showings here," he explained to Darren.

The fashion event that had always exhilarated Lesley in the past now made her feel like the quarry awaiting the final scene in a Stephen King movie. She glanced at Darren, wondering what he was thinking. He'd somehow found out she was working here in L.A. Did he intend to make her pay for what he considered her past sins? Was that what his showing up in L.A. was really all about? If that were so, she wondered how he planned to exact his revenge.

Lesley switched her attention to the last model as she made her grand entrance and paraded down the runway to join the others for the final review.

Arthur cleared his throat. "I suggest we get out of here and leave the haggling to the throng."

"You don't have to twist my arm." Darren smiled, then added softly, "How about you, Ms. Evans?"

"I agree with Arthur."

Once inside the conference room, Darren turned to Lesley. "Tell me, Ms. Evans, are you a transplant from back east? For some reason you don't seem to fit the L.A. persona."

What game was he playing? she wondered. "You mean because I'm not white, blonde, and tanned?"

Arthur gasped, clearing his throat. "Lesley, I don't think—"

"It's all right," Darren said. He turned to Lesley. "I didn't mean to imply that you had to be."

"I do have a tan. But I must confess that it has nothing to do with the climate," she replied smartly. "It's completely natural and permanent. Of that you can be sure."

At her flippant answer, Darren's dark penetrating stare seemed to bore into Lesley like a diamond bit drill into unyielding ground.

She shifted her attention to Arthur, wishing that he had told her who he was meeting and why. True, she was just Raiments' designer, but stilt, she felt entitled to know what was going on. Before she could voice her thoughts, the phone rang.

Arthur strode the few steps to the phone stand and picked up the receiver. "Arthur Rainville. Lola. Yes, dear. I'm kind of busy at the moment." His expression changed into a wobbly, embarrassed smile. "No, no. I'm never too busy for you, you know that."

He covered the receiver and looked apologetically at Darren. "I'm sorry, it's my wife. I'll only be a minute." Arthur fixed a took on Lesley and said, "Talk to him, will you, love?" and then turned away to resume the conversation with his wife.

Lesley shifted her gaze from Arthur to Darren. "Why are you really in L.A.?" she said in a low voice. "It's obvious you came for more than just Clare Benson's party."

"Is it? Does not knowing bother you that much, Ms. Evans?"

Not knowing? Not knowing what? Her heart slammed against her spine. Surely he hadn't guessed—no, it had to be his business with Arthur he was referring to. Many times over the last three years, Arthur had threatened, whenever he got angry or tired, to sell Raiments, but she'd never really taken him seriously. Maybe she should have.

And maybe she was jumping to conclusions. After all, he and Darren were both savvy men in the fashion industry. They could have just run into each other by sheer coincidence and started talking shop.

Yeah right. Get real, girl. You know better than that, the voice of reason interjected.

Lesley cleared her throat. "Why didn't you give me away to Arthur?"

"Give you away?" Darren tilted his head to the side and grinned. "I don't know what you mean, Ms. Evans."

Lesley gritted her teeth at his goading words and glared at him. They were like two street fighters circling and sizing each other up for the inevitable battle ahead. Surely if he was considering buying Raiments, knowing she was a part of the deal would make him change his mind, wouldn't it?

Wake up, Lesley. You know you're the only reason he's here.

Do I?

Darren smiled. "I think an explanation is called for. Don't you agree, Ms. Evans?"

She remembered that he had wanted to talk to her last night. Maybe she should have listened.

At that moment, almost as if on cue, Arthur hung up the phone and advanced toward them. "Sounds good to me. Lesley?"

"I…ah…" She bristled at the gleam of triumph in Darren's eyes. Ooh, she wanted to kill him, and Arthur too, for putting her in this position. Lesley bit the inside of her cheek and ungraciously answered. "Me too."

"That makes it unanimous, then." Arthur glanced at his watch. "It's past breakfast and not quite lunchtime. Why not have our little talk over brunch? I'll spring for it, of course."

Minutes later, they stepped off the elevator into the entrance foyer and were swept through the revolving glass and brass doors out into the murmuring hive of activity going on in downtown L.A.

Arthur decided to take them to a quiet Greek restaurant only a few blocks from the Mart.

As they walked across the street, Lesley, wedged between the two men, couldn't help noticing the way Darren's grey, expertly-tailored, Armani suit emphasized his tall, superb build and rivetingly virile masculinity. His caramel brown skin, gleaming with health and vitality, was bronzed as though he had recently spent some time in the sun. Probably Hawaii, Lesley thought. She knew that Taylor's had a branch office there. She wondered if he had gone there, whether it was with a wife or a fiancée?

When they stopped for the light, a warm breeze suddenly gusted, lifting and teasing a lock of Lesley's hair. As she raised her hand to sweep it away from her forehead, she saw Darren's slender brown fingers reach out as if to push the errant curl back into place, then quickly drop to his side.

Their eyes met and held.

Her insides shifted crazily. Oh, God, she'd forgotten how sexy the man was.

The light changed and the trio resumed walking. Lesley listened as Arthur regaled Darren with tales of his latest exploits and the expected success of his new fall line. Though she contributed a word here and there, she couldn't concentrate on the conversation.

She didn't know whether it was her apprehension, intuition, or the negative vibes coming from Darren, but she suddenly became alert to expect the worst from him.

Once they were seated in the restaurant, Arthur spoke to her. "It's not like you to be so quiet, Lesley. Well, it doesn't matter. The reason Darren is here in L.A. is to—"

"Please, allow me, Arthur." Darren grinned engagingly.

Arthur considered it. "All right."

Lesley's stomach churned uneasily as she waited to hear what Darren had to say.

"Ms. Evans, Arthur contacted Taylor's several weeks ago about selling Raiments to us."

She released a pent-up sigh. "I see." It was as she suspected, not just mere coincidence that Darren had shown up at the Mart. Taylor's didn't need to buy a company like Raiments. It was only because of her that Darren was even considering it. He had to have his pound of flesh. Damn him.

The waiter arrived with the menus.

Darren watched Lesley as though he were trying to gauge her reaction before he continued. She purposely schooled her expression, allowing nothing of how she was feeling about his revelation to show.

"Of course, we're prepared to make you an offer to continue as the company's head designer, Ms. Evans."

"Will the policies of Raiments remain the same?" she asked.

"We'll just have to see, won't we? There are bound to be changes and adjustments that Taylor's may feel are necessary. You understand." He shot her a sly, goading smile. "Arthur has been telling me a great deal about you."

"Oh?" She turned a questioning glance on Arthur.

Darren laughed softly. "Professionally speaking, that is, Ms. Evans."

Arthur began, appearing not to have noticed the subtle innuendo in Darren's voice and manner. "I've been telling you for ages, Lesley, that I wanted to retire. You couldn't do better than to work for Taylor's. They're very much interested in a line of inexpensive clothes for the busy career woman who doesn't have a lot of money to spend on her wardrobe. I've shown him your croquis of the projected winter line. He's impressed."

"I guess I should be grateful for that." Lesley picked up the menu and glanced through it.

"Don't be like that, Lesley," Arthur pleaded. "Take pity on an old man married to a younger woman who is eager to be with me and to see the world. It's time I retired and left it to you young people, anyway. I don't have the same get up and go I used to. Besides, it's a golden opportunity for you to showcase your talents."

What could she say to that? She knew Lola constantly complained about the time Arthur spent away from her. She knew Arthur was tired of the day-to-day hassle involved in running Raiments. She couldn't blame him, he certainly didn't need the aggravation at this point in his life.

She just hated the idea of seeing it all go to Taylor's. She'd really poured a lot of herself into the business. If only she could afford to buy Raiments herself. She and Arthur had discussed it, but she guessed that he couldn't or didn't want to wait any longer.

"Lesley, you make me feel like Benedict Arnold. Darren has assured me that he would deal fairly with you."

"And I believe him. The only thing left is to sign the papers on Monday."

"It's all but settled then." Lesley looked into Darren's eyes and realized it was a mistake. The cat-that-cornered-the-mouse gleam seemed to say, you haven't got a prayer of escaping me this time, so don't even go there.

She didn't care; she refused to let him intimidate her. Stiffening her back, Lesley looked insolently at him, but said to Arthur, "Only time will tell if your feelings are dead on."

The narrowing of Darren's eyes when she impugned his character should have made her feel triumphant, but for some reason it didn't. She just felt numb and completely devoid of emotion.

No one said much of anything after that last exchange. The dark, rich Greek coffee and the roast turkey and Greek salad-filled falafels were eaten in silence before heading back to the Mart.

Relieved that her ordeal was finally drawing to a close, Lesley could hardly wait to leave the conference room and head for home.

"Can I give you a lift, Ms. Wells, I mean Evans," Darren said smoothly, with just enough bite to irritate. "I don't know why I want to call you that."

"I'm totally clueless," she shot back. "Maybe I remind you of someone. Whatever. I have to say no to your kind offer of a ride. I have my own car."

"Don't forget to bring those new sketches on Monday, Lesley," Arthur interjected into the lull of the conversation.

"I won't." She eased toward the door. "See you Monday, then. Nice to have seen you again, Mr. Taylor."

"Please, since we will eventually be on more intimate terms, call me Darren." He opened the door for her.

Lesley graced him with a perfunctory nod and edged past, careful not to touch him. She felt Darren's eyes on her back as she moved toward the elevators. When she turned to face him before the doors closed, she saw the savage expression on his face. It read like a neon sign: I'm not hardly through with you. I haven't got started yet.

"Join me for a drink, Darren," Arthur suggested. "You know the offer of my guest room during your stay in L.A. is still good. My wife Lola and I would be pleased if you would take us up on it."

"Thanks, Arthur, but I'm happy with my suite at the Bonaventure."

Arthur grinned, shaking his head. "You bachelors do love your freedom, don't you? Ah, those were the days."

Darren smiled and said, "I'll take you up on that drink, though."

THREE

Even though her legs were quaking badly by the time the elevator reached the parking levels, Lesley managed to make her way to her car parked on level C.

Her fingers shook when she inserted the key in the ignition. Taking several calming breaths, she willed herself to overcome the feeling of doom that had fallen on her like a downpour of leaden rain drops. She started the car, left the Mart parking building, then headed out into the heavy, afternoon freeway traffic.

It was imperative that she get a grip. Darren was a ruthless man. And, though unjustly, she'd been cast in the role of his most despised enemy.

Lesley halted her trip into anxiety. The past was the last subject she wanted to delve into right now.

She turned on her signal tight, indicating her intention to exit the Santa Monica Freeway which was mere blocks from her house. Within minutes she pulled her car into the drive of her small but comfortable West Los Angeles home.

Lesley lowered her forehead to the steering wheel, reveling in the feel of the cool plastic surface on her heated skin. But try as she might, she could no longer keep at bay the memory of the first time she'd met Darren Taylor...

She had decided to go to a fashion gala after the party. Moments after she arrived, Darren Taylor saw her and walked over to her.

"You're Lesley Wells, aren't you?"

"And you're Darren Taylor." The pictures of him she'd seen gracing the fashion industry magazine covers and newspapers in no way did him justice.

Darren grinned. *"I never thought the competition would be this lovely."*

"How did you expect the competition to look?"

"Whatever I thought, you're definitely not it. Care to dance, Miss Wells?"

Without giving her a chance to say no, he swept her into his arms, gliding smoothly across the dance floor.

"Are you always so overbearing, Mr. Taylor?"

"If you mean, am I always a take-charge man, the answer is yes. And call me Darren."

She shook her head at his arrogance.

He grinned. *"I take it you don't completely approve."*

"Would it matter if I didn't?"

"You're a clever piece of work, aren't you? I think you and I are going to be good together."

"Oh, really? How do you figure that? I'm sure our families will be less than thrilled about the prospect of a Wells and a Taylor dating each other."

"My family doesn't tell me who I can see."

The music stopped. He guided her over to a couch by the windows.

"Tell me, Lesley, do you design, or are you involved in the business end of Wells of Fashion?"

"I guess I won't be betraying the family by saying I'm a very junior designer."

He eyed the dress she wore. *"You designed this?"*

"As a matter of fact I did."

"I'd say you're a very talented lady."

Lesley knew it was a stunning dress. It was a short, midnight black sheath with one tulle sleeve and a glittering banner of gold sequins draping her bare shoulder.

"Too bad you aren't a Taylor employee. We could always use another talented designer in the family."

"I'm happy where I am, thank you." She laughed.

"I'm happy to be here with you, Lesley Wells."

Lesley beamed herself out of her momentary journey down memory lane, back to the present. It all happened a long time ago in another life when she and Darren...

You were right. You definitely need to get a grip, girl. Dread flooded her system with the speed and devastating power of snake venom. She'd struggled to make a life for herself these past six years. Why did Darren have to come crashing into it like a wrecking crew primed to destroy?

She felt eyes watching her and glanced out the windshield into a pair of familiar, dark brown eyes staring at her from the front window of her house.

The nerve-frazzling tension test Lesley's body almost immediately. Seeing her child restored her composure. The worry on her daughter's face changed to delight before that expressive face disappeared from its place at the window.

By the time Lesley got out of the car and locked the door, Dara Ann was out of the house and running toward her. Lesley stooped down, opening her arms, waiting for her daughter to launch herself into them.

"You're home early, Mama. Somethin' wrong?"

Millie was right: Her child was a sensitive, amazingly perceptive person for all of her five, nearly six, years.

"No, I'm fine. Aren't you glad for the extra time we can spend together?"

"Well, yes, but—"

"No buts, just plant one of your special kisses right here." She pointed to her right cheek.

"Oh, Mama." Dara giggled, tightening her arms around her mother's neck. "I love you."

She squeezed her daughter tight. "I love you too, baby."

After a few moments when Dara wiggled uncomfortably, Lesley realized she was practically crushing her in her embrace.

"I'm sorry, baby. We mothers get carried away sometimes."

"Can we have pizza tonight?"

"I walked right into that one, didn't I? We just had pizza Tuesday night, Dara Ann. It's only Thursday."

"It is?"

"Yes, but you want pizza tonight anyway. Right?"

Like dawn spilling over the horizon, a heart-stopping grin spread across her face, an expression so like her father's it was sheer torture for Lesley.

After all these years, she would have thought that she had gotten over Darren. But just the sight of him had resurrected feelings she'd thought were long since dead and buried.

"Alt right, just this once."

"Oh, thank you, Mama," Dara said, taking her mother's hand and pulling her into the house.

Millie came into the living room wiping her hands on her apron.

"I've just popped a tuna casserole into the oven."

Lesley studied the sudden guilty expression on her daughter's face.

"Tuna casserole, hmm?" She smiled at Millie. "Thank you."

"No problem. I've got to be getting over to the church. I volunteered to help organize the bake sale next week."

Lesley shook her head as she looked at her daughter. The little imp had done it again; maneuvered her into getting her way. Her child was definitely a person who knew what she wanted and how to go about getting it. Like her father.

At the contrite expression on her child's face, Lesley restrained the laughter that bubbled up in her throat.

"You mad at me, Mama?" Dara asked, casting an innocent pleading look at her mother.

"I should be, you know. What you did wasn't very nice. Millie went to a lot of trouble to prepare dinner for us."

"I'm sorry. But I can't stand that nasty old casserole. You gonna make me eat it anyway?"

"No, I guess not. But next time—"

"I know," she answered in a chastened voice.

Lesley walked over to her desk in the far corner of the room.

"You're not going to draw those pictures tonight, are you?"

"I'd planned to after I tucked you into bed for the night."

"Oh," she sighed.

Lesley frowned. "Why?"

"No reason."

"Does It bother you?"

"No. Mama, where is my daddy?"

Lesley blinked at the sudden jump from one subject to another.

"The other kids at school have daddies. When they ask me about mine, I don't know what to say."

Lesley dreaded the revival of this particular conversation. Dara was becoming more and more aware of that one missing element in her family life, just as Millie had said. The older Dara got, the heavier the burden of guilt grew over Lesley's heart.

She knew she wasn't being fair denying her daughter the information she craved so desperately, and now, knowing that Darren might become a part of their lives. But what could she say, short of the truth? It hurt just thinking about Darren, thinking of that last soul-destroying conversation they'd had six years ago.

"Mama, you gonna tell me about my daddy this time?"

Lesley sighed, walked over to her and went down on her knees before her child. "Baby, it's hard to explain. Before you were born something happened between me and your father. It had nothing to do with you. It was a grown up thing and—"

"That means you don't wanna tell me about him. Right?"

"Oh, Dara baby, I—"

Two fat tears rolled down her daughter's cheeks.

Lesley pulled her into her arms. "Don't cry, baby." No matter how she felt or how much it hurt, Lesley knew what she had to do. She had to take the first step toward bridging the gap between Dara and her father. She picked her daughter up, carried her over to the couch and sat down; then reaching across the armrest for her purse, she opened it and took out her wallet. Wedged between pictures, one of Dara and another of herself, was one of Darren.

"This is your father."

The child's gaze adhered to it like glue.

"His eyes are glittery like mine, and his hair's curly like mine, too."

Lesley struggled to make her voice sound normal when inside she was as far from feeling that way as it was possible to feel. Why had her life turned out like this? What had she done to deserve it?

She should have put more effort into finding a husband for herself, a father for her daughter, but every time she had gone out, none of the men seemed to measure up. Their kisses never raised a three alarm fire through her system the way Darren's did. He'd spoiled her for other men. Damn him.

Now, he had intruded into her life with the suddenness of an earthquake, and might prove to be just as devastating to the life she had so carefully built for herself and her child.

Why couldn't you have stayed in Philadelphia, Darren? Why did you have to come and find me here?

The pizza Lesley ordered came, and she and Dara tucked into it hungrily. Later, after having bathed and put her daughter to bed, Lesley browsed through her mail. There was the usual packet from Cheerful Children's Wear, along with a check for services rendered. She'd moonlighted designing children's wear for them the last three years. Arthur had allowed it because children's wear wasn't a part of his line, and there was no conflict of interest professionally.

If—when—Taylor's took over, she wondered what Darren would think of her sideline. As far as she knew, Taylor's wasn't interested in children's wear. He couldn't possibly object to it. Or could he?

Lesley put the packet down. What was she going to do? She definitely didn't want to work with Darren or have anything to do with Taylor-Made Creations. Once those sale papers were signed, it all would be over.

She didn't want any of Raiments' policies to change, but the injection of Taylor's into the picture made it inevitable. What if Taylor's decided to just absorb Raiments into their business like water soaked up into a giant thirsty sponge? Raiments had a moderate, but profitable, following here. Surely they wouldn't knock a good thing. She couldn't allow Darren's presence to get to her this way. She had to think.

Lesley knew Arthur had to be a little anxious and uneasy about selling. Maybe there was a chance that she could use that to get him to hold off on his decision. Benson Apparel had been interested in buying Raiments at one time. Maybe...

But then there was Lola, who was really pushing him to do it right away.

Lesley was securely perched on the horns of a dilemma. Once Arthur signed those sale papers, she would be neatly trapped. There had to be a way out of this predicament.

She thought about her family. Wells would love to get a plum as lucrative as Raiments away from Taylor's. Acquiring Raiments could go a long way toward mending the rift between her and her family. No. She couldn't do that, no matter how much she didn't want to work with Darren. He already hated her for what he believed she had done to him, and would expect her to pull something like that. There was no way she'd give him the satisfaction.

The one subject that she'd purposely avoided, her feelings for Darren, refused to be put off any longer. She'd loved him once. But what were her feelings for him now? By buying the company she worked for, he was in essence saying that he intended to step into her life, if only in a professional capacity. But if he found out about Dara that would certainly change. Her insides knotted in apprehension at the thought.

After Dara was born Lesley had felt justified in not telling him he had a daughter because he had hurt her so very badly. But later when the hurt had lessened, she knew she should have told him. Last night she could have. What would he say once he knew about Dara? Knowing Darren as she did, he'd want Dara.

But Dara was her life, and no one was going to take her child away. No one.

FOUR

Monday morning at 8:55, Lesley got out of her car and straightened her clothes. She'd chosen to wear a linen suit she'd designed. The right lapel on the red jacket, made from black and white zebra striped silk, was folded back. The blazer-length jacket tiered over a slim black skirt.

She checked the white velvet bow attached to the end of her raven black French braid to make sure it was secure. She knew she looked both chic and professional. This particular outfit was a hit in the career woman's wardrobe line she'd created.

Lesley felt that she had to look her best if she were to match wits with Darren. So far, he'd been playing with the gloves on. Knowing him as well as she did, she didn't expect that to last long.

She walked through the door of Raiments at exactly nine o'clock sharp.

"Is Arthur in yet, Karen?"

"No, I'm sorry, he isn't. He called fifteen minutes ago to say he'd be late. Is there anything I can do for you?"

Disappointed, Lesley smiled and said, "I wouldn't say no to a cup of coffee. When Arthur gets in, let me know."

"Sure thing."

Lesley moved on down the hall to her office. She dropped her portfolio case on the desk. Of all the days for Arthur to be late, he chose today. Sinking into her chair, she swiveled it around to look out the window.

"It must be true what they say about the early bird catching the worm."

Lesley tensed at the sound of that all-too-familiar voice. She swung around in the chair to face Darren. He stood leaning against the doorjamb with his arms folded across his chest and an infuriating grin plastered on his face. She felt like punching out a few of his perfect white teeth.

"Which one are you?" she said with sweet-voiced sarcasm.

"Excuse me?"

She ignored his words and asked. "What are you doing here, Darren? The meeting isn't until ten o'clock."

"I thought I'd get here early so I could talk to Arthur alone," he said, gazing at her as though he could read what was on her mind. "You didn't by any chance have the same idea? Ah, I see that you did. It won't work, Lesley."

"What won't work?" she demanded.

"Give me a break."

"Why should I? You never gave me one," she said tightly.

"You're not on that, 'I'm innocent, Your Honor' kick again, are you? Because if you are—"

"What?"

"Forget it."

"I don't think we should, since you obviously think you have all the answers."

"Look, I don't want to argue with you this morning, sweetheart."

"Oh heaven forbid!"

"Lesley—"

"Just get the hell out of my office, Darren."

He laughed. "Your office?" He glanced at his watch. "In little more than an hour I'm going to own this place, and you'll be right where I want you," he said, moving to leave the office.

Lesley looked around for something to throw at him. Finding only a pencil, she threw that.

Darren dodged the projectile and, grinning, said, "Tsk, tsk. You always did have a bad aim." Then he walked out.

Lesley swiveled her chair around to face the window. "Ooh the nerve of the man!" she muttered.

Sometime later, the sound of voices outside her office pulled Lesley out of her unladylike musings about Darren. She walked out into the hall. Oh, no! Arthur had brought Lola to the office with him. So that was why he was late.

"Lesley. I haven't seen you in ages," Lola smiled, gushing fondly.

"It hasn't been that long. Only a couple of weeks. How've you been, Lola?"

"Not so good," she pouted. Then her eyes lit up. "But I'll feel ever so much better once Arthur sells Raiments and we start traveling abroad. I can hardly wait to see Hawaii and Fiji. It'll be like having a second honeymoon." Lola inched closer to Arthur and pinched his cheek. "Won't it, Pookie?"

Arthur's face turned hectic with embarrassment. "That's right, honey bunch."

Lesley resigned herself to the fact that all was lost.

"You're looking kind of down, Ms. Evans," Darren inquired. "Aren't you feeling well?"

"I feel fine, Mr. Taylor," she grated out.

"I thought we agreed that you would call me Darren."

"Did we? I'm sorry, I don't remember agreeing to that."

"All new relationships are hard to get started. Sometimes those that aren't so new are even harder to resume. Don't worry, sweetheart, you'll get the hang of it." Darren looked at his watch. "It's almost ten o'clock. What do you say we get the business of signing the papers out of the way?"

"Nothing could make me happier," Lola said, squeezing Arthur's arm and kissing his cheek.

Later, while Darren, Lola and Arthur were in deep conversation, Lesley slipped away to her office and closed the door. Her hope had melted like butter left too close to the stove. What was she going to do now? The papers were signed. Raiments now belonged to Taylor's. Where did it leave her? What plans did Taylor's—Darren specifically—have for her future? The future of Raiments?

She walked over to her desk, picked up her sketch pad and thumbed through her designs. They were some of her best work. Where would these fit in the vast conglomeration of Taylor's? She flopped down in her chair. Arthur had a point about it being her golden opportunity, if she chose to make it one. When everything was out in the open, she wondered if Darren would let her.

The cheery, contented voices of Lola and Arthur filtered into her office. At least some people were happy. She heard a knock at the door and in walked Arthur and Lola before she could ask who it was.

"We—Lola, Darren and I—want you to come out to lunch with us." Arthur smiled imploringly.

"I've got a lot of work to do."

"I say it can wait until after lunch, sweetheart," Darren said from the doorway. "I am, after all, the boss now."

"Come on, Lesley. Pookie and I want you to celebrate with us." Lola batted her heavily-mascaraed eyes.

Lesley groaned softly under her breath. There was no way she could refuse. "All right." She closed her portfolio case, and placing it back on her desk, rose from her chair.

"How does Casa Maria sound?" Arthur suggested.

Arthur placed an arm around Lola's waist as they advanced toward the doors of Casa Maria. Lesley trembled when Darren cupped her elbow as they followed them into the restaurant. She wanted to jerk out of his hold and scream at him not to touch her, but she didn't want to make a scene.

As though sensing her mood Darren tightened his hold.

The host approached with a welcoming smile on his face. "Would by the windows overlooking the garden please you and your party, Mr. Rainville?"

"That'll be fine, Miguel," Arthur answered.

Relief washed over Lesley when Darren released her elbow as they reached their table. A waitress in a colorful, traditional Mexican full skirt and embroidered-white peasant blouse came to take their order.

Lesley loved Mexican food, but the thought of eating any of it today made her stomach churn. She chose instead a simple salad.

"Is that all you're going to have, Lesley?" Lola asked.

"For some reason I'm not very hungry today." She glared at Darren. Usually the relaxed atmosphere of Casa Maria put Lesley in a good mood, but not this time.

"It must be the anxiety of facing the unknown," Darren said in a subtly taunting tone.

"The unknown?" Lesley queried.

"Whenever a company changes hands there is bound to be that feeling of not knowing where you'll fit into the new scheme of things. If you'll fit in at all. Or if you even want to. Do you want to fit in, Ms. Evans?"

"Of course she does, don't you, Lesley?" Arthur asked.

She remained conspicuously, defiantly silent.

"I'll just have to use my powers of persuasion to convince her that being on the Taylor team is the right place to be. Won't I, Ms. Evans, Lesley?"

Their food arrived.

Seconds later, as they prepared to eat their meal, Lesley's insides tightened with exasperation when she caught Darren grinning at her as he raised a forkful of delicious-looking chicken enchilada to his mouth. It was amazing how he could make even eating a sensual experience.

Lesley noticed that Arthur was smiling as he watched the exchange between her and Darren. She couldn't help wondering what he was thinking.

When the waitress returned to ask if they wanted drinks, Lola answered. "You can bring me one of your wonderful strawberry margaritas. You want one too, Lesley?"

"No, I'm afraid not. I have to work when I get back to Raiments. I'll need a clear head."

Lola looked to Arthur to convince her. "Just one won't hurt her, will it, Pookie?"

"Lola, I don't think—" Lesley began.

"I think it'll be all right, Ms. Evans," Darren interjected.

"And what you say goes, right?"

"I am the boss, sweetheart," Darren said in an and-don't-you-forget-it tone of voice.

"All the same, I think I'll pass."

After they all returned to Raiments, Lola went home but promised to return for her pookie at four. Her "pookie." Lesley shook her head and ambled on back to her office.

Not long after Arthur and Lola had gone for the day, Lesley was summoned to Darren's office. She found him sitting behind Arthur's desk when she walked in. Though it irritated Lesley, she didn't comment on it. What could she say? Technically, Arthur no longer owned Raiments.

"There are several things I need to talk over with you." She took a seat. "Oh?"

Darren frowned, not missing the hostility in Lesley's voice. "Your future at Raiments might depend on how gracious you are to me, sweetheart."

"What is that supposed to mean? I'm gracious to everyone. And don't call me that."

Darren noticed that her eyes never wavered. She certainly didn't lack grit. He had to admire that about her. By the time he was through with her, she was going to need every granule. No one thwarted a Taylor for long. Those who tried usually failed, eventually getting what they deserved. Lesley Wells was definitely overdue in the payback department.

He took in the delicacy of her face, the coffee dark eyes fringed with long black lashes, dominating a slender, brown-sugar oval face. Her prominent cheekbones and finely-boned facial structure bespoke her exotic West Indies ancestry. That slightly upturned nose and full, sassy mouth definitely looked kissable, in fact, begged to be tasted and enjoyed. And oh, how he had once enjoyed it.

His thoughts were getting him off the subject he'd gotten her here to discuss. Her very presence was distracting. In the past he'd paid a very high price for letting that happen, and he didn't intend to make that same mistake again.

"I've been considering moving Raiments to Philadelphia by the end of the year."

Lesley shot to her feet. "You can't do that."

"But I can."

"Raiments and L.A. are…are…" she groped for the right word to get her point across "…synonymous."

He ignored her outrage. "If I decide to move the company, you'll be coming with us if you want to keep your job."

Coming with him—to Philadelphia! Was he on drugs? She had no intention of returning there ever, not after the pain and humiliation she'd suffered. The pain he personally dealt her.

"If you were wondering where you would fit in, I can put your mind at rest. I have the perfect place for your special talent."

"Darren, you never let me explain—"

"The here and now is all that concerns me, sweetheart." For a moment he thought he saw, along with the frustration and anger, hurt glimmering in her dark eyes. He must have been mistaken, because after that peering into her eyes was like trying to gaze through a window with the shade pulled down.

"I want to make one thing clear, Lesley." He walked around the desk and sat on the edge of it. "Raiments belongs to Taylor's now. If it's too much for you to handle, you'd better bail out now, because if you wait too long, you might find yourself without a parachute."

"Who's to say I won't find a better job somewhere else?"

"You're so cool, self-possessed and confident. You weren't always that way, though, were you, sweetheart?" He took her hand in his. When she tried to pull it away, he increased the pressure. "In fact, I can remember a time— no, many times—when those dark eyes of yours turned into pools of desire urging me to drown in the infinite depths of your beautiful body. And oh, how I could lose myself in you. Who knows? History just might end up repeating itself."

"You wish. You may own Raiments, Darren, but you don't own me." She smiled with acid sweetness.

"I wouldn't say that. I distinctly remember hearing you cry out, 'I belong to you, heart, body and soul, Darren,' when I made love to you."

Lesley gasped and her face heated at the memory of those unforgettable moments of passion between them.

Darren slid a long, slender forefinger along her jaw line. He smiled when he saw the pulse beating wildly at her throat. Then he raised his eyes and looked deeply into hers. "You aren't so unaffected after all, are you, sweetheart?"

She slapped his arrogant face, then blazed a defiant look at him, awaiting the form his retaliation would take.

Darren had expected a number of reactions, but not this one. Before, he'd always been able to guess what she'd do. But this new Lesley was proving to be definitely more of a challenge than the old.

Lesley took a step back. When nothing happened, she was puzzled. What was he up to now? She got angry. Just who did he think he was?

"Taylor's isn't the only cog in the fashion industry wheel, Darren," she said finally. If he thought he could intimidate her into submission, he'd better rethink his strategy. She'd had offers from other houses to design for them. Arthur had often complained about some of them trying to steal his thunder, as he called her. She'd stayed with Raiments not only out of sheer enjoyment, but also because of the debt of gratitude she owed to Arthur. When she had first arrived in L.A., desperate to find a job, he was the only one who would give her a chance, considering the cloud she'd left under when she'd fled Philadelphia. And she certainly couldn't use the Wells name as a point of reference.

"Maybe not, Lesley, but I can make it damned hard for you to go anywhere else. And don't think I can't. Of course, you could always go to your people."

Lesley flinched. The dig really hurt. He knew she could never go back to work at her family's business. Wasn't it enough that he'd practically forced her to leave Philadelphia six years ago? No. He had to come to L.A. to torment her here, and now he was trying to coerce her into going back there! Never!

"Will that be all, Mr. Taylor?"

When Darren saw the pain in her eyes, he felt like a bastard. What he'd said about her going to her family was a low blow. "Yes, that'll be all."

A plan began to form in Lesley's mind during her drive home. Tonight wouldn't be too soon to work on it. If Darren could be made to see the advantages of allowing Raiments to remain in L.A., maybe, just maybe, he could be maneuvered into the realization that it was better for the company if she remained here with it.

Lesley barely touched her dinner that evening. Millie noticed and commented later, after Dara had been put to bed, and they were in the living room.

"You didn't like the casserole?"

"It was fine, Millie."

"Something is bothering you. Why don't you tell me about it?"

"I'll have to tell Darren the truth now. He just bought Raiments, and wants me included in the deal." Lesley rose from the loveseat and walked over to her desk. "Although I love designing for Raiments, I can't work with Darren."

"He lives back east. I don't see—"

"Millie, he wants to move Raiments to Philadelphia. There's no way I'm ever going back there."

"You said someone framed you. Maybe you ought to go back and try to clear your name."

"That wouldn't be where it ended, even if I could find the guilty person after all this time. I have a feeling that Darren has his own reasons for wanting me to go back, that buying Raiments was just an excuse. Proving my innocence doesn't enter into it."

"Maybe he still cares for you."

"Believe me, that's not it. He wants revenge. I can't let him involve Dara in something like that."

"How do you intend to stop him, if he's anything like you've described him?"

"I don't know, Millie. I could leave California, but I don't want to do that. He'd only find me again. No, I'll have to stay and face the music."

"Whatever you decide, I'm with you all the way. You and Dara are my family."

"Thank you, Millie. I don't know what I'd do without you."

Lesley had spent half the night working on her plan to thwart Darren. When she finally did climb into bed and close her eyes, unbidden the memory of Darren's touch came back to torture her. She'd always loved the feel of his long slender fingers touching, stroking, intimately caressing her.

Oh, God, why can't I forget?

No! She exerted every ounce of control within her to push those ancient longings back into the abyss where she'd flung them. This was still a war of survival, and she didn't intend to be a casualty this time.

FIVE

The following day Lesley learned that Darren wouldn't be in the office until later that afternoon. She couldn't help wondering why. What was he up to? Was he doing this to throw her off balance? He couldn't possibly suspect what she was planning, could he?

She casually asked Raiments workers how they felt about the change of ownership. Most were concerned that they would lose their jobs. And the rumor that the company might possibly be moving to Philadelphia had many of them upset and anxious.

It was as Lesley had suspected. The uncertain climate at Raiments would work to her advantage. She went to George's, one of her favorite restaurants, to have lunch. It was quiet at this time of day, and she could lay her plan out on the table and study it. There were still details she needed to iron out, but she could see no reason why Darren wouldn't go for it.

Just as Lesley put her papers back into her portfolio case, she heard a familiar voice, Clare Benson's. Several tables away, she and Darren were having lunch. Lesley suspected that more was going on than simple courtesy and friendship. Was Darren already starting to cut off Lesley's options by convincing Benson's, and maybe other prominent fashion houses in L.A., not to hire her? Surely he didn't wield that kind of power! Not in California. She was just being paranoid.

Lesley waited as long as she could, but she had to get back to work, so she rose from her seat; unfortunately, the only way out was past their table. With an annoyed sigh she headed for the door.

"Lesley," Clare called out smiling, urging her to join them with a wave of her hand. "It is you, I told Darren I thought it was."

"Why don't you join us, sweetheart?" Darren added in a low intimate voice.

Lesley flinched at the endearment.

A surprised look came over Clare's face as she watched the exchange. Then a slow, knowing smile replaced it. Lesley knew what she was thinking. The look on Darren's face said he was enjoying himself. Damn him.

"I have to get back to work."

"Since you work for me, I say when you have to be back. Sit down," he said softly, but the demand was clear in his tone.

Lesley wanted to tell him to go to hell and stomp out of there, but she knew better than to try that.

Darren eyed Lesley's portfolio case. "What mysterious project are you working on?"

"Oh, just something I thought would be right for Raiments."

"Hmm, it sounds interesting. Let me have a look."

"It's not ready to be seen by anyone yet. I really do need to be getting back to work, Mr. Taylor." She got up from her chair. "It was nice seeing you again, Clare."

Lesley couldn't get out of there fast enough. If Darren had seen what she had been working on... She still wondered what he had been talking to Clare Benson about. Surely he wasn't going to buy them out, too. Clare hadn't acted differently toward her, so that had to mean he wasn't trying to sabotage her professionally, at least not yet.

Lesley was preoccupied the rest of the day and ended up taking work home.

During the rest of the week Lesley waited for Darren to call her into his office. When he didn't, she grew more anxious to present her proposal to him. He just had to go for it.

Monday morning arrived. Lesley was ready to present her plan to Darren, only to learn that he had flown to San Francisco, she was told, on Taylor business. What kind of Taylor business? she wondered. Maybe he would forget to come back, she thought hopefully, but knew better than to pay into that particular fantasy.

Lesley had just put her portfolio case on her desk and sat down when she heard a knock at the door. She tensed, having a good idea who it would be on the other side, before Arthur opened the door and walked in. She thought she would feel awkward with him now, but found that wasn't the case.

"Lesley."

"Yes, Arthur?"

"I'm going to miss you. You've been like a daughter to me for the past five and a half years." He reached out his arms to hug her.

She got up from her chair, skirted the desk, and rushed into them. "I'm going to miss you, too." After a moment, "You'll have Lola."

"I know, but that's different. You'll be all right, won't you?"

"Of course I will," she said, easing out of his embrace.

Lesley saw the assessing look on his face and walked back to her chair.

"You haven't accepted the reality yet, have you?"

"I know Raiments belongs to Taylor's." She took the papers out of her portfolio case and looked them over. "I don't know what else you could mean."

"Yes, you do." He gazed at the papers. "What is that you're working on?"

"Leave it alone, Arthur."

"All right, I will. No matter what you've taken it into your head to do, I promise you it won't work. Darren Taylor owns this company now, and he has his own agenda. Nothing you do or say will change that. Accept it and go on from there."

"You don't understand."

He looked sadly at her. "But I do. Change is inevitable. That's life, Lesley. You either come to grips with the reality or risk being destroyed by it if you don't or can't. Remember it was this old man who told you that."

"You're not old. But I'll remember." Arthur just didn't understand what was at stake for her. Although Arthur's disapproval made Lesley uncomfortable, she had no intention of giving up on her plan.

Arthur sighed. "I see my words have fallen on deaf ears. Take care, Lesley."

"When are you and Lola leaving on your trip?"

Arthur's expression brightened. "Not for a few more weeks yet. There are still a lot of loose ends I need to tie up before we go."

"Will you be coming into the office?"

"On a limited basis only, and then just to show Darren around. Since Raiments isn't nearly as big an operation as Taylor's there are quite a few differences he needs to be made aware of." Arthur looked hopefully at her.

"You want me to help with it, don't you?"

"Would you? For me." Lesley was silent.

"Think about it, please?"

Darren returned to Raiments a few days later and called a staff meeting. Lesley was curious about the two women who were with him. She couldn't help wondering what, if anything, they had to do with his trip to San Francisco. Was Darren going to make an official announcement about his plans for Raiments at the meeting? Didn't he realize, or did he even care, what would happen to all the people who had no desire to relocate to Philadelphia, but still wanted to work for Raiments?

After all the introductions and the day-to-day business had been dispensed, and it looked as if Darren wasn't going to bring up the subject of Raiments' future, Lesley stood and gained everyone's attention.

"Mr. Taylor has informed me that the move to Philadelphia for Raiments is definite."

Murmurs of worry and concern buzzed through the room.

Darren glared warningly at Lesley. She ignored him.

"I have compiled some figures to present to Mr. Taylor."

Darren advanced toward her. "Lesley, Ms. Evans, I—" Lesley cut him off and quickly spoke. "In these statements are the production and sales figures. We have all done excellent jobs. And it is reflected here." She held up a file folder. She saw the disapproving look on Arthur's face, but continued her spiel. After finishing outlining her proposal, she gazed challengingly at Darren.

He didn't hesitate to take it up.

"As Ms. Evans has so aptly pointed out, Raiments has a very profitable following here on the West Coast."

Lesley's confidence began to seep away as he continued to speak.

Darren stepped over to the phone and picked up the receiver. "Karen, show the two ladies in my office in here, please."

Minutes later, Lesley watched them enter the conference room. One was a fortyish-looking woman dressed in a blue business suit and the other a young, eager, career-girl type.

Darren began. "I have, since my ah, discussion with Ms. Evans, re-evaluated my decision regarding Raiments. I intend to open a new branch of Raiments in Philadelphia, making it the head office, and still keep the one here open.

"If any of you care to join Ms. Evans on the East Coast, there will be jobs waiting for you."

Darren smiled and then gestured to the two women. "I'd like you all to meet Serena Gower, the new CEO of the

Los Angeles branch of Rainville's Raiments. And the new head fashion designer, Kelly Thomas."

The women smiled and nodded.

"I had intended to introduce them to all of you later in the week, but there's no better time than the present. I know you will join with me in welcoming them to Raiments. They will assume their duties effective June 4th. If there is no further business, you may all return to work. All except you, Ms. Evans."

Mortification infused Lesley's mind. Darren had ruthlessly but smoothly spiked her guns. She could feel her face heat with temper, and was sure it showed.

The buzz of conversation receded as the staff shuffled out of the room. Darren instructed Karen to show the newest addition to Raiments' staff around the company. Besides Darren and Lesley, only Arthur remained.

Arthur looked to Darren. "You will be gentle with her, won't you?"

"Don't worry, I won't be too rough on her. When she moves to Philadelphia and settles into the new branch office, everything will work out. Don't let us keep you from meeting your lovely wife. I'll take care of Ms. Evans." Darren smiled genially at Arthur, but looked reproachfully at Lesley.

As she watched Arthur leave, Lesley prepared herself to face the wrath of Khan. She was the first to break the silence. "You're always on top of everything, aren't you, Darren? I should have known you'd have all your bases covered."

"Yes, you should have. Sit down, Lesley," he said in a soft, yet steel-lined, voice.

She hesitated.

"I said sit down."

Lesley defiantly dropped into a chair.

Darren walked the few steps to where she was sitting and pulled up a chair. "I hate deceit as much as I detest disloyalty. In what category do you fall, Lesley? Don't stress yourself, sweetheart. You fit into both." He took her hand in his.

When Lesley attempted to pull it away, Darren's grip tightened.

"Relax," he said softly before letting her hand go.

Her eyes conveying the fury she felt, Lesley molded her lips into a militant slash.

"If you're smart, you won't ever try anything like this again."

Lesley stood up. "Darren the Great has spoken. Who do you think you are? God?" she asked in a cold, controlled voice.

Darren stood and smiled down at her.

Lesley's mouth went dry at the sudden blaze of emotion she saw in his eyes. Her heart rate speeded up. Sensing that the threat had changed, she shrank back slightly.

"Darren, I—"

He grasped her upper arms and pulled her close to his chest. "You know, I almost went out of my mind wondering what happened to you over the years: where you were; what you were doing; who you were doing it with."

Lesley swallowed hard, her heart beating almost painfully in her chest.

Darren cupped the back of her head, bringing her lips a mere breath from his. As he gazed deeply into her eyes, he could feel her body tremble, he assumed from fear. Cursing under his breath, he suddenly released her.

"That'll be all for now, sweetheart." Then he strode from the conference room.

Lesley ran her tongue over her lips. They felt as though he had actually kissed them.

"Damn him," she cried, then threw the report she had so carefully compiled to the floor. "Damn you, Darren Taylor."

Lesley was too angry to inflict herself on anyone in the lunchroom, so she sent out for lunch and ate it in her office. She definitely hadn't felt like going out to eat. Darren had been one step ahead of her all the way. How had he guessed what she would do? She wondered if that day at George's she had somehow given herself away without realizing it. From the way Arthur had stared at her when he left, he'd felt sorry for her. She would never forget that pitying look in his eyes.

Darren had certainly made sure that there would be no place for her in the L.A. branch of Raiments by hiring Kelly Thomas. She hated to think what her position would be in the new branch if she were crazy enough to go back to Philadelphia with him. If she went back! What was she thinking? There was no way she was going back there.

Even if she did go, Darren had every right to reduce her status to that of assistant fashion designer or sketcher to the assistant. But no, he wouldn't waste her talent that way. No, not Darren Anthony Taylor II.

Lesley knew she had alternatives other than moving to Philadelphia, but she didn't want to get pushed into considering any of them. Her problem was that she liked designing for Raiments. And Darren knew it. Why couldn't he just go back to Philadelphia and leave things in the hands of the new CEO? And forget her. "Even if he did that, Kelly Thomas was set to take over Lesley's job. And what about their daughter? What was she going to do about that? At the moment she couldn't decide which way to turn.

If she stayed in Los Angeles there was always Cheerful Children's Wear, a company practically begging her to officially join them. Although she liked designing children's clothes, her first love was creating elegant styles for women. And her goal was to someday design fashions for men. Johnson Attires and Elite Ensembles were also interested in her. Even Gala Garments had been impressed by her work and made her an offer.

The trouble was that the top two fashion houses in the fashion industry who could utilize her particular skills happened to belong to either her family or Darren's. If push came to shove, she could always go to Europe, but she loved the States and didn't want to move to a foreign country. She wanted her designs to stay in America, display an American label.

Over the next few weeks, she had a lot of thinking to do. All too soon Arthur would be gone and there would no longer be a buffer between her and Darren. Why was Darren doing this to her? It had been six years. Surely his need for revenge wouldn't compel him to force her into accepting his offer.

But when she thought about the look of triumph in Darren's eyes the day he announced that he was buying Raiments, she compared it to a vengeful junkyard dog who had been beaten because he let someone steal from the yard he was guarding.

"Brooding, or still plotting and scheming, Lesley?" Darren taunted from the doorway.

"Neither."

"Yeah, and "I'm Prince Charles. Why don't you bow to the inevitable, sweetheart?"

"You'd like that, wouldn't you? Well, it ain't gonna happen." She pushed herself to a standing position. "And stop calling me that."

He grinned. "Calling you what?"

"You know very well what." Lesley reached for her purse and portfolio case.

"Running away again, sweetheart?"

"Certainly not. If you would look at the clock on that wall," she pointed to it, "you'll notice it's quitting time."

"What, no overtime?"

"You can go straight to hell, Darren."

"Only if you'll agree to be my companion."

I'm leaving now."

"Oh and, sweetheart," he said as she reached the door, "you have a good evening now." He waved his hand for her to precede him out the door.

❧❦❧

That night, after pulling Dara to bed, Lesley sat down to look over some sketches for Raiments' special line, but found she couldn't concentrate. Her mind kept drifting to the past. From as far back as she could remember, her life had been a struggle. She'd hated being referred to as Lesley Wells, pampered youngest daughter of the successful Wells fashion family. Especially since she wasn't anything like them. She had always felt like a shirttail relative.

Her mother, Meredith, an outstanding designer, was the only daughter of investment magnate Judson Crenshaw. At the age of thirty-five, Lesley's father, Curtis Wells, had ascended to the presidency of Wells of Fashion over his two older brothers.

Together, he and her mother had made the Wells name a fashion statement. And they had expected their children to be an extension of their combined energy, talents and good looks.

Lesley's beautiful sister, Jasmine, had been the top model for Wells, and then later its fashion coordinator. Her brother, Brett, had been groomed from the cradle to take over the reins of the business. That left their near-sighted, overweight, withdrawn daughter, Lesley. For most of her teenage years, her mother chided her constantly to wear contacts and go on a diet. She'd taken her to one dermatologist after another about her skin problem. To her beautiful mother, having an ugly duckling for a daughter was a disgrace.

Her father insisted that she be a straight A student in school. Anything less was unacceptable. She tried to be what they both wanted her to be, always seeming to fall short.

Contacts irritated her eyes, making it impossible to wear them for long periods of time. She tried every diet known to man, and none of them worked. Diet pills made her sick, and strenuous exercise gave her sciatica problems. As for the grades, she never got anything higher than a B.

Lesley finally talked her parents into letting her go to the University of Connecticut, where she majored in design. Miraculously, over the next few years, she dropped the extra weight, her skin problem cleared up, and she found contacts she could wear all the time without them irritating her eyes.

She got more than she bargained for when she met Darren. She had to keep reminding herself that she'd barely escaped the gigantic mistake of marrying him. If she had anything to say about it, history wasn't going to repeat itself.

SIX

Darren paced back and forth in his hotel suite. He'd outmaneuvered Lesley, but it had left a bitter taste in his mouth. She'd shown him the lengths she was willing to go not to have anything to do with him.

If, as she had said six years ago, she was innocent, then why hadn't she stuck around to face the charges against her? Unless there was nothing to defend, and she was guilty as hell of stealing the designs from his family's business and handing them over to her family.

He hated the words industrial traitor. But at the time they seemed the right label for Lesley Wells. Since nothing had changed, why did he still desire a thief and a traitor? He shook his head because he couldn't understand it. When he had touched her in his office a week ago, she had inflamed his passion.

After all this time, that ache to feel her satin-smooth skin and kiss those ripe, sassy lips should be gone and the sight of her should leave him cold, but it didn't. All he wanted to feel for her was contempt, but he didn't.

What would it prove by forcing her to return to Philadelphia when she didn't want to go?

If there isn't the slightest possibility that he could be wrong about her, what good would it do to drag her back there to dredge up the past?

It would do him a lot of good, because he had to know for a certain whether she was a traitor of the worst kind, dammit.

Was she planning to thwart him again? What would her next move be? He had to think of every possible angle, because he knew she would. Her determination to stay in L.A. was every bit as strong as his that she return to Philadelphia. But she was up against a Taylor. There was no way she could win. He couldn't understand why he wanted her to try.

Once he got her back home, then what? He didn't know the answer to that question.

Several days later, when Lesley came into work, Karen informed her that Arthur wanted to see her in the conference room. Lesley sighed, curious to know what he wanted. Whatever it was, she was sure it had something to do with Darren.

She went to her office and put her things away, then headed down the hall to the conference room. She found Arthur busy skimming travel brochures.

"Karen said you wanted to see me."

He looked up from a brochure of Fiji and smiled. "Sit down, Lesley." When she had done so, he cleared his throat. "I wanted to talk to you about Darren Taylor."

"I knew it." Lesley shot him an exasperated look.

"Now, Lesley, I know you don't want to talk about him, but we have to. It's important that you be nice to the man. Your entire future as a designer could hinge on it. Remember that you have that beautiful little daughter to raise."

"Taylor's isn't the only fashion house in America, Arthur."

"If he decides to use his influence, you won't be able to get a designer job in any of the more exclusive houses."

"I can always go to Europe."

"You don't really want to do that, do you?"

"No. What you're saying is that I either play the game his way or I don't play?"

"I wouldn't put it exactly that way."

"I would." She crossed her arms over her chest.

"Look, Lesley, you know I love you like a daughter. Darren has asked that you personally show him around Raiments. He wants to familiarize himself with the inner workings of the company. In the long run it'll help the employees adjust to the change of leadership if you help Darren."

Lesley knew he was right. She didn't want to make the adjustment any harder for her co-workers than it had to be.

"All right, Arthur. What exactly do you want me to do?"

"That's my girl. This afternoon I want you to take Darren on a tour of the production department."

Lesley kept an eye on the clock. The hands seemed to have wings on them. Afternoon came much sooner than she wanted it to. It was almost one o'clock. If she didn't go to Arthur's—no, Darren's—office, he'd come looking for her. She was sure of that. With a resigned sigh, she headed for his office.

Darren looked at his watch when he saw Lesley walk in. "You're right on time. I thought for a moment that I would have to come after you."

"I'm sure you would have enjoyed that, but I decided not to give you the satisfaction of exerting your authority over a lowly peon like me."

"Lesley."

"You already know what the production process involves. I don't see why I have to take you on a tour."

"Because I wanted you to. Taylor's owns this company, don't forget. Technically, you're still employed by it, by me. That's reason enough, don't you think?"

"Humph."

Lesley preceded him out of the office and on to the design room. "You all know Raiments' new owner, Mr. Darren Taylor."

After he'd spoken to everyone, she guided him on to the production room. "How's it going?" Lesley smiled at Saul Epps, the pattern maker.

"Great, Lesley." He smiled back and continued translating the designer's sketch onto paper.

Darren felt a stab of jealousy. Lesley had never once smiled at him like that since he'd been here, never once treating him to the warm shower of her affectionate smile; instead she dealt with him as though he were a complete stranger, an enemy. He didn't like it. He didn't like it worth a damn.

They moved on to the pattern grader, who was in charge of sizing the design; next, the spreaders, who laid out the fabric, then the markers, the cutters and assorted assemblers. He couldn't help noticing that she had a friendly cheerful word for every one of them.

Although she flattered them outrageously, she had genuinely kind words for the sewing machine operators, the finishers and cleaners on down to the pressers as well.

Darren realized that Lesley still had that special charisma to dazzle people. Knowing she could be just as devious with it angered him.

"That about does it for the tour, Mr. Taylor."

"Lesley! Dammit, I've told you not to call me that," he said in a low voice so only she could hear him. "It's not as though you've never intimately known me, is it?" He looked her over as a man appraises a beautiful woman. The telltale throbbing at her throat betrayed that she wasn't immune to that masculine form of flattery.

"Darren." She said his name softly, but with a tinge of menace.

At that moment he wanted to kiss her mouth and taste the special sweetness he knew he'd find there. What was his problem?

"You've been very helpful, sweetheart." Seeing her flinch whenever he used that endearment annoyed Darren. It hadn't always been that way. There was a time when… No, he wouldn't go there. Soon she would have him questioning his own sanity. His annoyance at Lesley increased as he watched her go into her office. With a heavy sigh, he headed for his own.

"Karen, see if you can get me Clayton Colby at Gala Garments on the phone," Lesley urged anxiously before cradling the receiver.

She sat back in her chair and waited. Clayton Colby had been impressed with her summer after-five designs and had asked her to get in touch with him if she ever considered changing houses. She'd laughed off his offer at the time, feeling smug and secure in the knowledge that she would never leave Raiments. She wondered if it was too late, if he was no longer interested.

Darren had put her in an awkward position, making her feel surrounded and trapped like a young gazelle separated from its mother, left as prey for a ferocious tiger. She didn't like it, and wasn't going to stand for it. There were other houses she could design for, places the Taylor reputation and connections didn't reach and influence.

The phone buzzed. Lesley picked up the receiver. "Mr. Colby. Gala's last showing was fantastic."

"It's kind of you to say so. It's good to hear from you. That dress you wore to Clare Benson's party was simply exquisite."

"Thank you, I agree that it was. There are others in that line just as exquisite. I have more floating inside my head." She laughed.

"You're a true artist, Lesley. What can I do for you?"

"The reason I'm calling is that I'm considering leaving Raiments and wondered if Gala could use another designer."

"If you'd only contacted me sooner. Just a couple of days ago I was talking to Darren Taylor—you've heard of him." He cleared his throat. "He's the head of Taylor-Made Creations. Anyway, he put me on to one of his designers who is moving out to the West Coast. We hired Blaze Everett yesterday. Do you know of him?"

"Who doesn't? He's an excellent designer. I thought he was one of Taylor's top designers. I can't see him leaving them."

"Well, actually he was set to move to Taylor's Hawaiian office, but Darren decided to promote one of the assistants there to the position. And since he knew I was looking to replace Deborah Markham, he contacted me. I'm sorry, love, but I'll keep you in mind if it doesn't work out with Everett. That's all I can promise. I would love to have gotten you instead. Not that Everett isn't good. You have that certain flair for elegance that's rare these days. Look, love, I have to go. My flight to New York leaves in less than two hours. You know what the traffic going to LAX is like."

"Yes, I do indeed. Thank you, Mr. Colby, for your time. Have a good flight."

Lesley hung up the phone and sat staring at it. Was it just a coincidence that Blaze Everett had been considered for that job at Gala? Or had Darren set the whole scenario in motion? It reeked of his sheer ruthlessness. However, she wouldn't let this put her off trying some of the other houses in the country. Even if she had to leave California and take a job in either Dallas or Chicago.

She wasn't going to allow Darren to control her life or manipulate her into leaving the States. He'd see that she was a strong, mature woman with responsibilities, not the same naive fool she used to be. Despite him and his influence, she'd find another designing job.

Lesley had just come back from lunch when Karen handed her messages, and a reply to a fax she'd sent earlier. Hopefully the answer from Johnson Attires was the one she wanted. The president, Sheridan Winslow, had always complimented her every time he saw her about the coats she'd designed for Raiments' winter collection. He'd offered to pay her a very upscale salary to join them.

She sat down at her desk to read the fax:

Sorry, we have all the designers we can handle, but I'll keep you in mind if we have any openings. You might try Taylor's. I hear Blaze Everett is now with Gala Garments. Good luck to you. A designer with your talent won't have any trouble finding a spot.

Taylor's again? Or was it the heavy hand of fate slapping her down again? Was she just being paranoid? Seeing Taylor's influence everywhere? Why was she letting Darren get to her like this? If she wasn't careful, he'd turn her into a basket case. She had to think positively. Her next inquiry would be the one for her.

"You look worried about something, sweetheart."

Lesley's mind cleared immediately at the sound of Darren's voice.

"I'm not worried about anything, just thoughtful, that's all."

He walked into her office. "Thoughtful about what, I wonder."

"You have an office, Mr. Taylor, would you please…"

"Here's your hat, what's your hurry? When are you going to accept my offer to be a part of the new branch of Raiments?" He picked up her fax and shook his head. "Still scheming, huh, sweetheart? You should really—"

She snatched the fax. "I'll never give in or out."

"Oh, I remember a time or two when you willingly surrendered to me."

"Would you please get the hell out of my office."

"The truth hurts, doesn't it? You'll have to face certain painful home truths eventually, Lesley. I'm just trying to make the transition easier for you."

Yeah, right, she thought, gritting her teeth as she watched him stride out of her office with that provocative walk of his. Why couldn't he just leave her the hell alone?

A week after her disappointing fax inquiry, Lesley gathered the staff into her office as soon as Arthur had gone out to lunch with Lola.

"It sounds like a good idea to me, Lesley," said Giezel Garcia, Raiments' assistant designer.

"Where do you think we should have it?" Clyde Belden, the design room supervisor, asked.

Several others from the design room and the production department murmured their agreement to that question.

"Have what?" Darren asked from the doorway.

Lesley frowned, murmuring to herself. She should have locked that door.

"Why, the bon voyage party Lesley plans to throw for Arthur and Lola. Didn't you know?" Giezel looked at Lesley.

Darren smiled. "No, I didn't. Evidently, it must have slipped someone's mind. I propose having it at my hotel, the Bonaventure. I'm sure we could reserve a lounge or ballroom for the occasion. I'll have Karen call to make the arrangements."

"Darren—" Lesley began.

"You don't have to thank me, Ms. Evans. I like Arthur and his charming wife. By the way, what date have you all decided on for the party?"

"June eighteenth. I hope you won't have gone back to Philadelphia by then," Lesley oozed out sweetly.

"Oh, didn't I tell you that I'll be staying in L.A. until the end of August? No? It must have slipped my mind." He looked at his watch. "I have a meeting with Serena and Kelly in a few minutes. If you'll all excuse me…"

Clyde and the others, with the exception of Giezel, followed him out the door. Lesley watched Darren's retreating back, wishing she had a dull knife to shove between his shoulder blades.

"He's so nice," Giezel remarked.

"Yes, isn't he?" Lesley turned away.

"You don't sound like you think he is."

"I'm sorry, Giezel. Don't pay any attention to me, I still haven't recovered from the shock of Raiments no longer belonging to Arthur, that's all."

"I know what you mean. But a boss like Mr. Taylor makes it easy. We're in good hands, I think."

The man seemed to instill confidence with the flick of his long, thick eyelashes or an arch of his well-shaped black brows. Or with that smooth, silver tongue of his. But then, that was one of the Taylor characteristics she'd once admired about him, and had to admit still did.

She wished there was some way to exclude Darren from the preparations for the party, but knew it was impossible. Why was he staying in L.A. so long? He'd bought Raiments. What other reason did he have, other than to torment her?. He must really want her to go back to Philadelphia pretty badly. Just what did he have in store for her if she went back there?

"What do you think of the new CEO, Giezel?" Lesley asked.

"So far, she seems remarkably capable. At first I thought she'd be stiff and staid, but she's not like that at all. She's easy to talk to."

"You like her, then?"

"Yeah, I do. Look, I'd better be getting back to the design room."

"I'll talk to you later about the details for the party."

Lesley had worn a comfortable pair of jeans and a cotton sweater to work. She took a critical look at her workspace in the corner next to a row of windows. There was a partially draped dressmaker's form and a worktable covered with spools of thread, scissors, needles and pins. She picked up her tape measure and draped it around her neck.

She had never been the kind of designer who was satisfied with relying on paper sketches alone. She participated fully in every aspect of production, from creating the original design to supervising the final alterations on the finished garment. She experimented with muslin or other fabrics, draping them on dress forms to perfect her creations.

Out of the four lines or collections a year she was expected to create, she'd completed three. There was still next year's summer line of dresses, as well as swimwear, to finish. Lesley frowned. Her replacement would... Lesley had already started work on Raiments' special line for Christmas. Of the seventy-five items that made up the line, she'd completed thirty-five.

Lesley looked around the room. Everything was so familiar. She was going to miss this if she had to leave it. Darren wasn't giving her very many choices. Sink or swim.

Which one did he want her to do? The former probably, she reflected ungraciously.

She considered the new fashion designer. Lesley had found that Kelly Thomas was very imaginative and sharp. Darren had contemplated everything. Or so he thought. It wasn't over yet.

Darren gazed into Lesley's office as he came from the production room on the way to his own. He saw her down on her knees picking up a thimble that had rolled underneath her worktable. He got a clear view of firm, rounded buttocks pushing against the back seam of her snug-fitting jeans. She'd worn her hair in a ponytail today.

She appeared almost child-like, but he knew only too well how much woman was concealed beneath those clothes. He lingered a few seconds longer before heading down the hall to his office. The scent of her perfume seemed to follow him. He wasn't as free of her as he wanted to be. Considering all the pain she had caused him, how could he still desire her like this? He wouldn't, couldn't, let it make a difference in his plans. For a Taylor, control was everything and he intended to keep it.

He had a few projects of his own to occupy him while he was in L.A. So why wasn't he following through with any of them? He was letting himself get distracted by leftover feelings for Lesley. His second love, researching, had kept him sane during those awful months and years after Lesley disappeared.

Darren sat back in his chair. Creating new fabrics was exciting. Almost as exciting as a pair of dark brown eyes. He shook himself out of his momentary reverie. He refused to think about how he and Lesley had once…

Stop it, man! What's the matter with you? Wasn't the hell she put you through the first time enough for you? You're asking—no—begging to be destroyed all over again.

He forced his mind back to the present. Lesley had thought to exclude him from the preparations for the bon voyage party for Arthur. Whether she wanted to or not, she was going to have to be in his company over the next few weeks. He smiled, remembering the priceless look on her face when he'd said he'd be extending his stay in L.A. until August.

You won't be able to get rid of me that easily, sweetheart. I intend to have an exclusive contract with you once we get back to Philadelphia. And make no mistake about it, you will be coming back with me, no matter what I have to do to bring it about. You won't escape me this time.

SEVEN

Lesley knew she would have to be pleasant, flexible and cooperative with Raiment's new CEO and the head designer, Kelly Thomas, in order to keep the efficiency and atmosphere of the design room flowing in harmony. It wasn't as hard as she had expected. But she couldn't seem to get past feeling as insecure as a baby bird forced to leave the nest to take its virgin flight.

She definitely didn't like the feeling, and she couldn't help wondering what it would be like in the new branch of Raiments. If—and that was an impossibly big if—she chose to go, which she had no intention of doing.

It worried her that she hadn't managed to get another job yet. Time was running out in more ways than one. Her guilt concerning their daughter urged her to tell Darren the truth. Fortunately for her, Arthur was so caught up in his preparations for his trip that he hadn't noticed the similarity in looks and names between her daughter and Darren. But there was always the off chance that he might mention something in passing to Darren, and she didn't want that to happen.

Maybe it would be better if she told Darren the truth now. But she was terrified of what he might do once he did know. No. She would wait until after the party for Arthur and Lola. Then she would tell him. Throwing this party would be her last official act as the L.A. Rainville's Raiments head designer. Arthur had always been her friend. She wanted to show her appreciation.

While the preparations for the party proceeded, Darren found reasons to be near Lesley, much to her annoyance. He insisted on helping with the decorations. She had to admit that he had some very good ideas, such as having early pictures of Raiments blown up and hung on the walls, as well as sketches and swatches of Arthur's many successes in the fashion industry over the years.

Lesley chose what to put on the cake. Instead of the usual candles, she had thirty miniature dress forms made into candles to symbolize the thirty years Arthur had been in the fashion industry.

The day of the party arrived. In the Cabaret Room, which they'd managed to reserve for the occasion, Darren watched as Lesley stood looking at the cake.

"A penny for your thoughts, sweetheart."

She brushed tears from her cheeks with the heels of her hands. "Sorry, Darren, you can't buy them."

"You're crying. Why?" he queried gently. It took a lot to make Lesley cry. Seeing her tears made him feel like taking her in his arms and soothing away the sadness he saw in her face.

"It's another chapter closing in my life."

"If only the chapter in the book we started had meant as much to you."

It had, Darren. You have no idea how much, Lesley silently added. "I don't want to talk about it," she actually said, the cold dismissiveness in her words effectively squelching the tenderness of the moment.

The sound of voices as people began filling up the room gave Lesley the perfect opportunity for leaving Darren's side. He frowned, wondering about her expression. *There is something you're hiding from me, sweetheart. I can feel it. And I intend to find out what it is.*

Lesley's breathing quickened. Being so close to Darren was almost more than she could stand. She'd sworn never to run from him again. Yet if she didn't, she had an uneasy feeling that he would in some way devour her. What was his real motive for wanting her to go back to Philadelphia? Why couldn't he leave well enough alone? Why couldn't he leave her alone? It was over between them.

Not quite. There is the matter of the daughter he doesn't know he has, the voice of reason insisted.

At one time she'd had a burning desire that he believe in her. But not anymore. He had completely shattered her trust. They'd lost something precious that could never be regained.

Not to mention the special moments with the beautiful child he helped you to create.

Lesley found Giezel. "Arthur and Lola should be arriving here any minute. You sure he believes it's a party to welcome Darren as the new owner?"

"Clyde assured me that he does. There's Saul now," Giezel said, angling her gaze toward the door.

Darren dimmed the lights, signaling everyone to silence. Seconds later Arthur and Lola entered the room. When they all cheered him, Arthur's face became animated with emotion as it always did when he was surprised or embarrassed. He looked to Lesley.

"I don't know what to say."

"You don't have to say anything."

He looked around the room. "You did this? All of you, for me? The next thing I know you'll all be singing, 'For He's a Jolly Good Fellow.'"

"That's not a bad idea," Clyde remarked. "How about it, everybody?"

They all sang several choruses of the song as Arthur and Lola made their way to the cake.

Lola sniffed, dabbing at the corner of her eyes. "You've all been so good to Pookie and me. I want you all to know we'll never forget this. Never."

Everyone gathered around for the cutting of the cake and then later began moving away to dance and enjoy the music and eat the delicious food Darren had catered in.

He had also hired the old-fashioned jazz band that played songs from Arthur's good old days.

Darren spotted Lesley sitting alone at a table and came up behind her. "You've made the man happy with this going-away party."

"He deserves it."

"You haven't told me what you've decided about the move to Philadelphia."

"Do we have to discuss that tonight, Darren?" she asked, sipping her punch.

"It seems as good a time as any to ask. Well?"

"You've tried your damnedest to insure that I don't have much choice. Why, Darren? Why do you really want me to go back? Do you really want to be reminded of all that went wrong between us? Why can't you just leave me alone? Why do you have to keep pushing?"

He moved closer until he was within inches of her. "If I only knew the answers to those questions. I can't forget what we meant to each other. God knows I want to. Seeing you again brought it all back. We shared so much. Why, damn it? Why did you betray me, betray what we felt for each other?"

Lesley trembled, closing her eyes. "I didn't betray you or our love. Why can't you believe that?"

"Why do you go on lying to me?" He sat down beside her and took her hand in his. "Why do I keep wanting you? Why can't I get you out of my system?"

"Lesley?"

"Arthur," she said in a shaky but relieved voice.

Darren let her hand go.

"Is anything wrong?" Arthur asked.

"No. Of course not." She smiled. "Are you and Lola enjoying yourselves?"

"Yes. I just wish you were." He glanced at a silent Darren, then back to an anything but pleased Lesley. "Both of you."

"We are. Dance with me, Lesley," Darren asked.

Lesley didn't want to accept, but she didn't want Arthur to know how upset she really was. "I'd love to."

Her reward was an approving smile from her mentor. As Darren swept her out on the dance floor, Lesley lowered her voice and said, "You con artists believe in cashing in on any advantage, don't you?"

"I don't know about con artists, but I do." He smiled, drawing her closer to his body.

Lesley tried to ease back, but Darren moved to bring them even closer. "It would have to be a slow dance," she muttered under her breath.

"You used to love being close to me when we danced, especially during that special dance of love, in fact you once told me you could never get close enough."

Lesley's face heated and a lightning response swept through her body. "You would have to bring that up."

"I haven't forgotten any of the tender words and sweet promises you made to me, then crushed under your feet."

"Darren, I—"

"The music has stopped. Would you like to get something to eat?"

Lesley flinched at the coldness that infused his voice. "No, thank you. I think I'll go and find Giezel."

Darren watched her weave her way through the crowd. She was lovely in her red moiré dress with its full skirt. Only the lapels on the plain shirt-waisted bodice were unusual in that they were covered with glittering, multicolored sequins. He didn't remember seeing anything quite like it before. He imagined it was one of her own designs.

She'd felt so good in his arms. Why couldn't he keep his thoughts and emotions focused on her betrayal? Why couldn't he keep the old shield of anger up? He was disgusted with himself. Why couldn't he stick to his objective? He should be seeing to it that Lesley paid for what she'd done.

"That look is so intense, Darren. Do you and Lesley have a thing for each other?" Arthur asked.

"No, we don't. Raiments is the only thing we have in common."

"If you say so."

Darren noticed the assessing look Arthur shot his way before walking away, and wondered if he'd guessed what was really going on between him and Lesley.

From her vantage point by the windows, Lesley absently watched the band play, deep into her own tormenting thoughts.

"You haven't told him, have you?"

"Arthur! I didn't hear you walk up." She didn't pretend to not know what he was talking about. "I figured that it wouldn't be long before you put things together. No, I haven't, and I'm not sure I should."

"That's up to you, of course, but think about that wonderful little girl. She deserves to know her father. A man deserves to know he's fathered a child, and be given a chance to show that he's capable of being the kind of father that child needs." He smiled. "That's all I'm going to say on the subject."

Lesley's eyes misted. "I'm going to miss you."

Arthur slid a comforting arm around her shoulder and squeezed. "And I'm going to miss you, too, Lesley."

EIGHT

Arthur and Lola left for Hawaii on Friday morning, the day of Lesley's interview with Randall Parkins of Elite Ensembles. She had made the appointment the week Darren had flown to the San Francisco branch of Taylor's. Before he'd returned to drop his bombshell. Before she had tried to match wits with the master.

Elite Ensembles was next to Taylor's and Wells in terms of elegance in women's evening gown fashions. Randall Parkins had gone to college with her father. While using that relationship might help her get the job, she knew she wouldn't.

Lesley chose a modified pinstriped, navy suit she called her power suit, one of several she'd designed specifically for women who wanted to hold their own in an interview or presentation in the corporate world. She was anxious, and felt that wearing it would lend her extra confidence. At least she hoped it would.

With her portfolio case under one arm, Lesley opened the office door of Elite Ensembles. She realized her palms were damp from nerves when her hand slipped on the door handle. This interview was crucial. After Elite, there weren't any more houses of its caliber left in the United States. She really didn't want to leave the country, not even to go to Paris, although she liked the city and its people. She and her family had spent a summer there before she'd met Darren.

"You must be Miss Evans," the receptionist said when Lesley walked in.

"Yes, I am." She smiled.

"You can go right in."

Lesley had her bright confident smile in place, ready to impress Mr. Parkins. The smile disappeared when she walked in and saw Darren standing beside Randall Parkins, looking over some papers.

Mr. Parkins met her at the door. "You know Darren Taylor."

"Yes, of course. We've known each other for a few years," she said tightly.

"Please, sit down, Ms Evans." Randall Parkins indicated one of the chairs in front of his desk. Once Lesley was seated, he walked around his desk and eased into his chair.

Darren gave have her a smug smile and took the seat next to the one Mr. Parkins suggested for her. At that moment she wished she could rip that smile off his face.

"It hasn't gotten around yet, but Taylor's and Elite have joined forces. We will be known as Taylor-Elite Ensembles in the near future. I made the appointment for the interview before finding out Darren had bought Raiments. He has assured me that he has plans for your special talents. So you need not worry that you'll be left out in the cold because he hired Kelly Thomas as the head designer for the L.A. branch. Darren's also said that if you didn't like designing for the East Coast branch of Raiments that you could join us here at Taylor-Elite."

"I felt you deserved to hear the news in person, Lesley," Darren said gently. "I really do want you to be a part of my East Coast venture."

Lesley, so angry and frustrated she could scream, was rendered temporarily speechless.

Randall Parkins smiled. "You were right, Darren, all she needed was to know how valuable you consider her to Taylor's."

"I'm—overwhelmed." Lesley quirked her lips into a slight semblance of a smile. "It's gratifying to know how much you care, Mr. Taylor."

"I don't like losing valuable people, Lesley." He glanced at his watch. "It's lunchtime. Why don't you let me take you to lunch?"

Lesley got up from her chair. "Really, I—"

Darren rose from his. "There is no reason why you can't come, is there? We can return to Raiments soon afterward if you have work that needs to be finished today. You have to eat, so why not join me?"

Lesley groaned inwardly. She'd decided to take a cab rather than drive and fight the traffic of the freeway to get here on time.

"I would join you," Randall inserted, rising to his feet, "but I have a previous lunch date with my wife. "I really have to go, I'm sorry."

A feeling of dread seeped into Lesley as she saw Randall Parkins leave the office.

Darren smiled at her. "Why don't you give it up, sweetheart?"

"I told you I never give up—"

Darren pulled her into his arms and kissed her, stealing her breath, catching her off guard so that she wasn't prepared for the shock of his hot mouth moving so sensuously over hers and didn't immediately resist. When she tried to push him away, he wouldn't allow it, and instead deepened the kiss until she went limp in his arms. Then he let her go.

Lesley backed away, almost falling over her chair. Darren reached out to steady her.

"I think we both need to eat something," he insisted.

"I don't think we should go anywhere together."

"We're going, Lesley. It's not negotiable."

She saw the stubborn expression on his face and decided she just couldn't handle a wrestling match with him right now.

Lesley tried to wipe the taste of him from her lips, then picked up her purse and portfolio case. Darren guided her out of the office.

Fifteen minutes later Darren and Lesley were seated in the Italian Kitchen. Lesley was reminded of how much he and Dara loved Italian food. She ordered a plate of Mr. Angeletti's lasagna; but Darren ordered the complete lunch special with pizza, salad, garlic bread and pasta in addition to the lasagna; he also ordered the wine.

"You really should have more than that. You're way too thin, sweetheart."

"Look, Darren, I—never mind." She flashed him a mutinous look. "Is getting me back to Philadelphia worth buying up half the fashion industry?"

"I told you I'd do anything it takes to get you there."

"Oh, I believe you now."

"If you continue to defy me, I might consider black-balling you."

Lesley's dark, angry eyes clawed him like talons.

"You have no ties left in L.A. now that Arthur is out of the picture. But you do have family in Philadelphia."

The waiter brought their food. As good as the food was, Lesley found that she had lost her appetite and picked at her lasagna.

"There's more to this, isn't there?"

Lesley looked up from her plate. "I don't know what you mean."

"Yes, you do. I'm going to find out what it is, sweetheart. So you may as well tell me now. I've been patient with you, but I want an answer to my offer."

"Your 'offer.' Is that what you call it? I call it blackmail."

"I think we'd better get back to Raiments," he said, taking one last swallow of his wine.

Lesley was finishing up the last of her pending projects when Karen buzzed to tell her that Darren wanted to see her in his office.

"Karen said you wanted to see me," she said upon entering.

Darren was seated behind his desk, pencil in hand, poring over a stack of papers, his gold-rimmed glasses resting on the bridge of his nose, his elbow parked on the armrest of his chair. Despite wearing glasses, the man still managed to look suave and sophisticated.

Darren looked up from the papers. "Yes, I wanted to see you. You've put me off long enough, Lesley. I want to know what your plans are. And I want to know now, today."

She felt her muscles tense automatically into a defiant pose at that particular tone in his voice. Although the pressure he had applied before was far from mild, she sensed that he intended to tighten the screws if she didn't give him the answer he demanded to hear.

"We don't always get everything we want," she answered.

A flush of irritation flooded his face. "Arthur mentioned that you had outside interests other than Raiments. They the reason you're so reluctant to give me an answer?"

Lesley's insides tightened into knots. Had he also guessed that he had a... She met his annoyed glance without flinching. "And if they are?"

"Sit down, Lesley."

She thought to ignore his directive, but changed her mind when she saw that implacable glint in his eyes.

Darren leaned back in his chair and watched her for a few moments. "I want to have the East Coast branch of Raiments fully operational by the first of the year. Arthur showed me your sketches for the summer line. You know they're the property of Taylor's. I won't allow you to—"

"To what?" The pulses at her temples pounded. "Are you accusing me of something?"

"No, I'm not, sweetheart. At least not yet. When and if I do, you'll be the first to know. I'm just giving you fair warning, that's all. And since you've insisted on being so evasive about your plans, I have to consider any and all temptations that might prompt you to do to Raiments what you did to Taylor's."

In a fury Lesley surged to her feet. "I didn't do anything to Taylor's."

He took off his glasses and tossed them on the desk. "You can drop the indignant act. It doesn't impress me."

"My supposed betrayal was the only thing that ever did. Right?"

Darren shot out of his chair and was around his desk in seconds. "Damn it, you know that's not true. I really cared for you, girl." He pulled her into his arms and pressed a convincing kiss on her soft lips, one that demanded an answering response from her.

Lesley stiffened in shock, and when she recovered, yanked her mouth free. Darren recaptured it immediately, parting her lips with sensual mastery. Her thoughts spun away, leaving her temporarily lost in his potent form of persuasion.

When he at last allowed her to breathe, she felt as though she'd been drugged. Her insides swirled and dipped. It was as she had feared; her attraction for this man was far from vanquished. It seemed to rage hotter than ever. She had to put some distance between her and Darren or risk being completely sucked into the whirlpool of his power all over again. She watched the stunned expression on Darren's face. If she didn't know better she would think that he…

Darren let Lesley go and slowly returned to his chair, his composure seemingly restored. "I'm still waiting."

Lesley took a cleansing breath. "You'll know when I do," she said simply.

"Damn it, Lesley, that's no answer."

"It's the only one you're going to get right now. I have work to do." Lesley fled from the room.

Darren sat staring into space, languishing in the aftermath of shock at his response to Lesley. He'd lost control. She was the only woman who had the power to do that to him. Why, after all that had passed between them, was it still true?

He raked his fingers through his hair, then picked up his glasses and toyed with the handles, swinging them around. While he was in L.A. he'd find some R and R. A city like this was bound to have more than the usual number of desirable women. Surely he'd find one that could obliterate these disruptive feelings he had for Lesley Wells.

Lesley flopped down in her office chair. The pressure Darren was attempting to exert over her made her more desperate than ever to find another solution to her dilemma. Telling Darren about Dara was one thing, but allowing him to take charge of her career, and her life, was another.

She looked at her design pad and thought of Clare Benson's offer to work for Benson Apparel. She wondered what Clare and Darren had been discussing that day she'd run into them at George's.

Lesley reached for the phone. There was only one way to find out. "Clare, this is Lesley Evans."

"That was a quite a party you and Darren threw for Arthur."

"Thank you." She cleared her throat. "The reason I'm calling is to ask if your offer to design for Benson's is still good."

There was a long silence.

"Darren told me you were relocating to Philadelphia to work at the new branch of Raiments he intends opening."

"I haven't made up my mind whether I want to make that move."

"Benson's would be ecstatic to have you join us, but I wouldn't want to offend Darren. You see, he's just become a member of the board of directors at Benson's."

"I see."

"If it's all right with him, I'd be more than happy to consider you for Benson's"

"Never mind, Clare, it was just a thought."

"Look, Lesley, if—"

"It's all right. Don't worry about it. Bye now."

Lesley closed her eyes and rubbed the bridge of her nose. She knew that Darren had purposely gained a board position at Benson's to cut off that alternative.

Benson's wasn't her only option, though. Cheerful Children's Wear came to mind. That's it! She'd call her friend, Ava Saxon. She just might know of a company that would hire her. If worse came to worse, she could always design for Cheerful. She reached for the phone. She needed to talk to Ava anyway.

"Mrs. Saxon's office, Rhetta speaking."

"Rhetta, this is Lesley Evans. Is Ava in?"

"I'm sorry, she isn't. She flew to Canada to attend a fabric conference. You want to leave a message?"

"Is Greg around?"

"Yes, he is, hold on."

Greg came on the line.

"Lesley. You've changed your mind and decided that you want my body after all."

"No, you idiot."

He sighed. "I knew I couldn't be that lucky. What is it, baby?"

"Do you know when your mother will be coming back?"

"In several weeks, I would imagine, since she's going on to Scotland from Canada to meet with a wool manufacturer."

Lesley sighed heavily. "It'll be too late by then."

"Too late for what?"

"It's not your problem, Greg."

"Anything having to do with you I'll make my problem."

"You know that all we can ever be is friends."

"I wish it could be more, but if friends is all there can be, I want you as my friend. Go out with me tonight. A little dinner and dancing can't hurt. I promise to be on my best behavior."

Lesley laughed. "All right. I need to get my mind off my problems for a while."

"Which problem are you referring to?"

"Darren Taylor."

"I thought so. He making your life impossible?"

"Most definitely. He wants me to move to Philadelphia and work for the new branch of Raiments he intends opening."

"You don't want to go. That's why you're looking for another job, isn't it? You know my mother would be delighted to have you come work for Cheerful on a permanent basis."

"I know, but that's not why I was trying to get in touch with her. I thought maybe she might have a line on a designing job."

"We're pleased with what you do for us, but that isn't what you really want to do, is it?"

"No."

"I'll look into it Monday morning and get back to you. But for tonight, let's just party."

"Why couldn't I fall in love with you?"

"Your little daughter loves me. Maybe if I keep racking up brownie points with the kid—"

"Greg…"

"All right. I'll be by to pick you up at eight."

"Where are you taking me?"

"Let it be a surprise. Wear that emerald green number you designed last year. If I can't have you, then I'm going to make every male in the place think you're mine."

"Oh, Greg. You do wonders for a woman's vanity."

After hanging up, Lesley gathered up her portfolio case and started out the door. She bumped into Darren. When he reached out to steady her, her heart pounded out a rapid tattoo.

"You're leaving kind of early, aren't you, sweetheart?"

"Are you going to require that we punch a time clock, Mr. Taylor? I've finished my work for the day. If you don't mind, I'd like to leave now."

His eyes narrowed. "Following up on another prospect?"

"Another prospect? I don't know what you're talking about."

"I just spoke to Clare Benson. If you're thinking of calling any other houses, I have to tell you that I've talked to all of those in your area of expertise in the Los Angeles, San Francisco, and Dallas areas. I don't believe they're taking on any new designers."

"Damn you, Darren," she fumed.

"You've damned yourself, sweetheart, when you dared to steal from me and my family."

Lesley wanted to rail at fate for the hand it had dealt her. She wanted to scream at Darren for being so eager to believe the worst about her. She wanted to hate him, but she didn't. How could she hate the man who had given her the beautiful gift of their daughter? She blinked furiously to stave away the tears that threatened to escape down her face.

"I really don't have time for this." And then pulling away from Darren, Lesley headed for the door.

Darren stared after her. He'd seen the pain flash across her face. Was there also frustration? What could it mean? After all, she was the one who had betrayed him, not the other way around. Why should he feel bad about exacting his revenge?

His shoulders slumped. He wasn't enjoying treating her like the enemy. He was tired of the whole situation. A friend of his owned one of the 'in' places in town to go. Tonight he was going to go out and enjoy himself. There were always single ladies who wanted to have a good time. He was sure his friend Malcolm could introduce him to a few. Surely there was one who could make him forget Lesley Wells.

That night Lesley searched through her closet until she came across the emerald green, crepe-back, satin sheath Greg wanted her to wear. She smiled. It was really an attention-getter. Whereas the jacket was plain, the dress definitely wasn't. On the front of it a lioness resided. A symbol of a fierce, primeval female strength and daring, as well as feline grace. It was the star attraction from Raiments' special party wear ensemble last year.

Lesley took the dress out and laid it on her bed, then walked back to the closet, bent down to the shoe rack and picked out a pair of gold sling-back sandals. Tonight she intended to be carefree and enjoy herself.

Dara came into the room. Her eyes lit up when she saw the dress lying on the bed. She walked over to it and touched the face of the lioness.

"I like this dress, Mama. It's just like the one you made for my doll."

"I'm glad you like it, baby."

"Where you going?"

"Out with Greg," she said, putting in her earrings. The large gold hoops were the perfect foil for the lioness dress. And tonight she felt like being flashy.

"Greg is fun, Mama."

"Yes, he is." She smiled.

"But he's not my daddy. Am I ever going to get to see him?"

"Yes, you will very soon."

"Promise?"

"I promise, baby," she said softly. "What are you and Millie going to do tonight?"

"She's teaching me to play chess."

When dealing with a mind like her daughter's, Millie had better watch out, Lesley laughed to herself as she finished dressing. Millie would soon begin to wonder who was the student and who was teacher.

She shifted her thoughts to her evening and the man who would be taking her out. One thing about Greg, he loved to have a good time. And he even had a reputation as a lady killer. She never understood her attraction for him, though. She really wasn't his type.

She'd once considered herself as Darren's. What was his type now? And why should it matter? The man was trying to manipulate her into a position where he could exact his revenge, whatever that was.

Dara raced to the door when she heard the bell.

"Hey, there," Greg said, scooping her up in his arms. "What's up, girlfriend?"

"Am I really your girlfriend, Greg?" Dara giggled.

"One among many, my little goddess. You are my number one girl, though."

"What about my mama?"

"The both of you tie for first place." He put Dara down and stared at Lesley. "You look fantastic, baby."

"Thank you."

After dining at the Olive Garden, Greg took Lesley to a club called "The Race Track." Lesley had never been there, but she'd heard of it. They had dancing and a live R & B band. The moment they walked in, a cocktail hostess dressed in a gold cap, glittering blue jockey shirt and matching short skirt showed them to an individual booth-type seating area. In the center of the place there was a huge dance floor decorated to resemble a real racetrack. To reach it dancers had to pass through the starting gates. The band and the DJ were situated in the press box.

When Lesley took off her jacket, she received envious where-did-you-get-that-dress glances from the women and I-could-eat-you-whole looks from the men. She and her dress were definitely a hit.

Darren was leading his date away from the dance floor when he saw Lesley and Greg. He remembered seeing her with that same guy at Clare Benson's party. Exactly what did he mean to Lesley? Could he be the real reason she didn't want to leave L.A.? The thought of that being true made him seethe with anger.

"Somebody you know, Darren?" his date asked.

"Oh, yes." He eyed the smoldering elegance of the lioness on Lesley's dress. Clever embroidery with a shimmering-orange floss outlined the lioness and gave the impression of animal heat. A forest of soft-brown, velvet trees flanked the sleek feline, showing clearly that she was in her element.

The most alluring thing about the animal were the two smoky topaz stones used for its eyes. As Lesley breathed in and out, her breasts emphasized them, causing the eyes to flicker and glow intensely as if issuing a challenge.

He strode over to Lesley's table. "Enjoying yourself, sweetheart?"

Lesley's smile faded. "Darren!" Her gaze passed from him to the woman at his side.

"Why don't you and your friend, Greg, is it, join Valerie and me at our table?"

"We're fine where we are, thank you," Lesley answered stiffly.

The waitress came with their drinks.

"Maybe you'll agree to dance with me later."

"You may have to take a number, Taylor." Greg grinned.

Darren's smile didn't reach his eyes, and they flashed angrily at Greg before he directed his date to their table.

"Goading him like that may not have been a good idea, Greg."

"You think I care? He can't touch me. We came here to party. Let's get on with it, pretty woman." He stood up and held out his hand.

Lesley smiled, shaking her head. "You're too much."

While she was dancing with Greg, Lesley felt eyes on her. She knew Darren was watching. Knowing that put her more into the partying mood. Several men asked her to dance after that, and she accepted.

After her last dance partner returned her to her table, Darren walked up.

"My turn."

"Maybe later, I'd like to catch my breath right now," Lesley answered, fanning her face with her hand.

Darren nodded and walked away.

"You were kind of rough on the brother, weren't you?" Greg remarked.

"I don't believe I'm hearing this."

"You've still got him under your skin, haven't you?"

"Greg, I—"

"You don't need to answer that question. From looking at him, I know who he is. He's Dara's father, isn't he?"

Lesley didn't answer.

"I realized it right away when I saw him again. He doesn't know about her, does he?"

"No."

"Are you planning to tell him?"

Lesley sighed. "I'll have to eventually; Dara has been asking about him."

"I won't ask why you haven't told him. Evidently it's something deep between you two. But that beautiful little girl of yours deserves to know both of her parents, Lesley."

"I know that, but—"

"Whatever the problem is between you and Taylor, you need to resolve it before you leave for Philadelphia."

"I haven't decided to go. I'm so confused, Greg."

"You need to get away to think. I'm moving out of my mother's beach house. Why don't you and Dara go there and chill. A week or two in Malibu will hook you right up. I know my mother won't mind if you use it."

"You're right, I do need to get away."

"Then do it. I have a spare key," he said, taking his keys out of his pocket, slipping the extra one to the beach house off his ring and handing it to her.

Lesley took the key, then leaned over and hugged and kissed Greg.

"Keep that up and I might get the wrong idea," he teased.

The next song that started to play was a slow one. Lesley saw Darren get up. So did Greg.

"I think you're going to have to dance with the man this time."

Darren approached and reached for her hand. "Lesley?"

She rose from her seat and let him lead her onto the dance floor. Because the song was a slow one, there was no way Lesley could keep a safe distance from Darren.

Seeming to know this, he drew her even closer, making her more aware of him with every beat of the music.

Lesley trembled when his cheek brushed against her hair and his thigh rubbed against hers.

"We always danced as though we were specifically created to do it together."

Lesley stiffened. "That was before—"

"Before you betrayed me."

She moved to draw away from him, and he tightened his embrace.

"You won't escape me this time, Lesley."

"You don't own me, Darren Taylor."

"Don't I? I'm the man who first aroused your body to passion, sweetheart. I know how to make you cry out in ecstasy."

"Let me go."

"Never. And don't try to run away from me. I'll find you wherever you go."

"What do you want from me? You obviously hate me for what you think I did to you."

"You're wrong, I don't hate you, sweetheart, but I do intend to see that you pay for what you did."

"At what price? Whatever there was between us is all gone."

"No, sweetheart, not quite all."

The music ended and Darren led her back to her table. Then he walked back to his own.

"I can see that you're really upset. What did he say to you, Lesley?" Greg demanded.

"Just take me home, please."

"That bad, huh?"

"I don't know how much more of this I can take."

"I'd say my offer of the beach house came right on time, wouldn't you?"

NINE

Lesley hadn't used any of her vacation time. She and Dara could spend it at Ava's beach house, she thought to herself Saturday morning as she watched her daughter eat her breakfast.

Saturdays were their special time together. Lesley spent the entire day doing things with her child. Sometimes they went to the park or to one of the many museums L.A. had to offer. Other times they went shopping at the mall or to the movies for a cartoon matinee.

Lesley had begun to realize how much Dara needed a father when she saw complete families doing things together. Dara noticed them, too. Guilt that she had deprived her daughter of that weighed heavily on Lesley's conscience. After she came back from her vacation, whether she decided to move to Philadelphia or not, she was going to tell Darren the truth.

When Lesley arrived at work Monday morning, it was to find that Darren wouldn't be in the office for the next few days. She wondered what he was up to this time. Whatever the reason, it was the perfect opportunity to take her vacation. Since she officially was no longer the lead designer for the L.A. office of Raiments, and hadn't officially accepted the offer to work for the proposed branch in Philadelphia, she didn't feel it necessary to ask Darren for the time off.

She would leave a message with Karen to give to him. July and August were the two off-season months in the fashion world, so he couldn't possibly object.

Her decision made, Lesley acted on it and went home early to tell Dara and to pack. She envisioned the fun they would have. Lesley loved the beach and so did her Dara. Back in Philadelphia she and Darren had spent a lot of time at the river. Like sand pouring through a sieve, her joy slid away. She'd shared so many cherished moments with Darren on the shore of the river.

Lesley forced herself to shove thoughts of him from her mind. For the next two weeks she would enjoy herself. Then she would give Darren her decision about whether to move to the East Coast branch of Raiments. And the most important thing she had to do was tell him he had a daughter.

"You think going to the beach is really going to help?" Millie asked Lesley as she helped her pack Dara's things.

"I hope so. I feel so stressed out, Millie."

"If you'd just tell the man the truth, you could cut your stress level in half."

"You don't know that. If I knew for sure, I wouldn't have a problem."

"I remember when you first arrived in L.A. and were looking for a place to stay."

Lesley smiled. "I remember. I had the price of a one-week stay in a cheap motel on Broadway. You were selling dinners for the church."

"Nobody was more surprised than me when you fainted at my feet."

"When I came to and found myself inside the church stretched out on one of the pews, I didn't know I'd find the best friend a person could ever have."

"You became the daughter Morris and I wanted and never had. When he died, you were there for me."

"We were there for each other, Millie. Dara thinks of you as her special grandmother. She loves you as much as I do."

Millie shot her a look of sympathy. "I want everything to go right for you, Lesley."

"I know you do. And it will. I just need this time away, that's all."

"I hope you'll be able to find a solution you can live with. You need peace, girl. And that little angel needs a family."

"I know, I should have tried harder to give her one."

"You couldn't just manufacture a father and a husband. Your heart has to be in it. And yours wasn't, and still isn't, Maybe it's a sign that you should face the past so you can get on with your life. Your happiness may lie with Dara's father."

"You don't understand, Millie."

Millie smiled sagely. "I think I do, but you have to come to that realization on your own."

When Lesley and Dara arrived at the beach house, Greg was still there packing his belongings. He turned and then held out his arms to Dara.

"Hey, girlfriend."

"Greg!" Dara trilled and launched herself at him.

"I didn't think you'd still be here," Lesley said. "If we're rushing you—"

"You're not. How about going down to the wharf for a bite to eat before I head back to my apartment?"

"Can we, Mama?" Dara begged.

With a pair of smoky brown eyes and a pair of glittering dark brown ones staring pleadingly at her, Lesley gave in. "Okay, give us a few minutes to change."

Darren intended to spend the next week at the beach house he'd rented for the remainder of his stay in California. The place was everything the real estate agent promised him it would be. He'd always enjoyed the beach. Before Lesley had… His thoughts strayed to her and the man he'd seen her with at The Race Track. He didn't want to think about her being with Greg Saxon. He'd seen him pass a key to Lesley, and her kissing and hugging the guy.

Lesley was going to Philadelphia with him. Whatever they meant to each other didn't matter. She would just have to forget Greg Saxon. He wasn't sure what he would do once he got her back to Philadelphia, but he knew one thing: she was definitely going.

Like the turbulence of a raging storm, the emotions the woman aroused in him could prove to be just as devastating if he let them. God, he needed to get a grip. Lesley Wells was making him crazy.

That morning he'd seen a woman from behind who looked liked Lesley. It brought back memories of throwing

Frisbees with Lesley at the beach on the Delaware River in Philly. He remembered the disappointment he'd felt when she turned around and it wasn't Lesley.

The woman seemed to never be farther than a thought away. Try as he might, the image of her in a yellow bikini refused to be banished.

"I've had enough, Lesley," he gasped, out of breath from running down a Frisbee she'd purposely tossed into the water.

"But you're so good at fetch and carry," she teased and ran.

"You're going to pay for that, woman." He gave chase, tackling her easily, much too easily. She wanted to be caught. He tickled her until she cried out for mercy. Then he kissed her.

"Your lips taste like salt water," he said. "I'm curious to find out if the rest of you tastes the same."

"We're on a public beach, Darren!"

"You're right, it definitely doesn't coincide with my very private intentions."

Her eyes darkened to the color of pitch.

"I love you, Darren."

"I love you too, Lesley." He kissed her deeply one last time before they headed arm in arm down the beach to his car.

Darren pushed himself up from the beach house steps and strode inside. He couldn't look out at the surf or hear the cry of a sea gull or feel the warming rays of the sun on his body without thinking about the times he and Lesley had spent together.

For the next few days he avoided the water and worked on the plans he had for the Philadelphia branch of Raiments. Soon becoming bored with his self-imposed isolation, he decided to go down to the wharf. He'd gotten the go-sign from his attractive next door neighbor, Regina March, and invited her to come along with him.

He'd forget about Lesley. Regina would make the perfect companion to help him accomplish that.

The sound of laughter assailed Lesley's ears. Surely she must be hearing things. It sounded very much like Darren's voice. She continued to talk to Greg about Cheerful Children's Wear and the plans he and his mother had for it while Dara sipped her strawberry shake.

"I'll be going to England in the spring on a buying trip. Now if you decided to join Cheerful, as its head designer you could come with me. You're sensible as well as knowledgeable about the fabrics needed for active children. Have you ever thought about trying your hand at researching?"

"I see Ava has enlisted you in her latest campaign strategy to get me to join the company."

"You know it wouldn't make her unhappy if you did." He smiled, lowering his voice to a cajoling entreaty.

"Oh, no you don't. I—"

Again the laughter. Lesley turned and locked gazes with Darren.

Darren nearly choked on his drink at the sight of Lesley in deep conversation with Greg Saxon. His eyes journeyed down to the head of the little girl sitting next to her. He wondered whose child she was. He couldn't see her face. Was she Greg Saxon's, Lesley's or theirs together? The question of just what Greg Saxon really meant to Lesley pounded at his brain with the force of a tidal wave.

"Someone you know, Darren?" Regina asked.

He didn't answer.

"It's like that, is it?"

"What do you mean?"

"If you want to cut this short just say so, I'll understand."

"No, I don't want to do that." He smiled at Regina. "Why not join me in another glass of wine?"

"What do you think?" Greg asked Lesley.

"Huh? I'm sorry, Greg, what were you saying?" Lesley asked.

"Forget it, you've got your mind somewhere else," he said, glancing back at Darren's table.

"No, I don't."

"Look, Lesley, I've got to be shoving off anyway." He put down some money on the table. "I'll drive you and Dara back to the beach house."

"Are you almost finished with that, baby?" Lesley asked her daughter.

Dara nodded.

"All right, then we can leave," she said nervously, knowing she and Dara would have to pass right by Darren and his companion.

Lesley grabbed up her purse, then she and her daughter moved to precede Greg out of the restaurant. When they reached the door, Lesley tripped. Greg reached out to steady her with a hand to her waist.

Watching them, Darren's anger blossomed, and he took a deep swallow of his wine.

"Who is she?" Regina asked.

"A woman who works at one of my companies."

"Is that all? I could have sworn there was more to it than that. Her little girl is a sweetheart, isn't she?"

"Yes, she is," Darren said absently, his thoughts on Lesley. "Getting back to what you said, no, not anymore."

"Right. I'm ready to go."

"Look, I didn't mean to ruin things for you."

"You didn't. Maybe another time?"

Back at Ava's beach house, Lesley stood looking out at the ocean through the giant, floor-to-ceiling window. Although it had turned chilly all of a sudden, she knew that more than just the weather was bothering her. She wondered who the woman was with Darren. They appeared to be enjoying each other's company. Was it just a coincidence him being there? Or was he living somewhere nearby? With her?

Why was she so concerned about that? Darren could do what he wanted, the same as she. He could see whomever he wanted, whenever he wanted, the same as she. This woman wasn't the same one she'd seen him with at The Race Track. Who he went out with was none of her business. Why then did the prospect of him being with other women bother her more than his finding out Dara was his child? He was nothing to her now and Dara was everything.

Ava kept her beach house well-stocked with food and drink, so they wouldn't have to go out to eat unless they wanted to. After feeding Dara and putting her to bed, Lesley decided to pour herself a glass of white wine, to relax, she convinced herself, but actually it was to dull the pain.

Would it ever stop hurting?

She suddenly became momentarily drawn back into the echoes of the past. Darren had taken her out to the dream house he was having built for them...

"I can see our kids playing in the sandbox and swaying in the swings. Can't you, sweetheart?" Darren asked Lesley.

Lesley enjoyed seeing the excitement on Darren's face when he was all fired up about something. In this instance about having a family with her.

"Yes, so can I. I envision Darren Taylor III pulling his sister's braids and getting into all kinds of devilment. Jordanna told me that was what you used to do to her when you two were growing up. It'll no doubt be a repeat of like father like son."

"Are you by any chance implying that I was a brat?"

Lesley kissed him. "I'm sure you were an adorable brother."

"You and my sister have grown closer lately, haven't you?"

"Yes. I like her very much."

"You never talk about your family."

"We haven't really been all that close in the last few years. I wish my relationship with my sister was as genial as mine with yours."

"Have you tried telling her how you feel?"

"I always feel intimidated by her for some reason. She's no dragon, don't misunderstand me. It's just that—I don't know."

"How about your parents? Will they be coming to the wedding?"

"I-I don't know."

"Have you even told them about us?"

"I've told them." She had, but she'd neglected to tell them Darren's last name. The looks on their faces when they found out wasn't one she relished seeing. Eventually they would have to know the truth before the newspapers discovered their plans.

All she needed was for an over-eager society photographer to snap a picture of them together. Thus far, she'd managed to avoid that disaster, but she knew it was only a matter of time.

She and Darren had walked over to the house site and stepped onto the foundation. From that vantage point in Palmyra, New Jersey, they had an unobstructed view of both sides of the Delaware River where the Betsy Ross Bridge spanned it.

"I love it here, Darren."

He pulled her into his arms and kissed her. "You know we're standing in our bedroom?"

"Now, Darren."

"Now, Darren, what? We're going to be so happy in this house. Our marriage will be the best on record. It can't help but be because I love you so much, Lesley."

"I love you more."

Lesley shook her head to clear it. That was a long time ago in another life. She wondered what he had done about the house. Had he sold it? Rented it? Or had he kept it? The house had been only half completed when...

Because of Darren her life was in turmoil again. She wanted to tell him about his daughter. But if she did he'd insist on visitation rights, or maybe even want custody. And finally he'd insist more emphatically that she and Dara return to Philadelphia, the one place she never wanted to go back to. Her decision about that was definite now.

Short of kidnapping her—or taking their child—there was no way Darren was going get her to agree to it. He would have to find a replacement for her at Philadelphia Raiments, that's all there was to it. There were probably several assistant designers at Taylor's who would jump at the chance.

The offer from Cheerful Children's Wear was beginning to look better and better. It was still a tough decision to make, though. She'd have to give them her best or not join them at all. It wouldn't be fair to Ava to give anything less.

Lesley was good at what she did for them, but it wasn't the spark she needed to ignite her creativity. It would mean settling. Could she settle?

Oh, God, I have so much weighing on my mind.

TEN

Early the next morning from the steps of the beach house, Lesley watched the beach come alive. Dara was still asleep. She reveled in the salt-sea smell of the ocean, the crunching sound the sand made under the sandaled-feet of passers-by. The soft, probing rays of the sun felt warm and seductive as they beamed gently through the thin material of her blouse to caress her skin.

When Lesley saw Darren jogging up the beach, her first impulse was to dash into the house before he got a look at her and pretend she hadn't seen him. She closed her eyes. No, she wouldn't hide. It was time she introduced the man to his daughter.

Darren's initial reaction to the lovely vision standing on the steps of the beach house was that it couldn't be Lesley. Then when he drew closer, he realized the woman was Lesley. He now knew that seeing her at the wharf was no coincidence.

When he'd checked in with Karen, he'd found out that Lesley had gone home early. He wasn't surprised when she told him the woman in question had taken her vacation. Not requesting it from him was her way of reminding him of her independent nature. As if he needed one.

The woman hadn't to date said what her plans were. He had to have some idea so he could eliminate any obstacles that might pop up. Again he had to ask himself why he wanted her to return to Philly. It wasn't just to make her face what she'd done, was it? God, he wasn't sure of the reason anymore. And maybe you're just not being honest with yourself.

His mind returned to the subject of the previous evening. Where were the man and the little girl? Was it possible the child was not theirs together? The thought that she might be had eaten into his gut like acid. Had it not been for Lesley's betrayal, they could have a child.

"Playing hooky, sweetheart?" he said as he approached the beach house.

He couldn't wait to start in on her, she thought, annoyed by his words. Lesley answered, "Certainly not. Not everyone thinks like you do, Darren," she added tartly.

"Touché. Technically you're still under my authority. Will I have to fire you, sweetheart? Or do you intend to quit?" He could clearly see that the implication that she was a quitter was too much. Finally he was going to get a straight answer from her.

"If you must know, I have an offer for another job. Until now I hadn't seriously considered taking it? Lesley sat down on the top step.

"But now you've made up your mind to go after it." Darren dropped down on the space beside her. "That's interesting. Do they know about what happened in Philadelphia? Ah, I see you haven't told them. What do you think they'll say once they find out?"

"It won't make any difference," she said, straightening her back.

"I wouldn't feel so smug about that, if I were you. No company likes a traitor in their midst, no matter how talented."

Lesley delivered a stinging slap to his cheek. "That's the last time I want to hear that word out of your mouth. I'm not, I repeat, I'm not, and have never been, a traitor."

Ignoring the last part of what she said, he replied, "You just like touching me, so you pretend it's in anger and affronted pride that you slapped me." He grinned. "It won't wash, sweetheart."

Lesley winced.

"The truth really hurts, doesn't it?"

"I guess you'd know more about truth than I would. Right?"

Just who was supposed to be punishing whom? he thought, moving his jaw around. He always said she packed a mean wallop for such a slender woman. Darren laughed.

"I don't see where any of this is funny, Darren."

"You wouldn't. I was just reminded of the time I conned Pete into sampling one of your kisses and you punched him in the arm. I only meant it as a joke, but you hadn't seen it that way. Remember?"

Darren could tell when Lesley's expression softened that she remembered the incident with his cousin.

She smiled. "I doubt if Pete ever forgave me for pulling a charley horse in his arm."

"What about me? You gave me a black eye."

"It wasn't intentional."

"You'd have a hell of a time convincing me of that. I'm the one who had to break out the ice pack and apply it to the abused area. But I have to admit that I enjoyed your loving effort to kiss and make it better."

Darren pulled Lesley into his arms and kissed her. It wasn't any peck on the cheek. He surged into it with a passion that stunned him. Suddenly he was drowning in the ocean of her sensuality.

It had been too long since he'd tasted her heady brand of intoxication. Her body stiffened, seeming at first to be paralyzed as if by a powerful electric shock it couldn't begin to make an instant recovery from.

Darren took full advantage and drew her more fully into his embrace. He felt her reflexive shudder to the intimacy. A confused look came into her eyes at the realization that she had responded so naturally, as though it were your ordinary everyday contact between lovers.

As if against her will, she gave a little lost helpless moan, the vibration catching him in a sensual tangle of emotional need.

Lesley tore her mouth away from his and inhaled deep gulps of air. She looked at Darren as though he had poleaxed her, then jerked out of his embrace, shaking her head. Tears spilled down her cheeks.

"Oh, God, why did you have to find me? Why?"

Emotionally overwrought, she got up, ready to rush into the house when the door opened.

"Why are you crying, Mama?"

As Dara looked at the man on the porch, Lesley knew the instant realization dawned in her daughter's eyes. And she groaned, then whispered. "Not like this."

"Lesley?" Darren's voice faded.

This time it was his turn to feel poleaxed, Lesley thought, because at that moment the same revealing light of realization that dawned on the child dawned on her father.

"You're my daddy, aren't you?" Dara smiled. "My name is Dara Ann Evans."

Darren swallowed hard and swayed unsteadily on his feet. He looked disbelievingly at Lesley. What he saw in her eyes was not smug triumph, but an emotion so raw and elemental he couldn't lend it any description. He didn't understand. But damn it, he would.

It was obvious to him on up-close inspection that the child was his. He looked to Lesley. She had some serious explaining to do, but not now. He wanted to meet his daughter.

"Yes, I'm your father," he answered gently.

For an instant, what to do, what to say barraged Lesley; then she cleared her throat.

"Dara Ann, this is your father, Darren Taylor."

Darren was in awe that this beautiful child could actually be his. Her eyes were the same shade of brown as his own. The hair coarse, but curly, was exactly like his.

"How old are you, little sweetheart?"

Lesley chewed on her lower tip and stole a look at Darren.

"Five, but I'll be six next week."

Darren shifted his gaze to Lesley. She had to have known she was pregnant long before she left Philadelphia. Which meant that she knew and purposely chose not to tell him.

Rage swept through him with the speed of a fire blazing through a dry forest as he continued to eye Lesley's anxious face. She'd kept this precious child from him all these years. To his way of thinking, it had to be the ultimate of all betrayals.

When he returned his attention to Dara, he had control of his emotions and let the instant love that radiated through him shine. But what did he say to this child as to why he hadn't been there for her?

"I've dreamed about you since Mama showed me your picture."

Tears stung Darren's eyelids. "What did you dream?"

"That you and me and Mama were a family." Dara looked at her mother. "I didn't tell her 'cause when I talk about wanting to get to know you she gets sad." Dara walked over to her father, tilted her chin, flickering her gaze up at him. "Can I give you a hug?"

Darren, surprised yet elated by her words, bent down and opened his arms. "You sure can."

Dara launched her tiny body into his arms. He closed his eyes and squeezed her tight, letting the baby-shampoo scent of her hair and the bubble bath fragrance of her body waft up his nostrils. After a few moments he felt her squirm uncomfortably in his embrace.

"I'm sorry, I didn't mean to hug you so tight," he said, releasing her.

"It's all right," she said matter-of-factly. "Mama does it all the time."

When Darren looked at Lesley, her insides lurched at the expression of longing and male pride on his face. At first when she'd seen the anger, it had unnerved her and made her worry as to what he would do now that he knew the truth. At least that part of the truth he'd let her explain. He had yet to listen to and learn what really happened six years ago. Would he ever be ready for that?

Dara left her father's arms and walked over to her mother.

"You gonna fix us some breakfast, Mama? I'm kinda hungry." She smiled at Darren. "You hungry, too, Daddy? Is it all right if I call you that?"

Darren coughed to clear the emotion clogging his throat. "You sure can, little sweetheart," he said, his voice husky.

Lesley smiled at Dara. "It's unanimous, then. Why don't you go wash up and get dressed."

Dara looked at Darren. "You won't go away, will you, Daddy?"

"No, little sweetheart, I won't ever go away again. I'll be right here waiting for you to join me—us." He glanced at Lesley.

Dara gazed in Lesley's direction with a look of leery suspicion, and though reluctantly did as her mother said.

"She's beautiful, Lesley. You've done a great job with her."

"I never wanted to keep her from you, Darren."

"But you have for over five years. Did you hate me that much, Lesley?"

She faltered under the accusation and hurt in his tone. "I think we'd better go inside and finish this."

Darren followed her into the beach house.

As he sat quietly at the kitchen counter, Lesley studied him as she took the makings for breakfast from the refrigerator.

"You're a lot of things to me, but I never hated you, Darren. I've always loved you."

He gazed up at her. "Well, Lesley."

"You've got to understand how I was feeling after the shock of the accusations lodged against me and the condemnation of your family. And most of all, from you."

"After finding out your family had the exact same designs as the ones you…the ones that were stolen, how else did you expect me to react?"

"You could have trusted in me and in my love for you, no matter what."

"I want her, Lesley."

She gasped. But before she could respond, Dara walked into the room and shifted her gaze from one parent to the other.

"Are you and Daddy mad at each other?"

"No, little sweetheart. We were just talking, that's all," Darren covered smoothly.

"Oh." Dara smiled up at Lesley. "Mama, are you going to fix us some special pancakes?"

"Special pancakes?" Darren asked.

"Um-hum."

Darren grinned. "What's so special about them, little sweetheart?"

"They're special 'cause Mama only makes 'em on Saturday morning. We sit down in front of the TV and watch our favorite cartoon shows while we eat 'em."

Lesley watched the expression on Darren's face. It was one a child would make after finding out he'd been left out of his own birthday celebration. She felt guilty. Arthur had been right. She should have contacted Darren right after their daughter was born. Better still, she should have told him about the baby when she found out she was pregnant.

Though she'd made a lot of mistakes, she hadn't betrayed Darren in the way he believed she had, Lesley thought as she mixed the pancakes.

Where did they go from here? What did Darren have in mind for their daughter? What did he have in mind for her? Of one thing she was sure: Knowing him as she did, there would be something.

Darren smiled. "Well, since it just happens to be Saturday, you want her to do just that, my little sweetheart?"

"Yeah, we can all watch cartoons together. Can't we, Mama?"

"Yes, we can, baby, just give me a few minutes to cook the pancakes."

"Where do you keep your syrup?" Darren asked.

"I'll get it, Daddy." Dara climbed up on a stool, leaned across the counter and reached up into the cabinet to retrieve the bottle.

During the morning array of "Teenage Mutant Ninja Turtles" to "Rug Rats," Lesley monitored Darren's actions and expressions, trying to gauge how he was taking things. He seemed genuinely fascinated by Dara. But he didn't give away what was he thinking. She pondered this as she did the last of the dishes.

A stab of jealousy at the instant rapport developing between father and daughter pierced her. Darren could so effortlessly charm any female over the age of one. She didn't know exactly how she felt at the moment A part of her wanted to go to him and melt in his arms. Yet another resented the ease with which he had insinuated himself into their lives. How did he feel about Lesley the woman?

Darren saw the worried look in Lesley's eyes. She had every right to be, but not in the way she imagined. A plan had begun to form that included the three of them. And heaven help her if she refused to go along with it.

Lesley intercepted the warning light in his eyes that signaled that Darren had made some kind of decision. As to what it might be, she didn't know, but she ached to find out. She could tell that he had no intention of revealing it until he was ready.

Darren swung his daughter up into his arms. "How would you like to go to Disneyland, little sweetheart?"

"Today! Right now!"

"Um-hmm."

Dara's eyes lit up like a flashing neon sign.

"Can we, Mama?"

"You've already gone there twice."

"But not with my Daddy, I haven't," she said proudly. "Mama, please." Seeing those devastating Taylor eyes Lesley always found so hard to resist flickering up at her was her undoing.

"Three is a charm, I guess," Lesley conceded.

"My rental car is back at the beach house. If after I've showered and changed, you want to go in it, we can."

"We can go in my car. It's no problem. Just let me get my purse."

In her bedroom Lesley sank down on the bed and sighed. They'd be spending the entire day with Darren. Was she ready for this? Ready or not, she had to go. She couldn't hurt that little girl in there, and Darren knew it. Maybe it wouldn't be so bad. She could see a mental picture of them walking through the amusement park hand in hand like a real family.

Her heart ached because she and Darren hadn't known any of that. The fairy tale life the two of them had once planned never materialized, and now... What about now?

Lesley grabbed her purse off the nightstand and went back into the living room. She volunteered to do the driving when they were ready to leave after stopping at Darren's beach house. Dara and her father couldn't be more pleased, because it gave them more time to get acquainted.

It was nearly two o'clock in the morning by the time the tired trio returned to the beach house. Darren carried their daughter into the house and on through to her bedroom. While he laid her on the bed, Lesley stood in the doorway smiling and hugging the giant stuffed replica of Mickey Mouse he'd bought for Dara.

Darren looked up in time to catch a glimpse of Lesley's smile before she moved into the room to put the stuffed toy on a chair.

"I'll undress her," she said, her voice soft with motherly love.

He eased off the bed, allowing Lesley room to work. When she had finished undressing Dara and slid the comforter over the sleeping child, a pang of loss at what he had missed clawed through Darren. He should have been included in his child's upbringing from day one, and he resented the fact that he hadn't been given the chance. He'd always wanted a child of his own. Now he had one. It wasn't too late to have the family he'd dreamed of. He could tell it was what his daughter wanted. Was it possible that Lesley could want it too?

He followed Lesley out of the room and caught up with her in the hallway.

"We need to talk."

"I know, but I'm dead tired, Darren."

He could see it was true. There were dark shadows beneath her eyes. She looked about ready to drop. He led her into the other bedroom.

Lesley glanced at the clock on the nightstand. It was too late for Darren to be walking down the beach at this hour. She gazed at the bed and then at him. Surely he didn't expect to...

Darren started taking off his shirt.

Lesley's eyes widened. "Surely you don't plan to—"

"Better get ready for bed, sweetheart."

"Darren, I..." Her voice faded.

"The bed's big enough for two. Don't worry. I won't attempt to jump your bones tonight, Lesley, unless of course you want me to."

Her face heated and she grabbed her nightshirt off the bed and headed for the bathroom, then turned.

"The couch is free." She didn't wait to hear his answer.

Darren laughed softly to himself. If he had his way that wouldn't be an alternative she would ever have to worry about. He knew Lesley was a very passionate woman. He was willing to wait for what he wanted.

What he craved was a Lesley who desired him as much as he desired her. He wanted his daughter, with her mother, but Lesley didn't have to know that. They were meant to be together, and he intended to see that it ended up that way. As to Lesley's betrayal, he would deal with that when the time came. Right now, all he could manage was one step at a time, one day at a time.

Darren lay beneath the covers in just his briefs when Lesley returned to the bedroom. Judging from the look on her face, Darren knew she hadn't expected him to be in her bed, but on the living room couch as she had suggested.

He grinned when he saw her eyes rove his exposed chest. He guessed that she thought he was naked underneath the covers and remembered how he looked that way. Let her remember. Hell, he hadn't forgotten a damned thing. The satiny-soft, enticing warmth of her skin and the beguiling scent of the perfume she wore or the silky texture of her hair that made him feel as though he were dipping his fingers in a pot of liquid black gold.

Lesley's stomach tensed at the sight of Darren's bare chest. She gasped inwardly, taking in the outline of the flat scrub-board stomach and then lower to where the sheet provocatively blanketed the ridge of his manhood beneath the covers. Was he really naked between the sheets? she wondered, swallowing hard as memories of the passion they once shared came flooding back to remind her of the man Darren was.

An aching desire began to tingle through her breasts and by the time it reached her loins, it was a sensual throb.

"I don't think that you should be—"

"Be what?" Darren said in a goading yet sexy voice.

On impulse she swept back the covers, and on finding that he wasn't naked, she didn't know whether to feel relieved or disappointed.

Darren noted the look of confusion and/or frustration that crinkled her brows. Then his gaze centered on her thin nightshirt. She was sexier in it than if she were completely naked. He desired her, God, how he desired her, but he knew it wasn't the right time. There were too many things left unresolved between them. They needed to get to know each other all over again before becoming intimate. He pulled her into the covers, enfolding her in the intimacy of his embrace.

He felt her stiffen. "Go to sleep, Lesley. When I make love to you there won't be a doubt in your mind as to what you want. You'll want me, need me as you've never wanted or needed me before."

Lesley remained silent, thinking as she lay caught in the enveloping web of his embrace. When Darren's even breathing said he was at last asleep, she mentally relaxed, even though physically her body still languished in the afterglow of aroused passion.

It seemed to her that Darren had committed to memory her responses to his lovemaking, recalling them to mind when he needed to, knowing exactly when to advance, when to retreat, how long to wait for surrender. She shivered, closing her eyes, summoning back in vivid detail how she used to respond to the glory of surrender to his passion.

Then the cold shower of reality splashed over her. Was he really waiting for that? After what he had done to her, surely he didn't expect her to just... Suddenly the bitter-sweet recollections of the pain and hurt he inflicted converged in force to remind her why they had parted in the first place.

He had known how much she loved him, and yet he had believed that she could betray him. Hot tears stung her eyelids, but she willed them away. She had more than just herself and Darren to consider. There was Dara now. What she needed, what was best for her, had to come first.

Passing up an advantage was not in Darren's character. She knew he certainly wouldn't hesitate where his child was concerned. Where would that leave Lesley? She didn't want to think about it. She eased out of the intimacy of Darren's embrace.

ELEVEN

The smell of coffee brewing the next morning invaded Lesley's nostrils, aromatically insisting she awaken.

Darren. She yawned, then glanced sleepily at the clock on the nightstand. It was almost eleven o'clock.

Eleven o'clock!

Lesley shot abruptly to a sitting position, swept back the covers and slid off the bed. She pulled on her robe and headed for the kitchen. When she reached the doorway, she found Darren busily at work fixing himself and Dara, who sat attentively observing him from her perch on a kitchen stool, breakfast.

A pang of jealousy shot through Lesley, and she turned away and headed for the bathroom. While she showered, she ran over in her mind the scene between father and daughter and wondered why she should feel jealous. After all, she'd had Dara to herself since she was born. Dara had been her whole life, her work coming second.

Why the resentment because Darren was spending time with his daughter? She couldn't be afraid of losing Dara, could she? Then why was the concept of sharing her with him so disturbing?

Darren observed the agitated expression on Lesley's face when she'd entered the kitchen and speculated about the cause. He'd been on his best behavior with her, so it couldn't be that. Should he reveal his plans for them? Or should he wait?

"Good morning." He smiled.

"Me and Daddy been up a long time waiting for you, Mama."

"I see you have breakfast all ready. It's nice to be pampered, but you really should've woke me up."

"Daddy said you were tired and we should let you sleep."

When Lesley looked to Darren with a tender expression warming her features, his insides shifted like the ground during an earthquake. Before he could bask fully in its heat, that look disappeared.

"Thank you," she said, frowning at the conspiratorial glances passing between father and daughter. "All right, what are you two up to?"

"Daddy thought we should have a picnic on the beach. After we went to his house to get his swimsuit and some more other stuff, we stopped at the deli on the wharf and bought a picnic basket."

Lesley glanced in Darren's direction. He knew the significance a picnic on the beach had for her. He was forcing her to remember what she had been missing all these years. As if she could forget the invigorating late evening swims and the midnight to dawn loving as they lay cozily wrapped in blankets on the sand. Yes, he was pulling out all the stops.

"Daddy said that you and him used to have picnics all the time before I was borned."

"He's right, we did," she uttered, an oddly softening note infusing her voice.

Darren felt his heart jerk at the wistful expression that seeped onto Lesley's face. What did it mean? Had she guessed what he really had in mind? Did she have any idea to what extent he was prepared to go to obtain that end? No, he was sure she didn't have a clue. She had no idea that he'd come across the sketches she'd done for Cheerful Children's Wear and now knew it was the job offer she was considering taking rather than joining the Philadelphia branch of Raiments.

Lesley saw the determined glint in his eyes and knew instinctively it portended trouble. Maybe not, there could be any number of reasons why he had that look. The thought deviled her mind like a rash at the peak of irritation.

"Are we ready to go, Daddy?"

Darren turned to Lesley. "We are, aren't we, sweetheart?"

She was trapped. Darren had slyly used their daughter to ambush her. And was now emotionally blackmailing her to do as he wanted. "Yes," she answered in a low, resigned voice.

Darren grimaced. Everything was going his way, yet why didn't he feel triumphant?

Lesley spread the blankets out on a fairly isolated strip of beach they'd found. She breathed in the smell of sunshine and salt, reveling in the soothing sounds of the wind and the surf as she watched the foaming waves wash over the sand. The beach always made her feel free and exhilarated.

Darren's breath caught in his throat at her reaction to her surroundings. By engineering this picnic on the beach he had effectively marauded his own heart. By conjuring up the joy they'd once shared, he'd also conjured up the pain they'd also suffered.

Dara wore a swimsuit underneath her tank top and shorts and couldn't wait to peel out of them and head for the water's edge.

"You know the rules, young lady," Lesley called out after her.

"Yes, Mama. I won't go out too far." She turned to her father and, frowning, cupped her hand over her eyes to deflect the glare of the sun. "Wanna come, Daddy?"

"In a minute, little sweetheart. I need to talk to your mother first, okay?"

"Okay." Without further hesitation she splashed giggling and sputtering into the cool, shallow water that spumed over the sand.

Darren arched concerned brows. "She a good swimmer?"

"Like a fish, like…"

"Like the both of us," Darren finished simply.

He quickly stripped down to his swim trunks, reached inside his bag and pulled out a red Frisbee, then rushed to join his daughter.

A yearning look accompanied the tears suddenly that welled in Lesley's eyes when Darren brought out the Frisbee and threw it to Dara.

"Come on, Lesley. We need you."

"Yeah, Mama," Dara urged. "Come on, we need you."

Lesley blinked back the tears, then abandoned her shirt and shorts to join them.

"No more, you guys, I'm wiped out," Lesley called out in a hoarse, breathless voice as she stumbled toward the blankets an hour later.

"Coward," Darren shouted.

"You'd better believe it."

"I think we should join your mother, little sweetheart," he called to Dara.

"Aw, do we have to?"

Darren quirked his eyebrows and screwed up his lips.

"Okay." Dara conceded defeat.

Darren smiled as he waited for her; then they both headed for the blankets.

Observing them as they ate, Lesley felt the beginning of a strong bond of family closeness that she'd always longed for since she was a child not much older than Dara. After she met and fell in love with Darren it was within her grasp, but she'd lost it. Did she dare hope that she could get it back?

Darren seemed to want it back too. Or was she deceiving herself? She was sure he had wanted revenge when he first came to L.A. But now, after coming to know his daughter, he'd changed his mind. Could she chance trusting him? He might be using Dara as a way to even the score. Darren could be ruthless, but could he be that cruel?

"You'd better get some of this, Lesley, before greedy here eats it all up," he said, ducking his head and stuffing his mouth full of potato salad.

"Daddy's the one eating it all." Dara giggled, throwing a stack of napkins at her father.

Lesley smiled; it was as though they'd had that genial rapport all along. What had she done by leaving Philadelphia? She had to keep reminding herself that the destruction of their relationship and her pregnancy weren't the only factors that contributed to her flight: Someone had gone to a lot of trouble to make her appear the traitor. That someone could be dangerous.

Darren studied Lesley for a moment, wondering what made her smile turn into a frown. He would give anything to know what she was thinking.

"We've had enough sun and surf for one day." Lesley gathered up the used paper plates and dirty napkins to put into a trash bag.

"Do we have to go?" Dara pleaded with her mother, then turned imploring dark eyes on Darren. "Do we, Daddy?"

"You're a little manipulator, aren't you, my little sweetheart?" Darren grinned.

"Like father, like daughter," Lesley said in a low voice.

Darren heard it and looked her way.

In a confused voice Dara asked. "What's a 'nipulater?'"

"Manipulator," he corrected her. "Let's just say it's a person who knows how to make people do what he or she wants them to do."

"Oh." She guiltily lowered her head.

"I get the feeling you know how to do that very well. Am I right?"

Dara blushed, but didn't answer.

Darren grinned. "I thought so."

They were so much alike in ways other than looks, Lesley thought. As they drove back to the beach house, she wondered what would happen once this idyll ended.

Back at the beach house, Lesley rushed Dara into the bathroom to wash away the sand that seemed to have escaped the rinsing spray of the outside shower faucet on the beach. She insisted that Darren use the stall shower off the den.

Lesley was in the process of making a pot of coffee when Darren came out of the shower with a towel draped around his neck. Her breath caught in her throat at the sight of his gleaming, still-wet hair and the beads of water that glistened on his bare chest. Her eyes instinctively dropped lower to where his shorts clung damply to his narrow hips and muscular thighs.

"Now it's your turn," he said in a low sexy voice. Lesley shook her head to clear it.

"What? My turn?" "To shower."

"Dara may come out before I'm through."

"If she does, I'll be here for her, as I intend to be from now on. Go ahead, sweetheart, we'll be fine."

Lesley made to leave the room, but glanced back at Darren several times on her way out. She wasn't sure she liked the takeover feeling his words suggested.

Darren was telling Dara a story when Lesley returned. His soothing soft tones, coupled with the gentle massage of his long slender fingers at her temple, had all but put the little girl to sleep. Lesley remembered the times he'd used those same fingers to elicit moans of pleasure from her when he'd made love to her. At the very thought of it, the nerves in the pit of Lesley's stomach fluttered like the agitated beating of hummingbird wings.

Darren's eyes drifted over her at that moment and his expression immediately changed, his eyes glittering dark and dangerous. Her mouth felt dry all of a sudden, and Lesley quickly headed for the coffeemaker. How well she knew that look. He wanted her.

"Would you like a cup?" she asked in an attempt to derail the sensual machinations she saw lurking below the surface, lying in wait to consume her.

"Yes, as soon as I put this tired little minx to bed. Then we need to talk." He gently gathered his daughter into his arms, treating her as though she were the most precious gift in the world to him. He draped her across his chest, letting her nestle her head lovingly in the cradle of his collarbone.

Now that the sensual nuance was gone from his voice and the look of desire seemed to have cooled, Lesley tensed, wondering what Darren had in mind to discuss. She paced back and forth before the floor-to-ceiling window in the living room, waiting for him to come back.

Darren entered the room and just stood watching Lesley for a few moments.

"Relax, and stop acting like Daniel awaiting his final appointment in the lion's den."

"Are you the lion lying in wait to—?"

"Devour you? No," he said, advancing closer.

Lesley took a step back. "Revenge, then?"

"Sit down, Lesley."

She gazed into his face, looking for any sign of what he intended for her. Seeing none, she let out an anxious sigh, then walked over to the couch and sat down.

Darren eased down beside her.

His clean, heady, male scent, mingled with the heat emanating from his body, seemed to reach out and stroke her senses. God, she wished he would put his shirt on. He was so close, too close, too dangerous. She couldn't breathe. Lesley tightened the belt on her robe. She wanted to move closer, but the urge to inch away for her own safety was greater.

"I have to admit that, at first, revenge was my sole purpose. I wanted to hurt you the way you'd hurt me. I wanted you to pay for your sins. Then I saw our daughter and knew that you had to have suffered already. It couldn't have been easy raising a child alone in a strange city. You've done one hell of a job."

"Thank you."

"You look surprised."

"Well, I am."

"I'm not a monster, Lesley. I do have feelings. I think I understand why you left the way you did. You were too ashamed of what you'd done and couldn't face up to the consequences of your actions, so you ran away."

Lesley shot to her feet. "That wasn't the reason. Your distrust and belief that I could betray you was the deciding factor that influenced me to leave Philadelphia."

"You talk to me about trust when you let me wonder whether you had ever really loved me." He circled her upper arms with his hands and pulled her toward him. "How do you think that made me feel, huh?"

Lesley moved her head to the side, away from the glowering intensity she saw in his eyes.

"When we discovered that the designs were missing and everything pointed to you as the guilty person, I felt hurt, used and betrayed. It's all irrelevant now because when I saw you again I wanted you, and I'm prepared to do anything to get you back."

"Even though you believe I betrayed you?" she said incredulously.

"Yes."

"I don't understand."

"Believe me, I don't want to want you, but I can't seem to help myself." He released her arms. "So I maneuvered things to force you to come back to Philadelphia with me. When you resisted, it made me more determined than ever to make it happen. Then to discover that you hadn't entirely destroyed all of my dreams—that you had given birth to our child, our beautiful daughter... I knew then that I didn't care what you had done. I wanted you, and I wanted our child. I wanted that life you'd cheated us all out of."

"But, Darren, I—we can't—"

"Are you serious about Greg Saxon?"

She wanted to lie and say that she was, but she couldn't.

"No. We're just friends."

"Then there's no problem. Right? No reason why we can't be a family."

"It's not that simple, and you know it. You might desire me, but you don't love or trust me anymore."

"We owe our daughter a family life, a normal family life, Lesley. I think we should get married. I'm willing to overlook what you did."

"Maybe I'm not willing to forgive you."

"Forgive me!" A muscle twitched in his jaw and his voice rose. Then he spit out, "Forgive me? For what? You were the one who gave free rein to whatever demon it was that drove you to steal from Taylor's in the first place. It was you who turned our lives into a living hell."

"No, I didn't, Darren. You were wrong to believe I was guilty back then, just as you are now. And you're badly mistaken if you think I'll let you emotionally blackmail me into marrying you by using Dara."

"I'm not doing that. We belong together, damn it." He hauled her to his chest and stared purposefully into her eyes, then lowered his mouth to hers. He groaned as he parted her lips, sliding his tongue between them, drawing from their sweetness.

Mouth to mouth, the contact affected Lesley like instant shock therapy treatment, and she was unable to resist the tingling excitement that undulated through her body, pervading her senses, storming her heart.

When Darren deepened the kiss her vulnerable inner self seemed to melt. The feel of his long slender fingers moving erotically over the thin material covering her breasts made her tremble and suck in her breath.

Lesley tore her lips from his. "Darren, please."

He swiftly recaptured her mouth, gently kneading her bottom lip with his teeth while at the same time his fingers loosened the belt on her robe.

"Oh, Lesley, my God, woman, how I've missed this, missed you," he murmured before covering a nipple with his mouth.

Her skin was on fire, her brain languishing in exquisite sensations as he lowered her to the couch. Her fingers slid in circular motions on his sweat-dampened shoulders and muscular biceps. His male scent penetrated her nostrils, driving her to the brink of madness.

Although her body clamored for more, her mind fought to escape this all-out attack on her senses. She should put a stop to this, but how could she when she so desperately wanted him to continue? This is crazy, she kept telling herself. How could she feel two such opposing emotions at the same time? What was happening to her? Was she losing her mind? What was she thinking?

You're not thinking at all right now, and you know it. You're feeling, Lesley, and enjoying everything he's doing to you.

That splash of reality was like a dash of cold water on the desire he'd kindled. This man could be an emotionally dangerous element that could wreak havoc with a woman's equilibrium. She had to keep reminding herself of that. The realization lent her strength to pull away from him.

"Let me up, Darren," she said in a low yet firm voice.

So carried away by his own emotions, he didn't hear her at first and continued to rain kisses on her breasts. When

Lesley repeated her words, they finally sank in. With a groan of frustration, he lifted his weight a fraction off her.

"You want me inside you as much as I want to be there, sweetheart. Why did you stop me?"

"Because we'd just be having sex?"

"Just having sex!" Her words were like a slap in the face. He raised himself completely off her, and surging to his feet, glowered down at her. Had what was beginning to happen between them meant so little to her that she would relegate it to just having sex? He was furious. It meant more than that to him, damn it.

"Go to sleep in your cold bed, Lesley. I'll take the couch."

She got up. "And do what? Stay in here and smolder?" she said as a parting shot before marching into the bedroom and shutting the door none too gently behind her.

He considered not letting her words pass, following her into the bedroom and seeing who ended up 'smoldering' as she put it. But he wouldn't do it. He knew it wasn't the way to convince her to marry him, although he wasn't exactly sure what it would take to convince her.

Then suddenly a thought came to him. There were many kinds of sweeteners. He'd venture to guess that there were just as many ways to sweeten an obstinate woman, and he intended to find the right one for Lesley. With that encouraging thought, he lay down on the couch and slept.

TWELVE

Lesley found sleep elusive. Her nerves were on edge and her body complained about being aroused and not allowed to experience relief. By the time she finally did manage to fall asleep, it was almost dawn, and she ended up over-sleeping the next morning.

When she entered the kitchen, Lesley found Darren and Dara sitting at the kitchen table with their heads together making plans for the day.

"We're glad you're up, Mama. Me and Daddy are going to the L.A. Zoo, and we want you to come with us," Dara trilled excitedly.

Lesley cast Darren a questioning glance. When he flashed her an angelic grin, she molded her lips into a parody of a smile. She knew what he was up to. He was still pushing her, using their daughter as the bulldozer. God, he was devious.

"You do want to come, don't you, Mama?"

"Of course I do, baby. Just let me eat some breakfast and dress. It's been a while since we've been around wild animals."

"Wild animals are the most interesting kind. Don't you agree, Lesley? They're never predictable."

"And the tame ones are?"

"Mama, you'd better hurry up so we can leave."

Lesley glanced at Darren, but said to Dara, "You're right, baby. I'd best get moving."

As they made their way from one animal cage to another, eating ice cream bars and drinking lemonade, Darren and Lesley became more aware of the importance of spending this time with their child. Seeing the joy on her face made being together all the more precious and meaningful, Lesley admitted, although she didn't approve of the way Darren had manipulated the situation.

Darren found excuses for putting his arms around Lesley, covering it with another one of the devastating smiles in his endless repertoire. He could tell by the look in her eyes that he hadn't fooled Lesley for a minute, even though she hadn't tried to move his arm away.

He stifled a laugh when they went into the snake house and Lesley cringed as a snake uncoiled against the window in front of them. She unconsciously moved closer to Darren.

Dara giggled. "It can't hurt you, Mama, it's behind the glass."

"I know that, smarty. I just can't stand snakes, that's all."

"If they got out my daddy would protect us. Wouldn't you?" Dara looked up at her father, an awing admiration lighting her face.

Lesley's heart lurched at the poignancy of the scene. Darren's parental pride and love for his child shone in his eyes, causing tears to push against her lashes. He shifted his gaze, unexpectedly catching her off guard, the heat in his look glowing hot and sensual. He wanted her. She wanted him too. Tingles of excitement passed through her body at his touch. The familiar intensity of unforgettable passion began to build between them like steam in a boiler. It was almost as though they were alone.

"They gonna get mushy?" a small boy who stopped close to Dara to watch asked.

"I sure hope so," Dara replied with feeling.

The children's voices brought reality rushing back to the pair. And although Darren removed his hands and Lesley blinked and moved away, the aura of passion remained, reminding them of how it had once been between them, but was no longer.

Lesley guessed from the momentary flicker of sadness in Darren's eyes that he hadn't planned what had just happened between them. Was it possible that he wanted her for herself, not merely because she was the mother of his child?

He doesn't trust you Lesley. When are you going to get that through your head? an inner voice chided.

When he saw the anguished look on Lesley's face, Darren suggested they leave.

Dara started to protest, but then subsided into silence as though she too had sensed that the rare moment of closeness between her parents had slipped away.

The ride home passed in silence. Lesley restricted her gaze to the side window while Dara slept on the back seat.

Darren sneaked glances at Lesley, trying to guess what she was feeling. Obviously, what had passed between them was still on her mind. He hoped that he had conveyed to her how much he wanted her and how much he wanted them to be together. But what if he hadn't? There was time.

After all, Lesley worked for him. He could extend her vacation if he wanted to, to accomplish his goal.

Lesley caught glimpses of Darren out the corner of her eye and wondered what he was planning next. There was no doubt in her mind that that was what he was doing.

By the time they reached the beach house, Dara had woken up.

"You hungry, baby?" Lesley asked.

"Can we go to the pizza place?"

"Don't you ever get tired of eating pizza? Never mind, don't answer that."

"Can we, please?" she pleaded.

"Sounds good to me," Darren put in.

"I'm obviously out-voted. Let's go to the Spaghetti Factory."

After they got back to the beach house, Lesley put a tired Dara to bed. When she returned to the living room, Darren was waiting with two glasses of wine.

"I'm not sure I should have any," she said, remembering how alcohol had always affected her in the past.

Darren smiled knowingly. "It's just one glass, Lesley. I thought that maybe you needed it to relax."

"What makes you think I'm not relaxed?"

"Admit it, what happened at the zoo threw you for a loop. It's all right. I felt the same way. The chemistry between us is still alive and well. Why deny it? Why fight against it?" He handed Lesley a glass of wine, and she reluctantly accepted it.

After a few sips she put it down. Darren poured himself another and watched Lesley pace back and forth before the window. He finished his wine and set the glass down next to hers and joined her at the window.

Lesley didn't hear him walk up, but she felt his presence as he came to within inches of her.

He turned her around to face him. Seeing no protest in the dark depths of her eyes, he bent his head and kissed her. She returned the kiss with ardor.

"Lesley."

"Darren, don't expect too much from that kiss."

He said softly, his voice having grown husky, "A kiss is only the first link in the chain. It takes a joint effort if things are to go beyond that point. On my part, I want it to, Lesley." He caressed her cheek. "What about you?"

She tensed. "Darren—"

He kissed her again, deepening it this time, stroking the sensitive insides of her mouth with his tongue. Feeling her body relax, he reveled in the low, arousing moan that escaped her throat.

When his fingers moved to lower the straps on her sundress and caress her naked breasts, Lesley found it impossible to resist and leaned into him. Just as she reached the point of surrendering to the urgings of her body, Darren lifted the straps back over her shoulders.

"It's been a long day, Lesley."

"Yes, it has." She sighed, disappointed that he'd put a stop to their lovemaking, but she managed to gain control over her chaotic emotions.

"I think it's time I went back to my beach house. But I'll be back first thing in the morning."

"What've you got planned for tomorrow?" she said, almost afraid to ask.

Darren grinned. "I think I'll let it be a surprise." He headed for the door. "Sleep well, sweetheart." Then he was gone.

As she watched him walk out to his car, Lesley frowned in confusion. Moments ago he had her at the point of no return and he knew it, but he hadn't pressed his advantage. Why? It wasn't like him to back away from what he wanted. And make no mistake about it, he had wanted her. So why? She just didn't understand him. She wondered if she ever would.

The next morning Darren arrived early and they had breakfast together. He noticed that Dara was very quiet.

"How would my two best girls like to take a trip with me to San Francisco?"

Dara's expression perked up as if by magic, then she looked to her mother. "Do we want to go, Mama?"

"I—"

"I'd like to show you both Taylor's San Francisco branch."

"Taylor's?" Dara asked. "What's that?"

Lesley turned to the sink, started washing the breakfast dishes and explained over her shoulder, "It's part of the company your father and his family own."

Dara's eyes widened. "You mean I get to see where you work, Daddy?"

"Ah, not quite. The main branch of the company is in Philadelphia."

"Can we go there, too?"

Darren saw the way Lesley's shoulders tensed. "It's kind of far away, but I hope to show it to you one day soon."

Lesley felt Darren's eyes on her back.

"That's in the future, though," he added. "Now, you two get a move on. Our flight is scheduled to leave LAX at twelve o'clock."

THIRTEEN

Lesley couldn't help being impressed by what she saw. She had to admit that the designers in the San Francisco branch of Taylor's were very talented, but Lesley felt confident that she was better and itched to put pencil to paper and rearrange some of the designs.

She looked up and saw Darren watching her. He knew what she was feeling. He was giving her a taste of what it could be like to design for the Raiments' East Coast branch. This had to be part of his scheme to get her to move to Philadelphia. Didn't it?

Darren crossed over to where their daughter sat in deep contemplation of her artwork.

"Could it be we have a budding designer in the making?' he asked Lesley.

Dara looked up at her father and grinning shyly, held up her drawing for his perusal.

"Do you like it, Daddy?' she asked.

"I certainly do, my little sweetheart,' Darren answered, holding it up. He stepped over to where Lesley sat at a desk reviewing the sketches of the projected spring line. "So what do you think?"

Lesley took the drawing and thoughtfully examined it. 'Yes, I like it. It's very good."

"If I get good enough, you think Daddy'll let me work for him someday?"

"It's possible, if you're still interested by that time."

"Your mother's right. I don't want to push you into anything. I want the talent, if it's there, to come naturally."

Lesley thought about how her family had insisted that she fit into a specific mold. She would never be that kind of parent to her child. And she could tell that Darren wouldn't either. She had to admire that about him.

He studied the look on Lesley's face and wondered what prompted it. Had he scored any points toward his goal of getting them back together, in every way?

Darren took them to dinner at Fisherman's Wharf. "See the sun starting to set behind the Golden Gate Bridge, Dara?" Darren pointed it out.

"The sun looks like a giant orange ball. It's so pretty I wish I could touch it." She sighed, "Can we go across the bridge, Daddy?"

"I don't see why not" He gazed at Lesley. "What do you say?"

Lesley saw the eager expectation on her daughter's face. "I say let's do it."

Darren smiled his thanks, then swung Dara up in his arms. A few minutes later he hailed a taxi and they climbed inside. As the taxi crossed the bridge, Darren captivated Dara with stories about the bridge, the history of the city, San Francisco Bay and the island of Alcatraz.

By the time the plane touched down at LAX, Dara, Lesley and Darren were three very exhausted people. After putting Dara to bed, Lesley headed for her bedroom. When she saw that Darren had fallen asleep in her bed, she just smiled, too tired to wake him up and insist that he sleep on the couch. She had to concede that the day had gone very well. Dara had enjoyed herself, and Lesley had to admit that she had too. So why didn't he insist on moving in and—and what? Now who was putting more significance on the relationship between them?

The next day, Dara's birthday, Lesley got out the doll she'd bought weeks ago. Though TV commercials had had Dara wishing for every doll they advertised, she'd finally settled on one with a recorder inside that could be programmed to respond to the owner's voice.

Lesley had considered having a party for her, and had even talked to Millie about arranging it, but at the last minute decided she wanted to keep her daughter all to herself. And then even that hope had gone awry. With the appearance of Darren everything had changed. At least it was a change that would make their daughter happy. She wasn't sure how she felt about it, though.

Lesley glanced at her watch. Darren wasn't back from running his errands. She frowned. It was almost two o'clock. Surely he wasn't going to disappoint Dara. Then she heard noises coming from outside.

"Mama, come quick. See what Daddy is doing."

Lesley opened the door and went out on the porch, completely stunned by what she saw. Darren had hired a clown, complete with jumping room tent and magic tricks. That wasn't all. A catering van arrived next. Then a van with Millie and other people drove up. Somehow, Darren had gotten all of Dara's school friends and their mothers and fathers together to make it a party.

The excited expression on her daughter's face told Lesley it was the best thing he could have done. She wondered where he'd gotten the names and addresses. It had to be from Dara, and Millie of course, but how had he done it so fast and without alerting Dara to what he had planned? Or Lesley from suspecting anything? She smiled. Darren really loved their child. Could he ever come to love her as unconditionally? Was it possible he could ever trust her again even? She found herself wanting that more than she'd ever wanted anything.

Dara proudly showed her father off to her friends. Her eyes twinkled happily before she closed them and made a wish and blew out the candles on her birthday cake. Lesley didn't need to wonder what she wished for. She had never seen Dara so happy.

A pang of guilt made her uncomfortable. Darren had been right, she had cheated their daughter. She remembered something Arthur had said as well, that a man deserved a chance to be a good father to his child, deserved to get to know his child.

It finally came time for Dara to open her presents. She'd worked her way through the gifts from all her friends, was now on the presents from Millie and her parents.

The new chess set from Millie made her smile.

"Thank you, Millie. I promise not to lose the pieces to this one." She hugged and kissed her special grandmother.

"Don't worry, I'll be around to see that you don't. Happy birthday, Dara."

The doll from Lesley received rave reviews, as did Darren's present, tickets for her and her friends to attend a matinee performance of "Peter and the Wolf" at the Music Center. If Darren was trying to prove that he could be a good father, he'd made one hell of a start today, Lesley realized.

Dara went straight to bed without an argument when they returned from the Music Center. Darren stared in awe at her from the doorway of her bedroom. "She is a beautiful child," he said to Lesley.

"I agree."

Darren placed his hands on Lesley's shoulders and gently guided her down the hall. "Let's take a walk on the beach."

"Dara might wake up."

"I didn't mean that we should go very far, only a few yards down the beach."

"In that case, all right."

The moon was full, its silvery light giving the sand a sparkling, sugary, fairy-tale quality.

Darren stopped and looked back at the beach house. "You gave me the most precious gift in the world."

"You gave her to me first."

He drew her into his arms, gazing soulfully into her eyes. Lesley was mesmerized. When his lips touched hers, she closed her eyes, glorying in the sensations he caused to skate through her body.

"We created a miracle, didn't we, sweetheart?"

"Of course I'm going to say yes. I'm her mother, and tend to be more than a little biased."

"Lesley." He moved his lips over hers in an arousing kiss.

She responded, returning it with enthusiasm.

"I think we'd better go back inside."

No sooner were they inside than Darren started kissing her again, taking little nips at the corner of her mouth. Then he moved down the silky-soft column of her throat. He undid the buttons on the bodice of her dress and journeyed into the shadowy valley between her breasts. She inched away.

He lifted his gaze. "Lesley?"

The look in her eyes was an invitation. Suddenly he was her Sampson, and she his Delilah, beckoning him to follow. And he did.

When they reached the bedroom door, Darren swept Lesley into his arms and carried her inside. He lowered her down on the bed, then went to work to relieve her of her clothes. As eager as he, she tried to help, but he pushed her fingers away.

"I want the pleasure of undressing you, girl."

"When you're done, I reserve the same right."

He slowly, methodically, peeled her dress from her, his fingers grazing bare skin as he went along. Lesley's little jerks and gasps with each touch excited him further. At last she was naked. As his gaze slid over her body, he groaned. He'd wanted her so badly for so long. Now that the time was here, he wanted to savor it like a fine wine, caress her silky-soft skin, get lost in the delicate bouquet of her body.

He felt a throbbing deep in his groin. And suddenly his clothes were a straight jacket he wanted desperately to escape.

Lesley halted his movements. "Let me."

She slowly removed one piece, then moved on to the next, taking her time. He thought he would go up in flames before she was through.

At last they were bare flesh to bare flesh. He enticed, nuzzled, and petted every inch of Lesley's body. She returned the action in kind.

Although aroused to the point of insane passion, Darren stopped long enough to protect them. Seconds later he slid over her body, parting her thighs, to thrust deep inside her. At first he encountered a resisting tightness, but her femininity yielded, deeply enveloping him in her welcoming heat.

Her pulsing sheath closed around him eagerly, embracing him like a tight, vibrating glove. The old magic was still as potent as it ever was, as though she'd never caused him any pain other than that of the pleasure/pain variety.

At the moment he didn't want to think about that other kind of pain. When he felt Lesley's body involuntarily arch upward, absorbing him even deeper, a breath-robbing groan escaped his lips and on instinct, he raised her legs around his hips, effectively melding his flesh more deeply in hers.

The sizzling sensations he wrought scorched Lesley's senses, sending up intense heat waves that obliterated everything except the urge to engage in the age-old mating ritual of woman and man.

Lesley's breathing grew labored as again and again his fiery passion stroked her inner core as if it were by a literal fire burning hotter and hotter, the flames blazing higher until they burst into a shower of sparks that glowed brighter than gem fire.

Caught up in the shuddering tremors of her release, his own exploded, hurtling him into a rapturous world of pure sensation.

Their combined heavy breathing subsided to deep, contented intakes of breath. The reality of what had so quickly flared to life and roared far beyond their control was sobering.

Lesley moved out of the intimate cocoon of Darren's embrace and lay with her head resting on her bent arm. He understood how she was feeling and didn't try to coax her back into his arms. The uncontrollable emotions that had taken her system by storm had also devastated his.

Darren eased up on an elbow. "Are you all right?"

"Yes."

"You sure?"

"Yes."

"Now you see that we should have been together all these years."

To her, his voice carried an accusing undertone.

"I don't want to go back to Philadelphia with you, Darren. And I'm not sure a marriage between us would work. Something elemental in our relationship was sabotaged and destroyed when you chose to believe the worst of me. The one thing I do know is that I don't want to hurt Dara."

"Let me ask you something?"

"What?"

"You so vehemently claimed you were innocent of the charges against you, yet you didn't stick around to disprove them."

Lesley scooted off the bed then looked back at him. "I was too hurt and dispirited by your attitude. You were my life, Darren." She moved to the window, hugging her arms around herself, gazing out over the moon-silvered ocean. "Nothing seemed important after that. But I'm stronger now. What you do or say doesn't have the power to hurt me like it did back then."

Darren left the bed and came up behind Lesley, placing his hands on her shoulders. "I know about Cheerful Children's Wear and that you're considering their offer to design for them. I could block it, you know." He felt her tense beneath his fingers. "But this isn't about power or control between us now, Lesley. I thought it was when I saw you at Clare's party and again at Raiments' fashion show, but I was wrong. I could use Dara to force you to marry me or sue for custody. But I won't. Do you know why?"

She shook her head.

"Whether I believe you or not isn't really the point. I'm now convinced that you really believe what you claim."

When Lesley opened her mouth to protest, he squeezed her shoulders. "Since you do, I know you'll come back with me and face whatever you have to face. You were never a coward, Lesley. Leaving things up in the air must have eaten at you like a corrosive acid all these years. Then there's your guilt at depriving our daughter of a family she so desperately needs, wants and deserves. And finally, you wouldn't be happy with merely designing children's wear. I'm sure you do it very well, but it's really not you, Lesley, and we both know it."

She expelled a weary breath. She knew he was right even though she didn't want him to be. More than proving her innocence was in question; there was the breach with her family. So many things to resolve, she thought, turning around and gazing into his face. And most of all there were her feelings for this man.

"You're so very sure about that, aren't you?" Bitterness tinged her voice.

"If you'll notice, I'm not gloating."

She bowed her head. "No, you're not. And you're right about my guilt feelings where Dara is concerned. She deserves a family with two parents. Since you undoubtedly won't consider living in California…"

"No, I won't."

"I have no choice, but to move back to Philadelphia with you. When do you want to get married?"

He didn't like the emotionless, resigned sound in her voice. He drew her into his arms and kissed her forehead, then her eyelids. After a few moments, he felt the tension slowly ebb from her.

"It'll be good between us, Lesley, I promise you."

"I'm wondering how you can make a promise like that."

He feathered teasing kisses on her nose, her lips, behind her ear.

A little moan escaped her throat and a tremor quaked through her. She closed her eyes.

Oh, Darren, what are you doing to me?

That he actually believed she was…made her smolder. For Dara's sake and his desire for Lesley, it seemed that he was willing to overlook her 'mental machinations.' When they returned to Philadelphia, she would prove to him that she wasn't delusional; that she was innocent. Lesley longed to see the light of trust burn brightly in his eyes again, craved it like a plant does the warming rays of the sun.

Darren noticed the momentary stiffening of her body and knew that determination he'd always admired about her had reasserted itself. When she opened her eyes, they were glowing with desire.

"I think I know the method you'll employ to keep that promise."

"Do you have any objections, sweetheart? If you do, tell me now."

"It doesn't change my feelings about what happened six years ago."

"I know. One day, maybe with the help of counseling, you'll be able to admit the truth."

"Darren, I don't need—"

Before she could finish what she was saying, he once again submerged Lesley in an ocean of pleasure. In minutes he had her to the point where she didn't care if she drowned in the ecstasy. For now they would give themselves up to the all-consuming passion raging inside them.

Lesley woke up the next morning and walked out to the water's edge. She gazed out over the ocean, barely aware of the buttery-soft glow of the early morning sun on the water, or the sound of the waves as they gently washed over the sand. What had happened the night before floated before her mind's eye. Lesley was convinced that Darren hadn't planned it. Maybe it was inevitable that they would end up making love, considering the chemistry and leftover desire between them.

Lesley certainly couldn't accuse him of using their daughter to force her to go back to Philadelphia. He hadn't done that. No. There was something deep inside herself that had ultimately persuaded her to go back and right the wrong done to her.

If she were to be the kind of role model her daughter could look up to and be proud of, she had to do this.

"Is it that difficult?"

Lesley turned at the sound of Darren's voice. "I had forgotten what an early riser you are. I thought to find space and time alone."

"Am I ruining it for you, sweetheart? I can go——"

"No, don't leave. I've reassured myself that what I plan to do is right." She sighed. "About Raiments——"

"We really should be getting back there, but not today. Next week is soon enough. There will be a lot to do before we leave for Philadelphia."

That one thought made her shiver and she shifted her gaze back to the ocean.

"If you're worried about your position after you become my wife, don't. Philadelphia Raiments will be your baby."

She sliced a quick-second glance his way. "What do you mean, 'my baby?'"

gazed up at the ceiling. Could happiness be within his grasp?

The sound of the bedroom door opening brought him out of his wandering thoughts.

"Dara!"

"What is it, little sweetheart?"

"Can I get in bed with you and Mama?"

Knowing they were naked beneath the sheets, Darren felt his face flame.

Taking his silence for agreement, Dara slipped out of her nightgown and crawled onto the bed. Darren was speechless.

"Why did you take off your nightgown?"

"You and Mama aren't wearing anything. It's all right, though. I've seen statues of people without any clothes on in the museum. My friend Amber says all parents sleep that way. Her mama and daddy go to bed like that every night."

Darren was as close to blushing as he'd ever come.

Lesley moaned softly and awakened. "Dara? What are you doing in here, honey?" She did blush. "Where's your nightgown?"

Lesley looked askance at Darren. He had a sheepish expression on his face.

"Can I get under the covers with you and daddy?"

"Darren!" Lesley exclaimed.

"Come ahead, my little sweetheart," Darren said.

Lesley scooted over and let her daughter in the middle. Then she smiled. They were all three actually bonding, according to nature. She'd read somewhere once that it was done in Sweden. The studies told of how it knitted the family closer together, letting the love flow, the impediment of clothing not standing in the way of bonding. Lesley wasn't sure she ascribed to that theory. Dara knew nothing about any of that, all she knew was that she wanted to be as close to both her parents as she could come.

It never failed to amaze Lesley that little children had no inhibitions about being naked. She realized only when society imposed its proprieties on them were they made aware, and sometimes ashamed.

In seconds Dara was asleep. The poignancy of their closeness as a family caused tears to well in Darren's eyes and drizzle down his cheeks.

Lesley reached out and caught one on her finger tip. She knew in that moment she was deeply in love with this man. Always had been, and always would be. The three of them were irrevocably bound by love.

Darren drew Lesley and Dara into his embrace and they slept.

Hours later Darren woke up, and though reluctant to give up the newfound closeness he'd shared with Lesley and Dara, he got up and dressed.

He was fixing breakfast when Lesley and Dara entered the kitchen. He'd thought to see signs of self-consciousness or embarrassment, but both his girls were smiling, literally glowing.

Both his girls.

It sounded so completely natural and fantastic. If he had anything to say about it, this family of his was going to be all right.

After finishing breakfast, they cleaned up the beach house before leaving. Lesley agreed that they should get married in the next few weeks. Dara was ecstatic when they broke the news to her, and could hardly wait to get home to tell Millie and her friends.

Lesley wasn't sure what the people they worked with were going to think about their marriage. She hadn't exactly been friendly to Darren at Raiments since he'd taken over. Surely they would find it strange that they were suddenly contemplating marriage, and she voiced her thoughts.

He smiled gently. "Whatever happens, we'll deal with it together, sweetheart."

Darren followed Lesley and Dara to their home. He found it small, but comfortable and cozy. When Dara took him on a tour of the grounds while Lesley went inside, he knew why Lesley had bought it. The backyard was large enough to accommodate a swing set, a sandbox, and provided plenty of running around room.

Millie was cleaning up the kitchen when Lesley walked in. "I got a better look at Dara's father a minute ago. He's a real hunk."

"Millie!"

She laughed. "Well, he is. Don't look so surprised. I'm not so old I can't appreciate handsome male flesh. They used to call them buff in my day. Doesn't matter what you call good-looking men, they're still fine. When am I going to get to talk to him?"

"You will later. At the moment he and Dara are bonding."

"What about Dara's mother?"

"What about me?"

"That man out there has placed himself in the middle of your world, changing it completely." Millie gave her a sidelong glance. "What do you think? How do you feel about him?"

"I still love him, but…"

"But you're afraid. I can understand that, considering all you've been through. You sure you're not just going along with the program?"

"Going along with the program? What do you mean?"

"Are you doing this because Dara wants all three of you together as a family?"

"I had to take that into consideration. Dara's happiness is very important to me, yes, but it's not only that, Millie. I've repressed my feelings about what happened in Philadelphia six years ago for too long. Darren is right; deep down I have been aching to go back. Somebody set me up, and I have to know who it was."

"Set you up?" Millie frowned. "You mentioned that you weren't guilty of what they accused you of, but not that someone had deliberately set out to make you specifically look that way. That means that whoever did that could very well be dangerous. You should tell your young man about this."

"I know he cares about me and loves our daughter, but he doesn't really believe in my innocence, Millie. He thinks I've deluded myself into believing it."

"How are you ever going to convince him?"

"I don't know. The only way I can begin to make any progress in that direction is by going back to Philadelphia."

"It could be dangerous."

"I know, but I have to do this, Millie." Lesley walked over to her. "I—Dara— What are we going to do without you?"

Millie smiled. "Moving all the way out to the East Coast is something to think about."

"I want you to come with us, but I can't ask you to give up your church and your other social activities."

Millie reached out to hug Lesley. "You're my family now, you and Dara. My only family. You and that beautiful child were a gift from God. If not for you, I don't know what I would have done with myself after Morris died."

"Then you'll think about coming with us?"

"I don't need to think about it. I want to go with you. That is, if your young man doesn't mind."

Lesley hadn't thought that he might object. She didn't think Darren would mind, but she didn't know that for sure. She'd have to talk it over with him.

Darren walked with Dara around to the front of the house, thoroughly enjoying being with this tiny person who was his child.

"Mama loves plantin' flowers." Dara pointed to twin flower beds on either side of the porch, then sadly looked away.

"Is something wrong, my little sweetheart?"

"Not 'zactly."

Darren led her over to the front steps, sat down, then pulled her up onto his lap and drew her into his arms.

"Explain the 'not 'zactly' to your daddy."

Dara smiled wistfully. "I didn't have you here when my friend Amber had a barbecue. Everyone else had their daddies there. Everybody except me."

"You had your mother, didn't you?"

"Yeah, but it wasn't the same as having a real honest to goodness daddy there with me."

"You're glad that I arrived to claim you, then?"

Dara smiled up at him and nodded.

"I'm glad, too."

Lesley came to the screen door and started to push it open, but stopped when she heard Dara broach her next question.

"Daddy, if I ask you something…" She paused.

"Something like what?" he prompted, smoothing back a straying strand of hair that had escaped from one of her ponytails.

"Why didn't you and Mama get married before I was borned?"

Darren thought for a few moments before attempting to answer her question. "There was a serious problem between her family and mine. Kind of like Romeo and Juliet."

She moved to make herself more comfortable on his lap. "Who are they?"

"They were two young people whose families couldn't stand each other, but Romeo and Juliet fell in love with each other in spite of it."

"You and Mama fell in love like that?"

"Well, kind of. Only Romeo and Juliet didn't live happily ever after. Unlike them, I want us to have a happy ending."

"I'll help you, Daddy."

"I know I can count on you, my little sweetheart." He kissed her cheek and squeezed her tight.

Lesley opened the screen door. "Lunch is ready, guys."

Darren studied Lesley for a few moments. He could tell by her expression she'd overheard. Tears glistened in her eyes and she fluttered her lashes furiously in an attempt to blink them away. He wanted to make love to her right then and there. Not only make love with her, but tell her how much he loved her. He had to admit that was how he still felt. Realizing she had struggled, and was still struggling, with the trauma of what had happened six years ago, that she'd blocked it out, certainly hadn't changed that. In fact, it endeared her to him all the more. He knew deep down that nothing or no one would ever alter his feelings for this woman.

When they went inside, Millie came into the living room.

Lesley cleared her throat "Darren, I know you and Millie talked on the phone, then saw each other at Dara's party, but you never really had a chance to talk. She's like family to me and Dara."

Millie smiled. "So I'm finally going to get to know my angel's father."

"And you're the one who ranks up there just below God, according to my daughter." Darren beamed. "You've taken very good care of her, I've been told."

"I've done my best Dara is a very special person."

"I agree, but then I'm her father and you know, fathers tend to be prejudiced."

Millie smiled at Dara, then looked back at Darren. "She and her mother are my family." Her gaze sharpened. "Anyone who hurts them will have me to answer to."

Darren picked up on the warning and shot her a respectful glance. "Then I'll have to make sure that no one does."

Lesley read approval in Millie's eyes for Darren. She respected Millie's opinion. The woman had never been the kind of person to pass judgment. She'd been a true friend to Lesley and a loving surrogate grandmother to Dara.

Lesley gazed across the room at Dara, who stood in the archway watching them, a radiant smile lighting her face. To see that happy expression on her child's face made all she was willing to do well worth any regret she might feel when they went back to Philly.

Darren intercepted Lesley's vibes and his heart went out to her. Although she was trying very hard to accept his intrusion into her life with grace and courage, he wanted more than that from her. He wondered if he'd eventually win back her love.

"Let's eat," Lesley said with a smile.

After they'd all eaten, Lesley had Dara help her with the clean up while Millie and Darren went outside on the porch. Once they were seated, Millie spoke her mind.

"I didn't get to say all that I wanted to say in front of Dara." She paused, then began. "My girl was in a bad way when I met her. I'm speaking about Lesley now. I'm thinking you're responsible for it." She held up her hand. "Now don't interrupt. Lesley is the best in my book. I have to tell you that she had the look of the walking wounded six years ago. I won't stand by and let it happen again. Do I make myself clear, Mr. Taylor?"

"Very, Mrs. James."

"Since you came back into her life, she's been tense, confused and anxious about your intentions. She says you believe that she betrayed you."

"There are other—I don't really think we should—"

"Don't worry, I'm not going to get into it with you. It's not my place. Only the two of you know what really happened and how best to deal with it. What I'm concerned about is Lesley's happiness."

"You don't have to be."

"But I feel I do. Happiness encompasses a lot of things. Dara is a major part of that happiness. Lesley loves that child, and will do anything for her."

"I don't doubt that for a minute, Mrs. James."

"Please, call me Millie. I wouldn't want you to do anything that would—"

"You can relax, Mrs.—Millie. I'd never try to take Dara away from her mother. They come as a package deal, I know that." He paused before continuing. "I want you to be a part of the package. My daughter adores you. Will you consider moving to Philadelphia with us?"

Millie smiled. "I was ready to present an argument you couldn't possibly have refused if you hadn't asked me."

"Lesley and Dara were lucky to have had someone like you to help them all these years. Believe me, I'm grateful."

"I was glad I was there for them."

"How soon can you be ready to leave for Philadelphia?"

"I'll need a few weeks to get my affairs in order. How soon are you planning on leaving?"

"Yesterday. Not for real." Darren laughed.

"I like you, Mr. Taylor."

"We hope to leave in a few weeks. Please, call me Darren."

Lesley watched her daughter weave her spell over her father, urging him toward her bedroom so he could listen while she said her prayers.

"That child could charm the clouds out of the sky," Millie remarked with a smile.

Lesley sighed. "Just like her father."

"I can see why you fell in love with him."

"You and Darren had a talk. What did you discuss?"

"My favorite subject I believe he means to do right by you and Dara. Maybe you were wrong about him."

"I don't think so, Millie. If you could have seen him when—there's no use rehashing that scene. His rejection hurt."

"I'm sure it must have." Millie put her hand on Lesley's shoulder. "Mr. Taylor—Darren has asked me to move to Philadelphia with you."

"He has? That's wonderful."

"There are depths to the man, Lesley. He may surprise you."

Lesley watched Millie head down the hail to her room. She wanted so badly to believe what Millie said about Darren. She wanted to believe that the feelings he had for her ran deeper than just concern, deeper than simple caring about her because she was the mother of his child, deeper than the sexual attraction and his desire for her body, deeper than respect for her designing ability.

She wanted so much more from their relationship and their coming marriage. She wanted his trust, not his pity. She wanted his belief in her restored. By going back to Philadelphia, did she stand a chance of accomplishing it?

FIFTEEN

"Sweetheart, if the burden is too heavy, share the load," Darren exhorted to Lesley from the doorway where he'd been watching the play of emotions move across her face.

"Darren," she answered, startled out of her momentary reverie. "Did Dara finally fall asleep?"

"Only after conning me into reading her a second bedtime story." He smiled, an awed expression lighting his face. "You know, being a father is really something special, Lesley."

"I know and I'm sorry, I—"

"I didn't say that to make you feel guilty, although I can't help resenting the fact that I've missed the most important years of my daughter's life."

"You sure it isn't more than just resentment you feel towards me, Darren?"

"I'm sure. I'll admit it was more than that at first, but that's no longer true. I don't want to dwell on the past. Our future together is all that's important now. I'm impressed with Millie, by the way."

Lesley shot him an inquiring look. "Did she give you a hard time?"

"In spades." He laughed. "She's as protective of you and Dara as any lioness is of her cubs. I'm glad you had somebody like her around."

"So am I. She's been like a mother to me," she said, her voice tinged with sadness. "More of a mother than my own ever was."

"Was your relationship with your mother always so strained?"

"Always. And strained is a nice word for it." She laughed bitterly. "I never seemed to measure up."

"When we get back, you do plan on contacting your parents?"

She sighed heavily. "I suppose I'll have to eventually, but not right away. I'm just not ready for that yet."

"They accepted and used the designs, Lesley, which means that they were just as responsible—if not for them you would not have felt the desperate need to prove yourself in the first place. And you wouldn't have... I don't understand why they should—"

"Have an attitude? When they discovered how I allegedly got the designs, my mother practically disowned me. Like you, she never believed that I hadn't sent them to Wells. She in essence accused me, her own daughter, of being a thief."

Seeing her growing agitation Darren said, "I don't think we should get into this."

"That's because you don't want to face the possibility that you might be wrong about me."

"Lesley, I—"

She put up her hand. "Maybe you'd better go."

"No." Darren drew her into his arms. "I don't want to leave things this way between us. We need to be alone to talk things out. Come go for a drive with me."

She didn't want to be at odds with him, now that they had reached some level of understanding.

Darren saw the struggle in her face and said, "I promise not to bring up the past if you won't."

"All right, I'll come with you then."

Darren noticed as he drove down Santa Monica Boulevard how tonight the moon silvered the beach sand and a cool off-shore breeze gently whispered through the tall, stately palm trees lining the street. Although Los Angeles had a lot to recommend it, he was anxious to get back to Philly, anxious to have his woman and his child with him where they belonged. As he sneaked secret glances at Lesley, he wondered when she would ask where he was taking her. He didn't have long to wait.

She turned to Darren at last and asked, "Where are we going?"

He smiled. "To the beach house I rented."

She wondered at that mysterious smile. "You have something specific in mind to talk about, or do once we get there?"

"If you don't want to go, we don't have to."

"I didn't say that I didn't want to go."

"I love spending time with my daughter, but I want to spend time with my daughter's mother. We really need some time alone, sweetheart."

"I want that too," Lesley said softly, realizing how badly she really did want it. She heard the desire in Darren's voice and it made her insides tremble with that same emotion. Just being near Darren made her a captive to his mesmerizing maleness. Evidently he could do what he wanted, and take her anywhere he wanted, and those feelings would never alter.

Relief swept through Darren at her answer. He was sure now that Lesley wanted him as much as he wanted her.

When they arrived at the beach house, Darren turned to Lesley and put a hand over hers when she made to unbuckle the safety belt.

"I want to know if you have any doubts about going back to Philadelphia. I know I haven't given you much choice."

"No, you haven't, but if I had decided that I didn't want to go back, believe me, nothing you've said or done so far could have forced me to. It was inevitable that I would have to one day go back. It may have taken me longer to see that but I would have eventually arrived at that conclusion."

"All this time I thought I was being the man." He laughed.

Her expression softened and she smiled. "You are the man."

Lesley realized immediately when Darren turned on the lights as they entered the living room his beach house was much more luxurious than Ava's, and yet he had never once insisted that she and Dara leave it to move in here with him. The place was huge, too much for only one person.

As if guessing her thoughts, he said, "I never shared it with anyone, Lesley. Regina, the woman you saw me with on the wharf, is just a neighbor."

While Lesley walked around the room, Darren turned the radio to an easy-listening station, then strode over to the bar. "How about a drink? White wine okay?" he asked.

"That'll be fine." She seated herself on the couch while he poured the drinks.

Minutes later he brought the glass of wine she wanted and the brandy he'd poured for himself over to the couch and joined her.

"Things'll work out for us, Lesley."

"I certainly hope so."

His eyebrows arched inquisitively. "You sound doubtful."

"There are so many things unresolved between us, Darren."

"All we need is time, sweetheart."

She should tell him they needed more than just time because as long as he believed she had betrayed him, no matter that he thought she was blocking it out, all the time in the world wouldn't heal the wounds they'd inflicted on each other. But she didn't. They'd promised not to talk about the past tonight, and she intended to see that neither one of them broke that promise.

All of a sudden Darren felt as awkward as a boy on his first date. He and this woman shared a child, a past, the same passion, for God's sake! He was at a loss as to how to go about restoring a relationship that had been so badly damaged.

Over the rim of her wine glass, Lesley glanced at Darren, studying the play of emotions on his face. She wondered if he could possibly be feeling the same uneasiness she was. Surely not Darren. He was always so confident about everything he said and did.

"Lesley?

"Darren."

They spoke in unison.

"You go first," he said.

Lesley placed her glass on the coffee table. "We've made love before, but—"

"You feel it too, don't you, sweetheart?" He put his glass down beside hers and moved closer to Lesley, then pulled her into his arms. He groaned. It felt so good, so right, holding her like this.

Lesley laid her head against his chest, breathing in his scent, basking in his warmth and delighting in his sheer masculinity. She wanted his touch. She wanted him. Period. She'd never felt this way about any other man, and she knew she never would.

Darren raised her face with a bent forefinger to kiss her. His lips melded to hers, causing a fountain of sensations to bubble up inside her. Suddenly her mind flashed back in time to a night and a state of mind very much like this.

She and Darren had gone to his apartment after leaving a party. The wine and the music had put them in a very relaxed, mellow mood. The feel of his body pressed against hers had heated her blood, sending it pulsing wildly through her veins.

After reliving that moment, she returned to the present, moaning softly because those same feelings were coursing through her now.

Darren asked in a voice turned husky in his growing passion, "What were you thinking just now, sweetheart?"

"The first time we made love."

"That sexy little red dress you wore to Jordanna's party that night gave me fits. I could see the look of desire on every male face in the room when their eyes lighted on my woman. I wanted to leave right after we got there and take you some place where I would be the only male around to enjoy your charms."

Lesley laughed. "But your sister had other ideas, didn't she?"

"I could have strangled Danna. That devilish girl knew what she was doing."

"You have to agree that we were more than mellow by the time we left the party."

"We certainly were. I knew we would make love. I knew we would be physically as well as emotionally bound by that love by the time the night was over."

"I knew it, too. I wanted you as much as you wanted me."

"Do you want me now as much as you did then, Lesley? I know I could seduce you into wanting me, but I don't want it to be that way. Be honest with me, do you want me, girl?"

"Oh, yes, very much." When he cupped her face in his hands and began kissing her lips, her insides burned; his touch was like fire. And as with each addition of kindling, each one of his soul-burning kisses built her desire until it reached flaming proportions. Even then it seemed to grow even hotter, if that were possible.

"Oh, Darren," she moaned. "The fire."

"I know, sweetheart. It's consuming me too." He slid the strap on her sundress off her shoulder. When he touched his lips to her bare skin, he felt her tremble. The desire streaking through him became a throbbing ache deep in his loins and a groan escaped his control.

He lowered the other strap and kissed the swell of her naked breasts. The fragrance of Envy drifted up his nostrils. He pushed the bodice of the dress down to her waist and eased the delicate globes of her breasts into his palms, moving his thumbs across the sensitive nipples. He heard her low moan of pleasure. It excited him even more as he replaced a thumb with his tongue.

A cry left her throat and Lesley arched her back sharply when his mouth closed around her entire nipple and he sucked strongly. The friction of his tongue on her nipple caused it to harden. His stimulation of her responsive flesh urged the love juices to flow deep into her core.

He eased her down on the couch. "Your breasts are like ripe rare melons, a delicacy fit for royalty and right now, sweetheart, you make me feel like a king."

"I want to be your queen," she uttered in a low sultry whisper.

"You already are my queen, Lesley." He gently grazed her nipple with his teeth. "And I adore you."

"Oh, Darren," she gasped, closing her eyes.

He stopped. When she opened her eyes, he could see they were glazed with eager anticipation and he asked, "Do you want me to continue?"

She stroked the sides of his face with her fingers and answered. "You know I do."

Darren moved his lips to the other nipple, delivering the same rapturous bliss. Her little whimpers of ecstasy made his aroused manhood harden even more.

He dropped kisses along the smooth flesh of her midriff. "I want to pay homage to every inch of your luscious body, my queen," Darren whispered. He tugged her dress down her hips, hooking his fingers in the waist-band of her panties and dragging them both from her body, tossing them to the floor.

His breath caught in his throat. "You're so beautiful, Lesley." Darren swept her up in his arms.

She gazed into his eyes and asked. "Where are you taking me?"

"Let it be a surprise, sweetheart."

Darren carried her out onto the enclosed patio, then flipped on the switch to the jacuzzi. He lowered her feet to the floor and for a few moments all they did was stand watching the water as it bubbled enticingly, inviting them to step inside.

Lesley looked at Darren's still clothed body. "We need to make you more comfortable."

"More comfortable?" His eyes twinkled wickedly. "You mean as in naked? You going to be my valet?"

"Oh, yes. it's a task I'm really looking forward to," she said simply, then started to undress him. Her fingers shook in her eagerness, but once his chest was bare, she sought his nipple and quickly closed her lips over the hardened nub.

Desire surged through Darren when he felt her hot moist mouth on his flesh and he cried out.

Before he could react to the stimulus, she slid her hands down his flat stomach, then lower, splaying her fingers across the front of his briefs, moving them back and forth so the soft cotton abraded his manhood. When she at last slipped her fingers inside, she felt him harden and shudder. Seeing his magnificent tumescence when he was at last completely naked made her heart pound wildly in her chest.

"If you don't stop looking at me like that," he whispered, "we'll never get to enjoy what I have planned for us."

"What do you have planned?"

Darren silently led her over to the jacuzzi. There were towels and bottles of oil arranged around it. To the right stood a brass candle burner. He lit the candle beneath, then placed several of the bottles of oil on the tray above.

Then he stepped down into the jacuzzi and held out his hand for Lesley to join him in the water.

She placed her hand in his and with each step she sank deeper into the delicious, bubbling warmth. As her body began to relax, a contented sigh left her lips.

"You like my surprise?" he asked.

"Yes, so far. This feels wonderful."

He turned her so his front faced her back and tugged her against his. "You feel wonderful, so damned wonderful," he muttered, lowering his lips to her shoulder, trailing kisses along her shoulder up the delicate curve of her neck to the sensitive area behind her ear. He slipped his hands around her body and cupped her breasts, teasing her nipples with his thumbs. He smiled when he felt her go limp, as though her legs had given out on her.

Darren said in a low sexy whisper, "I think we'd better get out of here and on to the next phase of my plan."

"The next phase?" she asked dazedly.

"Umm." He gently urged her out of the jacuzzi, then unfolded several of the huge, fluffy towels and placed them over the plastic cushions on the floor. He knelt on one cushion and held out his hand to Lesley, signaling her to do likewise. As he gently rubbed her skin dry, she mewled in contentment.

"All right, sweetheart, ease onto your stomach," he commanded softly.

As though in a trance she did as he said. "Yes, my lord."

"Am I your lord?" He lifted his brows in a sexy arch.

Lesley lowered her lashes. "What do you think?"

He didn't answer, just reached for one of the bottles of oil on the candle burner and uncapped it. He poured some onto his palm and rubbed his hands together, then positioning himself, placed his hands on her shoulders and began massaging the heated oil into her skin.

"Mmm, that feels so good," she murmured. Darren moved his hands to her shoulder blades and kneaded her back muscles, then worked his way down her midriff. He poured oil on her waist and rubbed it in, then spread some further down to her hips and buttocks. After a few moments he applied oil to her thighs and calves, massaging his way back up her body with smooth erotic strokes until she felt boneless.

"Do you like that, sweetheart?" "I love it."

"Now roll onto your back so I can do your front."

"At this moment you can do me anywhere, anyway you want to do me."

"Don't worry, I fully intend to."

Lesley closed her eyes and waited for him to begin.

He didn't make her wait long before he started applying oil to the space just above the swell of her womanly

Darren gazed at her firm breasts and jutting nipples, wondering if she'd breast-fed their daughter.

When Lesley opened her eyes, she saw his thoughtful expression.

"Did you breast-feed Dara?" he asked.

"Yes, I did. I wanted her to have every advantage I could possibly give her."

"God, I wish I could have been there to watch."

He worked the oil into her breasts, his thumb kneading the nipples until they peaked hard with desire. He could tell when her heartbeats began to quicken because her breasts quivered when she breathed.

When Darren started to work his way down her belly, kneading her hips and the front of her thighs, Lesley gasped. When he eased them apart and massaged the sensitive insides, her thighs began to tremble, then involuntarily open wider.

As he began to stroke oil onto her Mound of Venus, Darren gazed into her eyes and saw that her need was nearing its peak, so he stopped. He knew if he didn't, he wouldn't get to enjoy the feel of her soft hands massaging him because she'd be too far gone in her passion.

Lesley raised up on her elbows and said In a husky voice. "I want to do you now."

Darren eased onto his stomach.

As she applied oil to his skin, she enjoyed the hard, smooth contours and textures of his body. By the time he rolled onto his back she could see how aroused he was.

Lesley first kissed a nipple, then the rest on the way down his body, applying oil to his flat muscular stomach and his narrow hips and lean thighs. She brushed her hair across his groin and heard him groan. Before she could apply more oil, he hauled her on top of him.

"I want you now," he demanded.

"And I want you."

As his tongue caressed her lips, his fingers stroked the now oil-shiny slope of her hips and buttocks. Squeezing gently, he murmured thickly, "So soft"

Lesley lifted her chest up from his, and let her breasts dangle alluringly above his mouth.

Darren captured a taut nipple in his mouth and sucked. Her sighs of pleasure urged him on. He gently flipped her onto her back and starting with her mouth, sensuously trailed kisses down her body to her hips, then lower to the dark thicket concealing her womanhood. He slowly approached the opening leading to her dark cavern, his fingers working magic, entreating her to open for him like the words "open sesame" made the cave open for Ali Baba. Her thighs trembled before giving way. Seeing her womanly flesh open in welcome nearly drove him over the edge, but he managed to hold on to his control.

That control almost slipped when Darren encountered the wet, slick nub of her femininity. Although he was eager to feast, he also wanted her to thoroughly enjoy the pleasure he could give her. He moved his fingers over the excited nerve ending throbbing between her legs, again and again until he felt the nub swell and pulsate with need.

Lesley moaned, jerking her hips upward when he delved his tongue and his fingers into the heated depths of her. Wild pulsing sensations flooded her loins as he moved those fingers and that wicked tongue in and out, in and out, again and again.

"Oh, Darren," she cried out.

He continued to work her flesh even more frenziedly until she shattered.

"What are you doing to me?" she gasped, breathlessly satiated.

"Binding you to me in all ways. From the moment we met you were meant to be my mine, sweetheart, and I don't intend to ever let you get away from me. Do you understand what I'm saying?"

"Darren, I—"

He moved his finger against her again.

"Do you understand?" he repeated.

"Yes, I do, but I want you to understand that it cuts both ways."

"I wouldn't want it any other way."

"I want to give you a man's pleasure."

When her fingers closed around him, that hard part of him stood stiff and erect. Suddenly her fingers were moving worshipfully up and down his flesh. When her lips touched him there, a deep growl of pleasure flew from his lips.

"Enough!" He swiftly eased her away from him, immediately covering her body with his own, thrusting deeply inside her throbbing core to the hilt.

"Yes!" she screamed.

"Are you with me, sweetheart?"

"Do you need to ask?" she gasped.

He reversed their positions, placing his hands on her waist, lifting her onto his erect shaft, embedding himself deep, and as completely as possible. He wouldn't let her move for long moments, then began slowly raising and lowering her rhythmically on his flesh until she adopted his pace perfectly.

Staccato-like cries stole from her throat when the friction of his hardness moving inside her turned to lightning bolts of pleasure.

"God, I've missed this. I've missed it so damned much." He picked up the pace, scoring her entire being with scintillating points of ecstasy, stoking her need higher and higher.

Lesley cried out, "Ooh like that! Just like that!"

Uncontrollable passion thundered through Darren as the storm peaked, bursting over them both, unceremoniously dashing them onto the shores of love.

"You were fantastic, girl!" he exclaimed.

"So were you." She eased off his body and rolled onto her back, still gasping from her wondrous release.

Moments later Darren glanced at Lesley.

"What are you thinking?"

"About how, after all the time we've been apart, our lovemaking could still be this intense, this all-consuming."

"It's because we were always meant to be together."

Lesley wondered exactly how he meant that. He'd felt that way in the past. Now, believing she was guilty and was suppressing it... She wanted so much for him to believe her, to trust in her feeling for him, but she was afraid. Maybe the trust would come in time.

Yeah, only after you prove your innocence, an inner voice retorted.

What if she were never able to do that? What then?

Darren sensed her apprehension about the future. He wanted to reassure her that everything would be all right, but he knew she wouldn't believe him right now. They still had a long way to go. She had to admit to herself what she had done six years ago.

Darren gently eased Lesley into his arms and just held her. They needed this closeness. He stroked her hair and her skin, still gleaming from the massage. She was his no matter what, and he would allow nothing or no one to ever come between them.

SIXTEEN

The next few days went by quickly, Darren returning to his beach house every evening to change, then on to Lesley's house to be with her and their child. Sunday evening after they had put Dara to bed, he headed for the door. Lesley put a restraining hand on his arm, stopping him before he could leave.

"Stay, Darren."

"Are you sure you want me to?"

"Yes, I am. After that special night with you at the beach house and all the time we've spent together as a family since, I've been trying to gather up the nerve to ask you to stay here with us."

"You sure it isn't for our daughter's sake?"

"She figures in my decision, yes, but more than that, I want you to stay."

Darren turned to her. "If I stay, you know what that means. Can you handle that? I know it's only a matter of days before we get married, but you might want the time that's left to yourself."

"I thought I would mind at first, but now…I…"

"You want what?"

Lesley wet her lips. "Now I want you in my bed every night."

Darren could see how hard it was for her to admit that, considering the wariness she obviously still felt. Was there a chance she could really be innocent after all? And not… He frowned. Maybe it was just what he wanted to believe. It would make things so much easier between them if he did.

He pulled her into his arms and, for a moment, all they did was stand in the middle of the room locked in an embrace, her head pillowed on his chest, her arms wrapped around his waist, his cheek resting on the top of her head.

Lesley loosened her grip from his waist and urged him in the direction of her bedroom. Darren didn't hesitate to follow her.

"I think we'd better get up or we'll be late for work," Darren said, looking out the window the next morning as the sun came up.

Lesley sleepily snuggled closer to him. "Do we have to go to work today?"

"As much as I'd like to stay in bed with you all day, I think we'd better—"

Lesley slipped her fingers around his manhood.

"Sweetheart, we—"

When he felt her fingers moving up and down his length, he gave an animal groan and flipped Lesley onto her back and immediately covered her.

She wrapped her legs around his hips, arching her body into his, glorying in the sparks and delicious shudders he sent shooting through her femininity.

Darren groaned out his pleasure and began moving strongly between her thighs, thoroughly burying himself deeply in her hot center, letting the flames of passion consume him utterly.

Sensations of ecstasy jetted through her system, over-riding all thought, practicality or reason. Sheer bliss burst inside her brain like thousands of bits of light as he urgently stroked inside her.

Seconds later Darren's release blanked out everything but the delectable feelings erupting inside him, and he rejoiced in that same shower of pleasure as their bodies and spirits fused together, melting, falling into a titillating pool of rapture.

Darren didn't move for what seemed like an eternity, then said to Lesley, "I think we'd better get up before you kill me." He groaned. "But oh, what a way to go."

"You're right, maybe we'd better—"

Darren kissed her. "Maybe just one more time." "You sure you can handle it?" she teased. "Are you trying to tell me something, woman?"

"Since you can't seem to understand what I'm saying, maybe I should try body language."

"I definitely want to understand, so maybe you should."

Darren knew that Millie hadn't missed the look that passed between him and Lesley as they took their seats at the table. Her knowing smile said she recognized that well-loved look he'd put on Lesley's face.

Just as Darren looked at Millie and she winked back at him, Lesley glanced up in time to catch the exchange. Her face heated up at its significance.

Dara, seeing the genial look on her mother's and father's faces and the approval on Millie's, smiled happily at them all.

"Isn't anybody going to eat this delicious breakfast I've fixed?" Millie asked.

At her words the hungry trio dug into the fare with gusto.

After they'd finished breakfast and said their good-byes, Lesley and Darren made to head for the door.

Dara ran to her father and tightly gripped his leg to prevent him from moving, then fixing a pleading look on her face, said, "Do you have to go, Daddy?"

"Yes, I'm afraid so, my little sweetheart. But don't worry, your mother and I will be home right after work."

"Promise?"

Darren grinned. "I promise."

Curious glances followed Lesley and Darren as they entered Raiments twenty-five minutes later. Darren waited until Lesley had gone into her office before calling a staff meeting for ten o'clock.

"I know you're all wondering why I called this meeting," Darren began, his eyes skimming the room. He gazed lovingly at Lesley, then at the staff. "Lesley Evans has agreed to move to the Philadelphia branch of Raiments, but most importantly, she has consented to become my wife."

Stunned surprise infused all their faces at first, then moments later smiles and offers of congratulations and best wishes murmured through the room. Lesley's uneasiness about the announcement slipped away.

After the meeting concluded, Giezel Garcia cornered Lesley. "I don't understand. I thought you and Darren couldn't stand each other. Now all of a sudden you're getting married!" She laughed. "It must be true what they say about there being a thin line between love and hate."

"It's a long story, Giezel. One I don't want to get into right now."

"Well, whatever the reason you changed your mind, I want you to know I'm happy for you. This must mean that you're more comfortable with the idea of moving to Philadelphia. For a while there, I wasn't sure that you ever would be."

"Me either." Lesley sighed, thinking about the lengths she had gone to thwart Darren's plans, and what he did in kind to gain her agreement. She added, "But things have changed."

"I'll say they have. You don't have any more doubts now?"

Lesley said more confidently than she felt, "None."

Darren moved to the doorway of Lesley's office after seeing Giezel leave.

When Lesley looked up and saw him watching her, she smiled. "You surprised me. I wasn't expecting you to do what you did."

"I prefer the direct approach whenever possible," he said, easing his lean muscular frame away from the jamb and entering the room. "I don't believe in wasting time."

She wondered if there wasn't a hidden meaning in his words. "When do you we leave for Philly?"

"Not for a while yet. I want to give you and Dara time to tie up any loose ends. It's going to be hard for her leave all her friends."

"Yes, I know," Lesley agreed, "but she'll make new ones."

"Have lunch with me today, sweetheart. There's something I want us to do together this afternoon."

"Do? Like what?" she asked curiously.

He shrugged his shoulders, but didn't add anything more.

"You've got to tell me more than that, Darren. Can't you even give me a hint?"

"No." He grinned. "I want it to be a surprise."

Lesley knew from experience it would be useless to try to pry any more information out of him. But curiosity was eating her alive.

"Darren, I—I don't know what to say."

"Saying you like it would be good. You do like it, don't you?"

Lesley stared at the three-karat diamond engagement ring sparkling on the third finger of her left hand. "What's not to like." A sudden glitch of sadness descended and she blinked away the tears.

Darren frowned. "What's wrong, sweetheart?" Realization finally dawned on him. "You're thinking about the first time we were engaged and the ring I gave you back then, aren't you?"

Lesley couldn't say anything, her throat seemed to have closed up. All she did was nod.

"After you threw the ring in my face and left town," he paused, giving the remembered pain a few moments to subside before going on, "I took a walk down to the river and pitched it in. I never wanted to see it again or…"

"Or me," she finished. "That ring wasn't as elegant as this one, but it was special, Darren. It symbolized the love we shared."

"You're right, it did, but since we both managed to shred that bond I thought it only fitting that the break be clean, complete," he said in a voice grown rough with past pain. "Why think about that now? That's all behind us."

"Not quite." She flinched inwardly at the distressing truth she saw in his face. Would the pain of that particular truth ever lessen, let alone go away entirely? "You're right. Why talk about it now? After all, we're going to be married and start a new life together in four days."

Darren longed to tell her of his love, but he knew she wasn't in any frame of mind to listen. Even if she did, it wouldn't change the situation between them. He couldn't tell her what she wanted to hear.

Lesley was still attracted to him and yes, she definitely desired him. There was affection there too, but he knew she no longer loved him the way she had before. If, in fact, she loved him at all. He hoped that teamed with their daughter, affection, desire and commitment would be enough to build a marriage. Maybe she could grow to love him again in time.

"We'll create new memories, Lesley. This ring symbolizes a new beginning." He leaned over and kissed her soundly on the lips.

Back in her office an hour later Lesley sat staring out the window, then looked at her ring. The episode at the jewelry store when Darren had kissed her after placing the ring on her finger replayed in her mind. If he only believed in her innocence.

There was no use hoping for the impossible. She had to be realistic. His love for Dara and his desire to be a father to their daughter and his passion to have her, Lesley, in his bed were the emotional magnets holding their family together.

Will it be enough to sustain you in the months and years ahead?

If only they were truly bound by all aspects of what the word love really encompassed. Of course she'd have her daughter and her job as the CEO and top designer for Philadelphia Raiments as an added inducement. But she had a feeling that if the trust between them wasn't restored, somehow neither of those things would be quite enough.

There was still the matter of her own family, her feelings toward them and theirs toward her. Was she ready to attempt patching the rip in their relationship? Would they even want to see and get to know their grandchild? The hurt generated by the misunderstanding and her ever-continuing disillusionment with them was still there like a wound that appeared healed on the surface, yet ached and festered underneath. Then there was Darren's family to deal with.

"A penny for your thoughts."

"Darren! I didn't hear you come in."

"You were so deep in thought, I doubt if an earthquake would have caught your attention. Are you ready to go home?" he queried, glancing at his watch. "It's quitting time you know."

"Oh, is it? I hadn't noticed."

He laughed. Lesley joined in, even though his teasing was at her expense.

"We'd better get a move on," Lesley said, adding a wry smile. "Dara will be patiently waiting for us."

"Patiently? Our daughter? That little vixen. I wouldn't place any bets on it."

"I didn't think you and Mama would ever get here," Dara grumbled, chiding her parents the minute they walked in the house.

Lesley and Darren exchanged knowing glances.

"I never said what time we'd be home, my little sweet. heart." Darren scooped her up in his arms.

"Oh, Daddy," she kissed his cheek, then wrapped her arms around his neck, "I love you so much."

"I—" He looked at Lesley. "We both love you just as much."

"I'm so happy," Dara chirped contentedly.

He kissed her forehead. "And we intend to see that you stay that way."

Lesley picked up on the emphasis Darren put on those words and she looked at the expression on his face. She knew what he expected of her and she planned to do her part to cement the relationship with their child.

Later that evening Lesley watched Darren and Dara as they ate their dinner. They were having pizza—again of course, the father having proven to be as bad as the daughter when it came to that particular food.

She grew silent when Darren mentioned their trip to Philadelphia. It wasn't a subject she enjoyed talking about right now. There would be plenty of time to think about that.

Long after Dara had been tucked in for the night, Lesley and Darren lay in bed, arms and legs entwined, still intimately joined from their lovemaking. Darren brought up what he believed to be the reason for her earlier silence.

"There are a lot of ghosts hovering, waiting to disrupt our newfound peace, aren't there, sweetheart?"

"There's only one ghost, and since you believe I'm delusional instead of innocent, what's the point in discussing it?"

"Lesley—"

She deliberately arched her body into his and kissed him deeply. Using massaging strokes, she traced urgent fingers over his hips.

His groin muscles jerked in response to the stimulation and his breathing suspended somewhere between his throat and his lungs. Desire hot and heavy poured through him like molten lava down the side of a volcano, rushing his passion toward a hot climactic release.

"Lesley, we need to—oh, sweetheart," he groaned, thrusting involuntarily inside her femininity, answering her erotic arousal of his hard flesh.

"Later, Darren. Right now, love me. Please, love me."

Darren lost what remained of his control and with a desire-filled growl, surged deeper in her pulsating warmth.

Her answering cries of passion further inflamed him. And in the next thrilling moments, the fires of wondrous completion obliterated all thought.

As the days went by, Lesley moved ahead with the preparations for their wedding, never getting around to questioning Darren about why he insisted that she wear a traditional white wedding dress when they were just going to have a simple ceremony before a judge who happened to be a personal friend of Arthur's.

From the time she and Darren had agreed on a date for their marriage, Lesley started to work on her wedding dress, a three-hem length gown that tiered to just below mid-calf in the front. Lesley decided on an illusion neckline. The dress fastened at the back with a string of pearls cleverly woven into the fabric, making it appear to be a separate entity from the gown. The bodice from breast to waist was done in summer white, silk-lined gentian lace, the flared skirt made of satin, and the sleeves were fashioned in white tulle.

Giezel and company whipped it up in a matter of hours. For Dara, Lesley created a sweet confection of pink lace and satin similar to her dress, minus the illusion neckline. She trimmed it instead with tiny artificial baby's breath dyed a soft blue and cotton candy pink and fastened in back. She opted for billowy, chiffon puff short sleeves. Because she wanted everything to be perfect, she personally did the work on it.

SEVENTEEN

The morning of the wedding arrived. Lesley moaned softly, stretching, as she slowly opened her eyes to find Darren propped on an elbow looking at her.

"You're finally awake, sleepyhead." Darren lowered his head and murmured in her ear before sliding an arm across her waist. "You do remember what day it is?"

She smiled. "Most definitely."

He pulled the sheet away from her breasts and caressed them. "In exactly four hours you're going to officially belong to me. I'll have papers on you, woman."

She laughed. "I'll have papers on you, Mr. Taylor."

"Joint ownership," he said experimentally. "I like that concept."

In that moment she loved him so much. This man held her love and happiness in his hands. It was almost frightening to know the extent of his power over her.

Darren saw that vulnerable look on her face and his heart melted. How could anyone who looked like that possibly have done the things of which she was accused? He would never have believed it of the person he'd known six years ago. Lesley was basically an honest, trustworthy person. Sometimes the demons that drove people to do things out of character caused them to have regrets later; in Lesley's case, she had repressed her guilt, convincing herself she was really innocent.

He glanced at the brown, opaque, plastic garment bag hanging in the closet. He'd been tempted to sneak a peek at her wedding dress, but decided to wait until Lesley was inside it.

"When the time comes, I'm going to get dressed in the laundry room and give you time to make yourself beautiful."

"I saw you looking in the closet. You think you can wait until then to see my dress?"

"It's going to be a struggle, but I think I can manage it if I have the right inducement to make me forget."

"You mean this kind?" she said, kissing him. "Yes, but I need more."

"Oh, you do, huh?" She kissed him again, longer this time.

"This kind of inducement has a lot to recommend it."

An hour later Millie came into the bedroom just as Lesley was applying her makeup.

"Oh, no!" "What?" Millie asked.

"I messed up my eyeliner—again."

Millie smiled. "You wouldn't be having an attack of bridal nerves, would you?"

"Yes, I would." Lesley laughed.

Millie walked over to her and gave her a big hug. "It's a normal condition, I'm afraid. You should have seen me on my wedding day."

"How did you ever manage to get through it?" "I don't know, I just did, just like you will." "Where is Dara?"

"In her room primping."

"Maybe I should—"

"Dara is fine, calm down."

Lesley turned to Millie. "Am I doing the right thing?

"You love the man, don't you?" "Yes," she said softly. "Then you have your answer." "What would I do without you?"

"I don't know, but there is no need for you to ever worry about that."

Darren stood in the living room pacing back and forth, waiting for the women in his life to join him.

"Daddy."

When he turned, his eyes misted. Dara was the image of his sister Jordanna at that age. This very special little person was his child. He was still awed by her, and knew he always would be.

"You look beautiful, my little sweetheart."

"Thank you, Daddy. Mama's almost ready. She said she'd be out in a minute."

"Until she does, you going to keep me company?" He walked over to the couch and sat down, then opened his arms.

"Yeah," she answered and went into them. "Are you really happy about the wedding?"

"Yes. You and Mama and me are going to be a real family."

His expression turned serious. "Yes, we will."

Lesley cleared her throat. Darren looked up. His eyes widened in appreciation when he saw her.

"You look so pretty, Mama!" exclaimed Dara.

"Thank you, baby." She looked from one to the other. "You ready to go?" Their smiles were so alike it brought tears to her eyes.

Minutes later, father, mother, daughter and Millie were in the car headed for the judge's chambers. Lesley observed her husband-to-be as he drove. She had to admit that he looked incredibly handsome. He made a simple black tux look like the sexiest attire a man could wear.

She wondered why he was dressed so formally, but didn't voice her curiosity. She managed to tear her gaze away from his magnificent body long enough to notice the route they were taking.

"Darren, the courthouse isn't this way."

He flashed her a mysterious smile. "I know."

She arched her brows in confusion. "Then where are we going?"

"To be married."

"But Darren…"

He didn't answer her unspoken question, just continued to smile, keeping his eyes focused on the street, appearing to concentrate on his driving. She turned to Millie for an answer, but the woman only shrugged her shoulders and offered Lesley a blank smile.

A few minutes later, Darren pulled the car up in front of a red brick building that looked to Lesley like some kind of meeting hail. He escorted his bride-to-be and their daughter and Millie to the front door. It opened and a smartly-dressed Saul Epps, Raiment's pattern maker and resident father figure next to Arthur, took Lesley's arm and wrapped it around his own.

Lesley noticed that the specially arranged chairs that had been placed in a semi-circle and filled with smiling people were divided in two by a carpeted middle aisle that stopped several feet before a flower-decorated altar.

Lesley watched as Darren headed down the aisle and took his place at the front of the altar. Millie left her side and took her seat. Lesley's mouth gaped open in amazed delight at the elaborate wedding decorations. The dulcet tones of the wedding march from an organ softly flowed into the room.

Giezel appeared with an exquisite crown and wedding veil draped over her arm and placed them on Lesley's head. Giezel reached for a basket of delicate pink rose petals and handed it to Dara, who immediately commenced sprinkling them down the aisle to the altar. Lesley could tell that her daughter was well versed in how to proceed. She smiled at the poignancy of the moment.

As Giezel turned, tracing Dara's footsteps, Lesley also noticed that Giezel's dress carried on the theme of her own, but was the same shade as Dara's.

Saul squeezed Lesley's hand and flashed her a reassuring smile.

Happy tears splashed down Lesley's cheeks as Saul marched her down the aisle. When she joined Darren and their daughter at the altar, a wobbly smile graced her lips.

Lesley sniffed when the minister asked who would give her in marriage to Darren. Saul stepped forward and said he would. She always pictured her father saying those words, but she was glad Saul was around to do the honors.

She was barely aware of what she said during the ceremony. It must have been the proper response, for the wedding was soon over and Darren was raising her veil to kiss her. When he ended it, he reached down and lifted their daughter in his arms and they both kissed her. At that precise moment, a photographer appeared to snap their picture.

Lesley studied Darren, wondering how and when he'd had time to arrange this special wedding. He was definitely a resourceful man. But to do this for her—could it possibly mean that he loved her? Even though her heart pounded hard and fast at the gallant gesture, she reminded herself not to get carried away. He'd hurt her very badly once. Despite her apprehension, she found herself hoping that what he felt for her would eventually evolve into love. And that one day when the truth came out, he could forgive himself for not having believed in her.

"How do you feel, Mrs. Taylor?" Darren said gently.

"I don't know. I never expected—"

"Sweetheart, every bride deserves as many special touches as possible on her wedding day."

"Thank you."

"It was my pleasure." He grinned engagingly.

Well-wishers surrounded them for the next hour, and the photographer continued to snap a multitude of pictures. Millie walked over to Lesley and hugged her.

"Dara and I will be spending the week together at the house while you and Mr. Taylor have a proper honeymoon."

"Honeymoon? A week?" She turned to Darren with a puzzled look on her face. "But I thought—"

"It's all right, Lesley," Darren said. "Dara understands and approves."

Lesley stooped down on a level with her child and looked into her eyes. "You're sure?"

"It's all right, Mama," Dara assured her mother.

Lesley smoothed a defiant curl back from Dara's face. "If you're sure."

Dara kissed her mother's cheek. "I am." She smiled delightedly and threw her arms around her mother's neck.

Darren waited until Lesley rose to her feet, then gently squeezed her arm. "Time to go, sweetheart."

She gazed up at him. "I thought we were going to leave for Philadelphia following the ceremony. If we're not going there, then where are we going?"

He didn't answer, just flashed her another one of his mysterious smiles.

"I seem to be always repeating those words." When he remained silent, she said, nodding her head, "I get it, it's another one of your surprises. You certainly zapped me with the wedding one."

After one last kiss for Dara, Lesley and Darren made a dash for the car amidst a shower of rice and waved good-byes to their guests and their child and Millie.

Lesley soon found out that Darren had reserved the bridal suite at the exclusive Beverly-Hilton. A champagne dinner awaited them when they arrived. The suite came complete with a huge sunken tub and a heart-shaped, king-size bed.

As soon as the room attendant left, Lesley turned to her new husband and kissed him soundly on the lips.

"Thank you."

"You already said that," he teased. "But say it again, I like the way you express yourself."

She kissed him again, lingeringly this time.

"I'm really beginning to like this gratitude thing. Thank me one more time so I can really get into it."

"Oh, I intend to." Lesley removed his jacket, unbuttoned his shirt and slipped it off him, then kissed his nipple. "Here's a thank you." She kissed the other. "Then here's another thank you."

"Does your thank you extend to other areas?"

"It's possible."

"Do you intend to reward those other areas?"

"It's possible." She giggled, then backed away from him.

"Why you—come here, woman."

"Come and get me," she said in a provocatively teasing whisper.

He advanced toward her, she inched back, he inched closer. She backed back until she felt her legs touch the edge of the bed.

"You have nowhere else to run, sweetheart."

"I don't want to run, not anymore."

"I'm glad because I wasn't about to let you do it." He pulled her into his arms and rained kisses on her forehead, the bridge of her nose and then dropped sipping kisses near her lips without actually touching them.

"How were you planning on stopping me if I had wanted to, by teasing me into submission? Or ordering me?"

"As in me Tarzan and you Jane?" He laughed, pounding his chest.

"That's not even funny."

"Oh, I thought it was."

"You would."

He tasted her lips. "Mmm, sweeter than honey. Oh, and, woman, I've got a sweet tooth like you wouldn't believe."

"Oh, I can believe it all right."

Darren snaked his arms around her neck, unhooked the back of her dress, and then slid it off her shoulders. He breathed in the delicious scent of her skin and kissed one shoulder, then the other.

"You're beautiful, Lesley. Even when you have..."

"What? My clothes on or off?"

"Both," he replied before stopping the flow of her words with his mouth on hers. Darren lowered the dress to her waist and kissed the swell of her breasts. "I want you so much."

His touch and his words removed all thought, replacing it with the promise of sheer rapture. "And I want you, Darren."

"Show me how much, sweetheart."

Lesley undid the fastening on his pants. "I want to look at you."

"You want to examine the goods before you try them?"

"It's been a long time since I've sampled them."

"Yeah, right. A whole six hours is a long time?"

"Those short hours seem more like years."

"How you do go on. You missed me that much, huh?"

"Don't say anything else. I want to see you naked."

"You're a demanding little thing, aren't you?"

"Not another word. Show me some skin." She gave him a sultry smile.

He slowly lowered his pants, letting them fail to the floor, then kicked them away.

Lesley's gaze dropped to his briefs which bulged, telling her he was aroused and ready. "I want to see more," she demanded.

Darren grinned as he pulled his briefs off then tossed them on top of his pants.

Lesley gasped at the sight of his naked manhood. Her eyes traveled up his torso, ending their perusal at his sensuous lips. She gulped, "God, you're magnificent."

He didn't say a word, just unhooked her strapless bra and kissed a nipple, sucking it into his mouth. She moaned and her body shuddered. He let the throbbing peak go and peeled her dress and slip down her body, watching them pool around her feet. The next moment his breath caught in his throat.

Lesley was wearing a garter belt and stockings. He groaned. "You remembered."

"Oh, yes. I remembered how much they turn you on. I also remembered how much I liked seeing you get so hot and bothered when you did."

He knelt before her. After taking off her shoes, he moved up her body to unsnap the stockings from the long elastic suspenders and slowly roil them down her legs and off. His hands sensuously journeyed back up her calves and thighs. When he reached her femininity, he tugged the fragile panties down, letting them join her pool of clothing, then worked his way back up to her waist to unfasten the garter belt and watch it fail to the floor.

Now she was completely naked. Darren started from her waist, kissing his way down her belly to the upper part of her black triangle. He felt her thighs quiver when he touched her there. When his finger delved between the damps folds and caressed the sensitive pearl, he heard a gasp escape her lips.

"Darren," she whispered, her legs threatening to give out on her.

"Yes, sweetheart?"

"Make love to me now. I want—I need—"

He rose from his knees to stand over her. "I know what you want, and I know what you need. I'm going to take care of everything, sweetheart." He lifted her into his arms and after kissing her deeply, laid her in the middle of the heart-shaped bed, then joined her there.

Darren took the pins from her hair and ran his fingers through the dark silky mane, loving the feel and smell of it. He felt himself harden even more, his need making him ache with wanting her. He wanted to thoroughly enjoy his bride, every delicious inch of her. As she lay looking at him with that smoldering look in her eyes, his hardened flesh began to throb.

Lesley stroked his cheeks and walked her fingers down his chest, tweaked a nipple, then moved on down his ribs to his flat stomach and further still until she reached his shaft. She took his hard, throbbing flesh in her hand.

Darren nearly jerked off the bed. He murmured incoherent sounds when she massaged him. He'd been full of words earlier, but not any longer; talking was the last thing on his mind. He moved her hand away and slid his body over hers. Parting her thighs, he thrust inside.

"Oh, Darren! Darren," she groaned huskily.

As he began to move within her, he could feel the tight walls of her femininity envelope him like thick, warm molasses. Her inner muscles pulsated around his manhood as he moved. He couldn't help himself; he plunged to the hilt, then started moving in and out frenziedly.

Lesley moaned, rocking her head from side to side, raising her hips up and down.

Staccato-like groans of ecstasy puffed from his lips; soft pants and murmurs escaped hers. It didn't take them long to master the steps of this unique dance. The pulse of the dance speeded up, the ecstasy building to dizzying heights.

The music of love rushed them into a climax, dashing them together like cymbals.

"Yes, yes, like that, like that!" Lesley cried.

Darren gave a male shout of triumph and went still, letting the flood of passion overtake him.

At last the music ebbed and their hearts slowed, their bodies relaxed in the afterglow of their lovemaking.

Darren couldn't understand it. Each time he possessed her their lovemaking got better and better when he thought the last time couldn't be improved upon.

Her body was meant for his, Lesley thought, snuggling against Darren.

The next morning Darren kissed and caressed his new wife awake. "We have a flight to catch that leaves in a couple of hours," he whispered into her ear.

Lesley yawned and stretched against him. "Flight? What flight? Where are we going? We're not supposed to leave for Philadelphia until next week. I thought we'd be spending—"

"Our honeymoon in L.A.? In this suite?"

"Well, yes—but I take it we aren't?"

"Tip of the iceberg, my love. An awkward analogy I'll have to admit, considering we're in the heat of the hot southern California sun."

"Darren."

He pulled her into his arms and splayed his fingers over her back. "You'd better get dressed or we'll have to change our flight plans."

"Would that be so bad?" she said, her voice husky.

"No, but I don't want you to miss out on any of the things I have planned for you, sweetheart."

Lesley smiled. "Plans. I think I like that word. You're so unpredictable."

"Like a wild animal?" he teased. "The one thing I'm completely predictable about is seeing that you experience pleasure like you've never had before. I want every day of this marriage to be wonderful."

"I know it will be if you have your way."

"I want it to be your way too, Lesley. Get up, woman, and get dressed. Or do you want me to do it for you?"

"Can you do it without touching me?"

"You're a cruel woman, sweetheart. You know I can't. Maybe I'd better change our flight."

Lesley got off the bed. "I want to experience to the fullest the pleasure of these famous plans of yours," she said, then slipped into the bathroom.

"You want some company?" he called to her. "The door's not locked."

Lesley had promised herself and Dara many times that they would go to San Diego, but she'd never managed to make it down there the entire time she'd lived in Los Angeles. She'd heard that its beaches were splendid. As she looked out the window as they left the airport and headed in the rental car across the Coronado Bridge, she believed it.

"The water is so blue and the bay is fabulous!" Lesley exclaimed. "I can hardly wait to go for a swim."

"Actually I had something a little more intimate in mind for our first day." He wickedly arched his brow.

The Hotel Del Coronado came into view. The uniquely structured building reminded Lesley of a giant wedding cake because of the way it tiered, then spread out over the grounds. The palm trees and blue sky were the perfect backdrop. She could almost imagine what it would look like under a moonlit sky.

"There will be a full moon tonight, you'll get to see what it looks like for yourself."

"How did you know what I was thinking?"

"I'm psychic?"

"Darren."

"You actually spoke your thoughts out loud. And all right, I checked the calendar about the moon. Come on, let's go inside."

If she thought the Beverly-Hilton was romantic, Hotel Del Coronado was a Cinderella fantasy. Their suite, which included a beautiful garden terrace with jacuzzi, spelled Honeymoon Haven with a capital H.

The bellhop left their luggage and quietly exited the suite. Darren walked over to the bed and sprawled out on his back. Lesley eased her body over his and wrapped herself around him like a lazy cat.

"I expect to hear you purr any minute," he whispered in her ear.

"Oh, you will and more."

"More?"

She loosened his tie, then unbuttoned his shirt and pulled it out from his pants. She kissed his chest and laved a nipple with her tongue. He groaned in pleasure.

"Oh, sweetheart, what are you doing to me?"

"Heightening your sensual perception."

"You think you really need to?"

She felt his manhood throb against her thigh. "No. Maybe I'd better remove the barrier concealing your family treasure."

"The term is family jewels."

"What jewel do you think best describes your treasure? Ruby, no, topaz, no. Diamond, yes. You're a diamond in the rough, aren't you? I think you need a little polishing."

"Polishing?"

"Oh, yes," she whispered.

"And what do you plan to use as a polishing cloth?"

"You're bad."

"No, just eager to know the answer and to derive pleasure from the benefits."

Lesley removed his clothes, enjoying nipping the flesh she exposed as each piece came off. When Darren was completely naked, she gazed at his magnificently male body. She was glad that he took great care in keeping it in such wonderful shape.

"Are you going to look at me all day?"

"I could very easily, Mr. Taylor."

"I want you to do more than that, Mrs. Taylor. After you left Philadelphia I didn't think I'd ever be calling you that."

"Oh, you missed me then?"

"Yes, I missed you a lot." His expression turned serious. "I didn't mean to remind you of the time you've lost with Dara."

"And you, sweetheart." He drew her close to his body and kissed her.

At twilight as they walked along the beach, Lesley felt a special bond between her and Darren. He'd made love to her right after they arrived at the hotel and she had felt so connected to him. Now as they walked hand in hand along the beach, the sand beneath their feet making a soft crunching sound, that connection seemed to strengthen.

Did she dare hope that her dreams would come true? She'd hoped that once before and... No, she wouldn't think negative thoughts. Her life was what she made of it. They were bound to each other in a lot of ways; through affection, their child, their profession. But the day she gained Darren's complete trust would be the day they would truly be irrevocably bound. How she hungered for that day.

"What are you thinking, sweetheart?"

"About you and our life together."

"It's going to be fantastic. I intend to make sure of that." He squeezed her hand. "Look at that sky. I promised you a full moon."

A warm romantic feeling washed over her. "I never dreamed our honeymoon would be like this."

"How had you dreamed it would be?"

"Ordinary, I guess."

"There is nothing ordinary about the bride, it stands to reason that she should not have an ordinary wedding or honeymoon."

"I love your logic and the compliment." She gazed lovingly at him.

"Tomorrow we explore the Coronado Islands, and from there the South Bay, Point Loma and—"

"You're a tourist at heart. I remember your cousin Pete telling me that."

"He's right. If you don't want to go we can—"

"I want to go wherever you've got planned to take me. Being with you like this feels so good. Too bad we can't stay here forever. We could send for Dara and—"

He stopped walking and turned Lesley to face him.

"Our life together is going to be great. We don't need an island away from everything and everybody we know. It's going to be all right."

He kissed her deeply until he felt her go limp in his arms. "I think we'd better go to our suite and resume this conversation."

"Who can talk at a time like this?"

"Talking isn't exactly the conversation I had in mind either, more like body language."

"I'm a little rusty."

"Oh, girl, am I the instructor for you!"

Lesley awoke the next morning wrapped in Darren's arms. She breathed in his scent and sighed contentedly. Right now she felt so secure, but what about when they had to leave here and head to the East Coast, to Philadelphia?

"No frowns are allowed on this honeymoon," Darren commanded softly.

"You're right. Let's hurry up and see all those places on your itinerary so we can get back and take up where we left off last night."

"You're an eager wench, aren't you?"

"Eager for you."

It was almost evening when they returned to the hotel.

"Are you a little tipsy, Mrs. Taylor?"

"Just a little. You know I don't have much of a tolerance for alcohol."

"Señor Benardo let you taste only the light wines. Wasn't his winery something to see?"

"I agree, it was. What have you planned for tomorrow?"

"I thought we'd watch the racing or rent a yacht and go sailing."

"Oh."

"Don't you want to?"

"I'd really like to spend some more time in…"

"Bed?"

"Am I that obvious?"

"A little around the edges, but I don't mind, It's good to know that my new wife desires me like that. As I said before, I want to make you happy. If it makes you happy to stay in and make love, that's what we'll do."

EIGHTEEN

Lesley had to admit that Darren had made their honeymoon the sweet creation of a woman's most intimate fantasy. Her new husband had been sensitive to her every need, had thought of every conceivable way to please her, and yet what she wanted most of all he had not done; tell her that he loved her without reservation. Thinking what he did about her, she knew he wouldn't, but she couldn't help wishing.

The week they'd spent on San Diego's Coronado Bay had been wonderful, but she was anxious to return to their daughter, to begin their new life together, eager to start working on making her little family the loving family she wanted it to be. In just a mailer of a few weeks they would be leaving California, closing this chapter of their lives.

Before they left for Philadelphia, Lesley decided to take an afternoon off so that she and Dara could spend some time alone together, say their good-byes to the place they'd called home for the last five years. She wanted to know exactly what her daughter's feelings were about the move. So far Dara seemed happy, going along with every facet of the program without a complaint or a whimper, but Lesley sensed that all was not so right with her child's world.

There was a special park they sometimes went to along Santa Monica Boulevard, which paralleled the coastline for several miles. Lesley brought a picnic lunch and after finding a relatively isolated spot under a towering palm, spread out a blanket. She watched as her daughter looked out over the Pacific Ocean.

"The water is so pretty and blue today, Mama," she said in her wistful child's voice.

"You're going to miss it, aren't you?"

"Yeah," she sighed.

Lesley smiled. Her daughter was, after all, a California girl born and bred. She'd taught Dara to swim when she was a couple of months old, and she'd taken to the water like a duck. Lesley remembered the few times her own mother had taken her, her sister and her brother to the Delaware beach. Her father had always been too busy to come along with them.

Lesley knew instinctively that Darren wouldn't be like that with their daughter, that he would always make time, quality time for Dara She realized now how wrong she'd been to run away from him. And as Darren had said once she'd cheated herself, Dara and him of the time they could have spent together, time they could never get back.

Lesley allowed her mind to drift back in time to the day she'd given birth to Dara and how she'd wished Darren could have been there to share the miracle with her.

"Push, Lesley, that's it," the doctor encouraged.

She pushed with all her strength.

"Just one more time."

Lesley felt her cervix opening. For a moment she thought she would spilt in two. Then suddenly she felt the burgeoning pressure slip from her body. Seconds later, a loud wail pierced the silence of the delivery room.

"You have a beautiful baby girl Lesley" the doctor said with a pleased smile.

"A daughter." Happy tears streamed down Lesley's cheeks.

Minutes later the doctor handed her a tiny squirming baby. She knew in those few cherished moments the little person lowered into her waiting arms was her reason for going on.

Her thoughts had immediately wended back to Darren. She had longed to see the look on his face when he saw their daughter for the first time. As she gazed into her daughter's face, she saw Darren. Her hair was the same shiny black. She knew instinctively her eyes would be the same sparkling near-black color.

The only name that seemed to fit was Dara. She touched her baby's nose. God, she was his spitting image. She lovingly caressed her baby's cheek "Hi, Dara Ann. You're my precious little baby. You're all I'll ever have of a love I believed would last forever."

After she'd filled out the information for the birth certificate, she wondered if it had been wise to name her after her father if she intended to try to forget him.

Lesley blinked away the memory to reassure Dara about the move. "There are beaches in Philadelphia, if a little different from this. Instead of the Pacific Ocean there are two rivers, the Delaware and the Schuylkill, to have fun in."

"Are you and Daddy going to take me to play in them?"

Lesley smiled and kissed her daughter's forehead. "Yes, we sure will. You won't have time to miss California."

"Do you think I'll make new friends?"

Lesley hugged her. "I'm sure you will."

"Friends like Amber Carter?"

"Friends like Amber."

Dara and Lesley stripped down to their swimsuits and went for a quick dip in the ocean before polishing off their lunch.

"Want to take a walk along the beach?" Lesley asked.

"Yeah, and we can gather shells."

Lesley watched as Dara gathered sand dollars and a few tiny shells from the sand and put them in her beach bag. If only she could gather up the sands of her life as easily without feeling that it would all somehow dissolve with the rush of the tide.

The move to Philadelphia was a new beginning for them, a huge step forward in their future, but Lesley couldn't help feeling a little apprehensive about how it would eventually turn out.

What would she have to face when she got back home? The question of who set her up continued to plague her. Someone in Darren's family or his company had to be involved. Was her family as innocent as they claimed? There were so many unknowns, so many unanswered questions. Would she find the answers to her questions?

"You ready to go, baby?" Lesley called out.

Dara took one last look, and, smiling, took her mother's hand and they walked back to the car.

As she drove to her house, Lesley thought about where they'd be living once they arrived in Philly. Darren hadn't said. She was curious, but it was probably another one of his surprises. In any case she wanted her own personal things around her. She'd put her house on the market, but didn't sell all of her furniture, opting instead to store only the pieces she wanted to keep, later having them shipped to their new home.

Their new home. It was hard to think of Philadelphia as that after all the years in Los Angeles. Darren had not only ordered the equipment to open Raiments' Philadelphia branch and organized the transportation, but also arranged housing for those employees relocating to the East Coast.

Finally the day the Taylors were set to leave arrived. The employees threw a farewell luncheon for Darren and Lesley.

"I'm going to miss you, Giezel." Lesley slipped her arm around her friend's shoulder as they stood talking by the windows in the conference room.

"And I'm going to miss you, too," the other woman sniffed. "Do you think you'll be coming back for a visit?"

"I'm sure we will."

Final last minute good-byes were exchanged, and then the Taylors were on their way to the next phase of their new life together.

An hour later, after his wife and daughter were settled on the plane, Darren eased back in his seat and relaxed, stretching his arms and legs out in front of him. He closed his eyes and minutes later drifted into a dream-filled sleep. The day he would relive over and over again for the rest of his life came back with a vengeance to haunt him. He remembered sitting in his office waiting for security to escort the woman he loved inside as though she were some kind of dangerous criminal.

The intercom buzzed. "Mr. Taylor, Joseph from security is here with Miss Wells."

Darren's jaw muscles twitched and his anger burned like acid. "Send them in, Vera."

His heart lurched at the sight of Lesley. She appeared very distraught as she entered the room, eyes red-rimmed and face puffy as though she had been crying. Against his will he wanted to reach out and offer her comfort. It took all his will power not to give in to the impulse. Instead, he hardened his heart.

"You can leave her—I mean, Miss Wells—with me, Joseph."

"You sure? I can always wait outside."

"That won't be necessary."

The man shrugged his shoulders and left the room. As he watched the security guard exit the office, Darren took advantage of those few tension-filled seconds to compose himself and choose the right words to deal with the situation.

"Sit down, Lesley."

She peered imploringly into his face. "Darren, please, you've got to believe that I didn't betray you—you've just got to."

"Believe? Believe what?" he ground out ruthlessly. "Believe that the woman I love didn't steal from this company, in essence, steal from me?"

The hurt, vulnerable look in her eyes threatened to soften his heart. He cleared his throat and shoved the sympathy that struggled to take root to the back of his mind.

"I didn't do it, Darren."

"The original designs for our new line that were in our safe are missing. You didn't happen to pass them on to the competition, who just happen to be your family?"

"I don't know what you're talking about. I didn't take those designs, Darren. I swear by everything that is precious to me. Please, believe me."

"Oh, Lesley." He pulled her up out of her chair into his arms. "Darling, I love you. I know how you feel about your family and how you've tried all your life to prove yourself in their eyes. I'll cover for you; just tell me the truth."

He felt her stiffen, turn her face away, then look at him again.

"Cover for me? I'm telling you the truth. It's true that I've always felt that I had to prove myself to my family, but I would never do it this way, not by stealing from the man I love."

She stood looking at him for a few moments, something in her eyes seeming to shrivel and die. When she made to move away, she swayed.

"Lesley!" He reached out to steady her.

"Don't touch me. I'll be all right in a minute."

He noticed the way she leaned against the desk as if for support. God, how he wanted to take her in his arms and protect her with his love. He ached to feel the softness of her body enfolded in his embrace. Somehow he managed to resist the urge, though for the life of him he didn't know how.

"The designs were in the safe several weeks ago when I left you in this office to respond to an emergency. If you'll remember, in my hurry to leave, I carelessly left the door to the safe open."

She didn't respond to his words, just stared at him as though he were as transparent as glass, and she could see into his very soul.

"So you automatically assumed…" She closed her eyes, then ground out, 'All right, Darren, what are you going to do?"

"Do?' He raked his fingers through his hair. "Hell, I don't know." He skirted his desk and prowled angrily around the room. "So far we've been able to keep this quiet, but if the papers get hold of this, the scandal will finish what you've started. If you'd just bring the designs back…"

The look in her eyes made him feel like he'd just kicked a defenseless kitten. As he continued to study her, he thought, God in heaven, why can't I stop loving you.

"I can't return something I never took. Darren, there is something else I have to tell you, I—"

Just then the phone rang.

"Yes, Vera," he snapped. "Put him on. Listen, Dad, I—" His father's words demolished what was left of his heart. "I see. Thank you for getting the information to me so quickly. Yes, I'll handle it, don't worry."

He raised his eyes to look at Lesley. "You speak of love when you've sold us out to your family. That was my father. Wells of Fashion has just presented its collection. And they look amazingly like the designs that mysteriously disappeared from this company. Can you explain that?"

Her innocent look of horror and disbelief at his words almost swayed him. He stared at her, wondering what she would say next. He didn't have long to wait.

Lesley looked down at her left hand, then twisted her engagement ring off. Gazing directly at him, she said in an emotionless voice. "Here. I should have done this when you first accused me of betraying you." Then she threw it in his face. "So much for the love you claimed to feel for me. All it took was the

*loss of a few pieces of paper to make you a liar." With a pained,
soulful look, she turned to leave the room.*

"Lesley, wait. What were you going to tell me?"

"Do you really care?"

"There's the matter of charges."

*"Do your worst, Mr. Taylor. I'm surprised you've waited as
long as you have. You know, I just don't give a damn." With
that she slammed out of his office, out of his life.*

Darren came awake with a start and glanced over at
Lesley as she sat dozing in her seat, her arm protectively
draped across their daughter. That day spelled the destruction of his dreams for a happily-ever-after with the woman
he loved.

He remembered wondering what she was going to tell
him before the phone interrupted. He now realized what it
was.

Oh, God, Lesley my love. How I must have hurt you.
His soul was mired in turmoil. He was now married to the
only woman he'd ever desired to be with, and who
happened to be the mother of his child.

Over the last few weeks, he'd had a chance to observe
Lesley up close and personal. And he hadn't seen her do or
say anything that would indicate she was a traitor. He'd
certainly put enough pressure on her by thwarting her
efforts to find another job.

Lesley had raised his child and done one hell of a job.
Millie, who worked for her, was really like a mother to
Lesley, protective of her as a mother hen of her chicks,
trusted and respected her.

Then there was Arthur, who'd trusted Lesley with his business over the years. Darren knew she could easily have stolen from him at any time, but she hadn't.

He squirmed uncomfortably in his seat.

Finally, bastard that he was, he hadn't allowed Lesley to explain six years ago, and as recently as a few weeks ago, he'd practically labeled her delusional; in essence insulted and called her a liar. If that wasn't enough, he'd had the audacity to suggest she needed counseling.

Despite all he'd done to her, she'd agreed to marry him—which meant she had to love him to do that, even though he was undeserving of it.

As far as he was concerned, she was innocent.

If he'd destroyed her love, he had only himself to blame. He should have had more faith in her. God, he hoped in time she could forgive him, because he didn't know if he'd ever be able to forgive himself. The only way he could begin to redeem himself was to expose the one who'd really stolen the designs and clear her name.

Hearing Lesley yawn brought Darren out of his reverie. He couldn't help gaping at her; he loved and admired this woman, and at this moment desired her above all else.

When Lesley opened her eyes, it was to find Darren staring at her. She felt her face heat up.

"I hope that flush means you were dreaming about me. I can hardly wait to get you home, Mrs. Taylor."

Into your bed you mean, a taunting little voice inside her head sniped.

Although he was smiling, being his usual charming self, Lesley noticed something was different about Darren. She couldn't put her finger on it; but there was something.

"Are you feeling all right, Darren?" she asked.

"I'm fine. Why do you ask?"

"I don't know. You just seem—never mind." She glanced at Dara who was rubbing her eyes.

"Daddy, when are we going to get to Phididelpha—"

"Philadelphia, my little sweetheart," Darren corrected. He looked at his watch. "We should be arriving there in about two hours and thirty minutes."

"Will I get to meet my aunts and uncles and grandparents?"

"Yes, you sure will."

Lesley's insides tightened into knots at the thought of confronting their families. She dreaded facing Darren's parents almost as much as she dreaded facing her own. She hadn't seen his parents since they'd been told she was a thief. They had obviously believed, as did Darren, that she was guilty of industrial espionage, using her relationship with their son to accomplish her goal. What must they think now that he had married her?

Would Jordanna, Darren's sister, look at her with contempt? She hoped not. They were once as close as sisters, closer in fact than Lesley was to her own sister, Jasmine. Her thoughts drifted to Pete Taylor, Darren's cousin, and his uncle Stewart. She felt apprehensive about the reception she was likely to receive from that part of Darren's family.

"Why don't you sleep a while longer, my little sweetheart?" Darren said to Dara, "I want you to be rested by the time we land." He smiled when she closed her eyes in sleep almost immediately.

"Lesley, are you all right?" Darren asked.

"I'm fine." She looked away.

Darren put his hand over hers. "Nervous?"

She looked back at him and nodded.

"It's going to be all right." He squeezed her hand reassuringly. "You'll see."

Despite the tone of reassuring enthusiasm in his voice, Lesley was not anxious to return to the scene of her humiliation.

NINETEEN

Darren studied Lesley as she eased back in the seat and gazed out the window, effectively shutting him out. What was she thinking? he wondered. He wasn't likely to find out until after they reached Philadelphia, if then, so he closed his eyes and minutes later joined his daughter in sleep.

When Lesley heard Darren's even breathing, she focused her attention on his face. That vitality he exuded when he was awake lay temporarily dormant as he slept. He looked younger and more vulnerable somehow. Her love for this unpredictable man swelled within her.

Oh, Darren I love you so much. If you could only come to love me again the way you used to. I would give anything to hear those three precious words: "I believe you."

No sooner had Lesley drifted off to sleep than the sound of the pilot's voice awakened her.

"We will be touching down at the Philadelphia International Airport in eight minutes. Welcome to Philadelphia, the cradle of the nation. Remember to fasten your seat belts."

Lesley's stomach heaved in anxious anticipation as though she were on a roller coaster waiting for the car to reach the summit, then plunge downward at astronomical speed.

How had she let Darren talk her into coming back here? She was sure that meeting his family again after all that had happened would be the equivalent of facing a firing squad at dawn. She glanced apprehensively at Darren. He wasn't gloating. What she saw was concern. But was it more for her or for their daughter? At that moment she was jealous of her own child.

Darren hadn't missed the anxiety he'd seen in Lesley's face. He wanted to reassure her that everything would be all right, but he couldn't completely because he wasn't sure himself how things would turn out.

On wobbly legs, Lesley accompanied her husband and child out of the plane and down the enclosed accordion-corridor into the terminal. At the gate stood Jordanna, Pete and another man she didn't know. She wondered who he was; probably a friend of Danna's or Pete.

The tension gripping her body eased when she realized that she wouldn't have to face Darren's parents and uncle just yet.

Jordanna smiled at Lesley, then held out her arms. Lesley went into them, closing her eyes and hugging her friend tightly.

"It's been a long time, Les." Jordanna smiled, a sheen of tears glistening in her eyes.

"Oh, Danna, it's so good to see you."

"Congratulations are in order, I hear," Pete added with a neutral look and voice.

"You're right, they are, cuz," Darren interjected lightly in an attempt to smooth over the awkwardness of the moment. He glanced at the other man, then back at his wife. "Lesley, I'd like you to meet my friend Ashton Price."

He smiled. "Pleased to meet you at last, Lesley." And he extended his hand. "Call me Ash, everybody does."

After a few baffling seconds, Lesley remembered why the name seemed so familiar. Darren had mentioned Ash a couple of times years ago when they first got involved. As she recalled, Ashton Price was a private investigator. Did she have him to thank for Darren having tracked her down? At the moment his scrutiny seemed casual, but she sensed that it really wasn't. She was sure that his assessing brown eyes rarely missed a thing. This Ashton Price was also a very attractive man. Why was he here to meet them? she wondered.

Jordanna lowered her gaze to Dara.

"Who do we have here?"

Jordanna shifted her gaze to Darren in a curious, questioning glance, then back to the little girl. He sent a message in a look that said I'll-explain-it-to-you-later She smiled, then dropped down on her heels to the niece she hadn't known she had until two minutes ago.

"You look so much like your daddy. Do they call you Dara by any chance?"

"Yes," the child said with a wondering look. "How'd you know?

Danna smiled. "It was just a lucky guess."

"I'm—my name is Dara Ann Ev—Taylor." She looked to her father.

Darren shot her an approving nod. He'd legally changed her last name at the time he applied for the marriage license.

"Do you know who I am?" Jordanna prompted.

"You're my Aunt Jordanna." Dara switched her gaze to the man standing next to her father. "And he's my cousin Pete. Daddy showed me a picture of him."

Pete's expression softened and he answered, "I sure am. Your father and I grew up together. I bet I know what picture he showed you: one of us together." He smiled, then added, "He's the closest thing I have to a brother."

Lesley watched Pete. His resemblance to Darren was striking, though his eyes weren't the same vibrant dark color, but a lighter shade of brown. He was also several inches shorter. Of the two Darren was more muscular. She shifted her gaze to Jordanna's head next to Dara's. Their eyes and smiles were almost identical. It pleased her to see that an instant rapport seemed to have blossomed between the two.

It would appear that Danna wasn't holding any grudges. Lesley sighed inwardly with relief. Could they revive their friendship? She hoped so; she knew she'd like nothing better.

"He's right, little sweetheart," Darren said. "We used to get into all kinds of trouble together when we were little boys."

Dara looked thoughtfully at her parents. "Maybe you and Mama can make me a brother or a sister."

Lesley cleared her throat and shot a quick-second glance at Darren.

"It may take a while since your mother and I just got back together."

"How long is a while?"

"Dara, I think we'd better talk about this another time, baby," Lesley suggested.

"Your mother is right, little sweetheart. What do you say we all get out of here?"

"Will you be staying in the penthouse apartment?" Pete asked.

"For the time being. I've already arranged for the house to be readied."

Lesley stared at Darren in shock. By the house did he mean the one he had been in the process of building for them six years before? Or was it another house he was referring to? Since he'd never said what he'd done about the other house, she assumed that he had sold it. Was it really possible that they were going to be living in their dream house? If they were, she wasn't sure how she felt about it, considering all that had happened between them.

Guessing at the look in Lesley's eyes, Darren said, "We'll talk about our permanent living arrangements later. For now, all we need to be concerned about is moving into our temporary place, the penthouse." He turned to his sister. "Where are Mom and Dad?"

"They wanted me and Pete to bring you back to the house. Since they don't know about Dara it will be a pleasant surprise for them."

Lesley winced, knowing she wouldn't be.

Thirty minutes later, Pete eased the family Mercedes through the gate to the semi-circular drive of the Taylor Mansion. Lesley remembered the many times she had come here with Darren when they were engaged.

She wondered who and why someone had deliberately set out to ruin her career and, most of all, her relationship with Darren. The thought of someone being that heartlessly cruel and calculating... Yet someone had been. Would she be able to find out the answer to her questions after all this time?

Darren sensed the conflict in his wife as he studied her profile. Was it the apprehension of seeing his parents, or another reason? He wasn't sure how his parents were taking the news that he had made Lesley his wife or how they were going to react to seeing her again.

A few minutes later he ushered Lesley and Dara into the entrance hall. Nadine and Darren Taylor senior came out of the living room to greet their guests. Lesley saw the tears shimmering in Nadine's eyes when they lighted on Dara.

Dara ventured forward curiously. "Are you really my grandmother?" she asked her.

Nadine walked over to her granddaughter. All eyes were riveted on them and no one said anything.

"Yes, I am. You look a lot like your father and aunt did when they were little." She smiled. "What is your name?"

"Dara Ann Ev—I mean, Taylor."

"How old are you, my dear?"

"Six. My birthday was last month."

Nadine held out her arms to her only grandchild. Dara went into them without hesitation. Tears stung Lesley's eyes when she realized how much having a family meant to her child and how eager she was to become a part of it.

"Lesley, how have you been?" Darren's father asked, his voice crisp and noncommittal, but not unkind.

Lesley cleared her throat. "Fine, thank you."

"Ash," Darren's father said, then glanced at his son and grandchild and inched forward to a place by his wife's side.

"I'm your grandfather. My name is Darren too. I see it and its derivatives are very popular names in this family." He shot his son a proud smile.

Darren grinned. He could tell his parents were hooked on their grandchild already. His little sweetheart had a way of wrapping herself around a person's heart at first sight. Now to work on his parents' opinion of his wife. He watched his parents lead Dara into the living room, then returned his gaze to Lesley. There were tears welling in her eyes.

"Are you all right, Lesley?" Jordanna asked.

"Yes, it's just seeing Dara and her grandparents together like that made me…"

"I understand. I feel it too.' Jordanna gazed thoughtfully at her brother.

Lesley knew this to be a time of truce with all the problems they had to face temporarily put on hold for Dara's sake, so that she could come to know her grandparents and they to know her, for them all to become family.

Her attention shifted to Pete, observing him as he stood talking to Darren and Ash. Could he possibly be the one who had set her up? It was hard to believe that he would do something like that, but someone had. When she thought about Pete's father, that was another story. She could believe anything about that man.

Just then, as if Lesley had conjured him up, Stewart Taylor descended the stairs. He did nothing to hide the contempt clearly visible in his eyes. Was he the one? She had no trouble believing that, but the one thing she didn't have was proof against him or anyone else, for that matter. But she intended to get it.

"Uncle Stewart," Darren called to him. "You remember Lesley, don't you?" He smiled. "Congratulations are in order. She's now my wife."

"Wife?"

"Yes, we were married a few weeks ago in Los Angeles."

"I wasn't aware that you even knew where she was. No one ever tells me anything in this family, including my own son," he said caustically, casting Pete an angry look, then gazing into the living room at his brother, his lips tightened bitterly.

"Finding Lesley was my primary reason for going to L.A."

"Oh," said Stewart in a less-than-gracious tone of voice. "I take it you resolved to your satisfaction her part in that 'business' six years ago?"

"That is not why I married her." "Congratulations, then."

Pete advanced toward him. "Father, I don't think—"

Darren glared at his uncle. "It's all right, Pete. Uncle Stewart and I understand each other."

Stewart walked into the living room and stopped just inside the doorway, his eyes riveted on Dara. Then he looked from the child to Darren; realization flowered.

"I'm beginning to see why you married her." "Are you my Uncle Stewart?" Dara asked.

"Yes, I am," he answered stiffly, staying where he stood.

Lesley flinched, knowing how sensitive her child was. Nadine moved closer to Dara and put a protective hand on her shoulder. Then Darren's father closed ranks, squeezing his granddaughter's hand reassuringly.

"Let's take her out to the garden, Nadine," he suggested.

Darren shot his uncle a warning glance. "Whatever the reason, Lesley and I are married now, Uncle. You may not like it, but it would be to your advantage to be civil to her and our child."

"I wouldn't think of being anything else." Stewart glanced at Pete. "Son, I need to speak with you and Jordanna about business." Without uttering another word, he left the room and headed down the hall to the study.

"I'm sure father didn't mean to be so—" Pete began.

"Rude?" Darren finished. "There's no need to apologize. This is me, Pete. I know Uncle Stewart as well as you do. He meant to be every bit as unpleasant as he was and more if I had let him get away with it, which I damn sure am not going to do."

Lesley realized in that moment how strongly committed Darren was to her and the marriage. Hope rose inside her like bread dough with yeast. If only everything would work out.

Darren smiled watching his parents and Dara. "Our daughter does have a way about her."

"Yes, she does," Lesley answered softly.

By the time they arrived at Darren's penthouse apartment, they were all exhausted both physically and emotionally. Deeply asleep, Dara barely moved when her father carried her into her room. Lesley looked around as she waited for him to return. The apartment was different from the last time she was here. Darren had obviously had a decorator come in and redo the place.

"How do you like it?" Darren asked as he entered the living room.

"It's very nice."

"Nice? Kind of a flat way of describing it, don't you think?"

"What do you want me to say?"

"That you like it very much or you can't stand it."

"Oh, Darren." She shook her head, wondering why they were mired in small talk. Lesley glanced in the direction of his bedroom and swallowed hard when she saw his huge waterbed.

Darren hadn't missed that look of uneasiness that raised the heat into her cheeks. Why had coming here had that effect on her? They'd been intimate here years before the marriage. Surely it wasn't the place. The apartment itself had been completely redone after she'd left. Except the bed. That had to be it. He smiled. He had to admit that they'd made a lot of memories, and possibly conceived their daughter, there. If he had his way, and he intended to, they'd make more memories before they moved into the house.

He liked the idea Dara had innocently posed about making her a brother or sister. He'd missed out on seeing Lesley pregnant and could vividly imagine how she must have looked in that condition. He'd love to have a son or another daughter with her, but that was sometime in the future. He wanted them to get to know each other again first, but he didn't want to wait too long to enlarge their family.

Darren crossed the room to the bar. "Would you like a drink, sweetheart?"

"N-no, yes." She smiled nervously.

"I"m not the wolf in sheep's clothing, Lesley. I promise not to devour you." He grinned wickedly and handed her a glass of brandy. "At least not yet."

"You're impossible. You know that, don't you?"

"Lighten up, sweetheart."

Strangely enough, after the first few sips, Lesley found herself doing just that.

Darren stepped over to the stereo and selected a soft romantic piece by Peabo Bryson, "By the Time This Night Is Over."

He turned. "Now, come here." He opened his arms.

She moved hesitantly at first, then slid easily into his embrace. Darren held her close.

"This is the moment I've been looking forward to all day." He felt her stiffen. "What is it, sweetheart?"

"I don't know."

"It's being back here in Philadelphia, isn't it? You'll get used to it."

She worried her bottom lip with her teeth. "I know you're right, but…"

"It's not the only thing, is it? When Pete mentioned the house, your mood changed."

Tears slipped down her cheeks. "We had such plans and dreams for that house, Darren. And then when everything fell apart…"

"We can still make our dreams a reality, Lesley. You, me and our beautiful daughter are going to have a wonderful life together. You'll see."

Only if I can prove to you that I'm innocent, then it would be.

"You're not convinced that you did the right thing, are you?"

"Are you? You still don't trust me, Darren."

"I'm turning the Philadelphia branch of Raiments over to you, lock, stock and barrel. Doesn't that show you the trust I have in you?"

"Well, yes, that kind of trust, yes, but—"

"No buts." He lowered his mouth to hers, halting the flow of her words.

The kiss, following so closely on the heels of the brandy, caused Lesley's body to tremble with desire. Darren eased his fingers inside her jacket and moved his thumb across the silky fabric of her blouse, causing the lacey bra encasing her breasts to abrade her nipples. When she felt her skin heat up and her pulses throb, she let out a low moan.

That moan was all Darren needed to hear. It sent exquisite messages of urgent need coursing through his body like electrical impulses through a hot wire. He groaned, continuing to kiss her with a desperation that shocked and excited him.

"Lesley, Lesley, sweetheart. God, how I want you."

"I want you too," she rasped, meshing her body with his.

Darren lifted her in his arms and carried her down the hall to their bedroom.

Lesley knew that even though the relationship between them wasn't perfect, she needed him more at this moment than she ever had before. He was a part of her that had been missing for so long. She needed to feel that sense of being one with him. She would just have to let tomorrow take care of itself.

TWENTY

Lesley came awake the next morning with a contented languor flowing through her body, a leftover from a night of intense lovemaking. When she felt warm eager fingers fondling her breasts and stroking another equally sensitive area, a soft sigh eased from her lips.

"Darren."

"Hmmm."

"It's morning."

His fingers moved more frenziedly against the source of her desire. "So?"

"So, maybe—" A gasp of ecstasy cut short her answer.

Darren covered her mouth with his own, sensually obliterating any idea she might have had to postponing their lovemaking. He felt her tremble, and when she parted her thighs for him to pleasure her further, he knew he'd accomplished his goal. And pleasure her he did, exciting every passion point, devouring every inch of her until she writhed in mindless rapture.

Then finally he slid his hard body over her soft one, guiding himself past the entrance into her warmth, burrowing deep inside her enticing depths. He hesitated, closing his eyes a moment, as though relishing having her in his arms, then he began to pay silent homage to her femininity with his worshipping manhood.

A complaining gasp escaped Lesley's throat seconds later when Darren withdrew, only to ease into a happy sigh when he drove smoothly into her pulsating core. Like an oar maneuvering in the ocean, his thrusting manhood moved rhythmically inside her femininity. He set a pace meant to move her to exhilarating heights of bliss and untold depths of ecstasy. And it did.

"Oh, Darren." She arched upward, rejoicing in his possession, completely lost in the joy of his devastating love-making.

I love you, Darren Taylor. I love you so much, she cried out silently in her mind as the tremors of her climax rocked her to the very center of her being.

"Lesley, my love," he shouted in male exultation as his release rushed through him, delivering the essence of himself deep inside her womb. As his senses slowly cleared, returning to normal, he realized that he hadn't used protection. Maybe Dara would get her wish sooner than she thought. And maybe it would help secure his marriage to Lesley, but dammit, he didn't want to hold her that way. He decided to be more conscientious about contraception in the future.

Darren studied Lesley. Her eyes were drooping closed. He smiled. She looked so like their daughter when she was relaxed like this. "Oh, Lesley, my love," he whispered against her sleeping face. "I love you."

The woman he held in his arms was his life and he would never give her up. What would she say if he told her he believed her? After practically calling a mental case, he was sure she wouldn't. But would it be the truth?

His past distrust had been indelibly etched in her mind. No, he couldn't say those words, not until he had proved his love by finding out who framed her.

Lesley awoke and smiled when she realized she was snug and safe in the haven of her husband's arms. However, a cloud of uncertainty still threatened to overshadow her happiness and rain on her parade. They were back in Philadelphia. It had been years since she'd been here. Was it too late to clear her name, and restore her reputation and gain Darren's love and faith in her? She hoped not.

She left the bed and slipped into her robe. Crossing the room to the huge plate glass window of the penthouse apartment, she looked out at the pre-dawn sky, observing the view without really appreciating its beauty. How could one place hold so many different sets of memories? Although there had been more good times than bad, the bad had a way of shading over the good, making her feel uneasy and afraid. What would happen over the next few weeks was anyone's guess.

"Come back to bed, sweetheart. Let each day take care of itself," Darren said sleepily.

"It's not that simple, Darren. About the house—"

"What about it?" He rose from the bed and joined her at the window.

"It was nearly finished when…"

"Call it a masochistic streak, but I had our dream house completed to your specifications. I haven't been inside it since it was finished, though. It'll be a virgin undertaking for us both. Are you ready for it?"

"I—I'm not sure."

"I'm not worried about you. This strong-minded woman I married is no coward. She can face anything." He drew her into his arms, then led her back to bed.

Was she that strong? Lesley wondered. She certainly hadn't been strong enough to withstand Darren's steely determination that she marry him and return here. But then what woman could resist such an onslaught? Besides, the fringe benefits were incredible when she thought about his exquisite lovemaking.

They lay in bed watching the sun come up. Somehow, that ordinary occurrence didn't seem so ordinary anymore. Did it portend brighter days they hoped to share in the future?

"You and Daddy awake, Mama?" Dara peeked her head around the partially open door.

"Yes, we are, my little sweetheart," Darren answered with the angling of his head, beckoning her to come in. "You're ready for breakfast, I take it?"

"Well…" she climbed up on the bed.

Lesley reached for her robe.

Darren stayed her hand. "Not to move, my love. It'll be my pleasure to fix breakfast this morning for both my ladies. After that we'll take Dara over to Mom and Dad's so they can get better acquainted, then we'll get on with the rest of our day."

Was there a hidden meaning in his words? Her insides knotted at the thought of facing yet another part of her past. What exactly did Darren have in mind?

The last place Lesley expected Darren to take her was Fairmount Park on the Schuylkill River. It used to be one of their favorite places to go when they were dating. They would go to the park to listen to the open-air concerts at the playhouse there. She thought as they walked that when they came back again, they'd bring Dara so she could watch the puppet theaters in City Hall Courtyard.

"I thought we needed time together, just the two of us, to relax and unwind. This was the one place I knew I could make that happen," Darren said gently.

Her face spread into a nostalgic smile. 'I remember the last time we were here," she said softly. "All the many times we came here, I'm still not sure we've ever seen it all." Fairmount Park was over six square miles, probably the largest park in America, she thought.

"Let's take a ride on the trolley." Darren pulled her in the direction of the trolley stop.

They made it just in time for the next departure. Lesley laughed at the clanging bell and dropped down on one of the wooden-slat seats.

Darren enjoyed seeing Lesley lighthearted and carefree like this. Suddenly it was as though time had rolled back the years. The fragrance of the azalea gardens wafted through the air as the trolley moved past Boathouse Row.

Darren smiled. "Pete always said we were nuts for wanting to do what the tourists come to Philadelphia for when we've lived here all our lives."

"I'll bet we know the city of our birth better than anyone else!" Lesley exclaimed with a happy sigh.

"You getting hungry?" Darren asked her two hours later.

"Starving, as in stomach rubbing against backbone."

"Can't have that, now can we? I just happen to know of the perfect place to remedy the situation."

Lesley's eyes misted because she knew the place he was talking about. Friday Saturday Sunday was classy but unpretentious. The cutlery and the china didn't match, flowers were rare, and the menu was set on a wall-mounted slate board. Penlights framed a row of rectangular mirrors set in wood paneling. The sound system was what Greg would call the bomb, she thought with a smile. An aquarium bubbled behind the bar, she remembered.

The smell of spicy Yum-Yum scallops assailed them when they walked through the door.

Yes. She was definitely back home.

Darren smiled when Lesley, with gusto, tucked into her dessert of cheesecake topped with fresh raspberries.

"You weren't kidding about being hungry, were you?" he teased.

"Being back home seems to have given me an appetite," she said, polishing off the last bite of the cheesecake.

"We'd better go. Our daughter will think we've abandoned her if we don't hurry and pick her up."

"I've gotten raspberries on my dress. We need to go back to the apartment so I can change."

"Before or after you've enticed me into ravishing you?" Darren grinned. "You know if we go back there that's what'll happen, don't you?"

"Yes, I know." She lowered her lashes seductively.

The day had been relaxing, Lesley thought as she snuggled close to Darren, who was sleeping soundly, his arm possessively draped across her waist. She knew he'd wanted her to truly feel that she was back where he believed she belonged. She was sure that he had very different plans for her for tomorrow. Today was his way of showing her that he cared. They both knew that she would have to face some difficult times.

"It's time to turn it off, sweetheart."

"Darren, I thought you were sleep."

"I can always tell when you're not with me in mind and spirit."

"I can't help feeling—I don't know—apprehensive, I guess."

"You're Mrs. Darren Taylor now. You'll get the respect that comes with that title."

"I know that should make me feel better, but it doesn't."

He drew her into his arms. "Give it time."

She breathed in his scent, reveling in his confidence and warmth, drawing from his strength. They had so much, but she wanted it all. She was going to work on that.

Lesley stood before the Taylor Building the next morning with Dara and Darren, a feeling of trepidation and deja vu bombarding her. Taylor's hadn't changed much. Her insides tightened when she saw Joseph, the security guard who had escorted her to Darren's office all those years ago, approaching them. She could tell by his expression that he recalled that awful day.

"Mr. Taylor." He stared at Lesley and Dara.

"I'd like to introduce you to my wife and daughter."

"Wife?" The man cleared his throat. "Daughter? Congratulations on your marriage, sir."

"Thank you, Joseph. I'm a lucky man."

Joseph reached for the special badges everyone was required to wear when inside the building.

Dara flashed a proud, grown-up smile as her father pinned the badge to the front of her dress.

Lesley realized this practice must have begun because of what had happened. The injustice of it came back to torment her. Just because she was Darren's wife now didn't put her above suspicion. If anything, it called more attention to her. Didn't Darren realize that? Of course he did, but it didn't seem to bother him.

Darren saw the suspicion in Lesley's eyes and wanted to allay it, but he couldn't, not yet. He'd started things in motion today and he had to see them through to their eventual conclusion. That meant letting her think he still thought she was delusional. It bothered him more than anything. And the feeling was hell.

Joseph was a good man, but he was a gossip. Darren knew that before they would make it up to his office the entire building would know about his marriage to Lesley and about their daughter. And each one would have his or her own opinion about it. But he didn't care what any of them thought.

As they made their way to the elevator, Lesley felt eyes on her back. She knew it would only get worse before the day ended. What had she let herself in for by coming back to Philadelphia, here to Taylor's?

Vera, Darren's secretary, tried to mask her shock and disapproval, but failed to cover it completely.

"Good morning, Darren."

"Good morning, Vera. You remember Lesley Wells."

She nodded.

"She's now my wife, and you will afford her every courtesy and respect. Do I make myself clear?"

"Very clear," the woman answered tightly, shifting her gaze to Dara.

Darren smiled proudly. "This is our daughter Dara."

The woman smiled at the little girl. "Pleased to meet you, Dara." As though it were an afterthought she added when she spoke to Lesley, "Allow me to be one of the first to welcome you, Lesley—Mrs. Taylor, back to Philadelphia." Vera cleared her throat and said to Darren, "Your uncle is in your office waking to see you."

He turned to Lesley and Dara "My sweethearts, would you mind wailing for me out here until I've finished with Uncle Stewart?"

"No, we won't mind will we, Dara?" The last thing Lesley wanted was to talk to Stewart Taylor.

Dara walked over to Vera's desk and watched her at work on a computer terminal. Vera invited her closer.

"You want to try it?"

Dara's eyes lit up. "Yes, can I?" She turned to Lesley.

"It's all right baby,' she assured her. Lesley watched as the secretary sat Dara on her lap.

After a few minutes Lesley picked up a magazine from a display table and thumbed through it. Although Vera was kindness itself to Dara, she could almost feel the hostility toward her emanating from the woman.

Did Vera hate her? As far as Lesley knew, she hadn't done anything to her to warrant that treatment. A distant memory floated to the surface of her mind. Jordanna had once mentioned that Vera had a king-size crush on Darren. Surely she couldn't be the one who had…

Thirty minutes later, the door to Darren's office opened and Stewart Taylor came marching out. On his way to the elevator, he glared venomously at Lesley and Dara.

"Our meeting is concluded," he spit out. 'You can go in now."

Lesley shivered at the chill in his voice.

"Lesley," Darren called from the doorway.

She watched Stewart until the doors of the elevator closed.

Darren stepped out into the outer office. "Uncle Stewart is Uncle Stewart. Don't let him get to you." He looked to Dara. "You think you could keep Vera company a few minutes, my little sweetheart. I need to talk to your mother alone."

"Yes," she answered and returned to what she was doing on the computer.

"It would seem that we've temporarily lost our daughter to the lure of computer technology." He laughed as he ushered Lesley into his office.

Lesley nodded an agreeing smile as she walked in.

As she sat down, Lesley wondered if Darren suspected even a little that his uncle could be the one responsible for the espionage. The birth of hope died. Of course he didn't. He believed she was blocking out her guilt, she had to keep reminding herself. His belief explained his seemingly nonchalant attitude toward his uncle.

"Vera will help you organize the files and records once they arrive from Los Angeles."

"Are you sure she'll want to help me?"

"If she wants to keep her job, she'll do as she's told."

She watched Darren closely. "What did you and your uncle talk about?"

"He's going to be the liaison between Raiments and Taylor's, and he was less than happy about it."

Lesley grimaced. Her stomach muscles jerked in reaction to the news.

"I know you and he have never really gotten along, but this is business, Raiment business. And since you will be overseeing its growth, you'll have to deal with him."

Why do I have to? Couldn't you get someone else? she wanted to shout at him, but restrained herself, barely. She got up from her seat and walked over to the window and looked out. "I see."

He wanted to take her in his arms and tell her she didn't have to deal with his uncle, but it was necessary to the success of his plan.

"Pete is going to give you a crash course in the responsibilities of running the business."

"You could do that, Darren. I'd rather it be you."

"I'm sorry, sweetheart, but that won't be possible. You see, I'm going to be busy with my research project."

"Research project?"

"Yes. I told you once how fascinated I was with researching new fabrics. After you left, I decided to get involved in that aspect of the business. Niven seems to think that I have a flair in that area of expertise. I've already turned many of my responsibilities over to Jordanna. She will become the new chairman of the board in my place at the new session."

Lesley frowned. "Who is Niven?"

"Niven Alexander is our new research scientist. You'll get to meet her very soon. She's in Ireland right now, deep in negotiations with a wool manufacturer there."

Her? Lesley was speechless. So many changes, so fast. What was Darren thinking? What was really going on?

"I haven't given you time to absorb all of this, I know, but it'll all become familiar to you in time."

"Darren, I—I'm not sure—"

"Don't worry, sweetheart. You'll have all the help you need to make the Philadelphia branch of Raiments a success. The major element in this equation is your talent for creating exciting, elegant fashions." He looked at his watch. "Listen, I've got a meeting in fifteen minutes."

"But I—" Lesley began.

"I've alerted Marsha in personnel. She should have several people lined up for you to interview for the positions of administrative assistant and assistant designer, starting tomorrow. If you're not happy with them, Marsha will get you more applicants to interview for the jobs.

Twenty employees from Los Angeles decided to move to Philadelphia to work for us. The rest of the personnel we'll need are being sought as we speak."

"Darren—"

"Got to go, sweetheart. Meet me back here at one o'clock and I'll take you to Dilullo's for lunch. My mother called to say she'd be coming by to pick Dara up and take her to lunch. I think she just wants to show off her granddaughter to all her friends. Oh by the way, Jordanna and Ash will be joining us for lunch." He smiled and hurried out the door.

Lesley stood watching the empty doorway for moment, then walked over to the window and looked out. She still couldn't believe what was happening here.

"Are you ready for the grand tour of your new enterprise?" Pete said from the doorway, Dara perched on his hip.

Lesley turned. "Pete?"

"In the flesh. Look what I found." He smiled at Dara and kissed the tip of her nose, then looked back at Lesley. "Don't look so surprised to see me. Didn't Darren tell you I would be helping you?"

"Yes, about five minutes ago. Pete, I—"

"Now don't go off. We've always gotten along in the past, haven't we?"

"Well, yes, but—"

"I never was convinced that you did what some members of the family think you did."

"No?"

"No. The whole thing was too neat, too pat. Danna doesn't believe it either."

"When you say some members, you meant Darren's parents and your father, don't you?"

Dara squirmed on Pete's hip. "What is he talking about, Mama?"

"It's nothing, baby."

"Lesley," he went on, "they don't know you as well as we do."

"You don't need to try to spare my feelings." Pete had purposely forgotten to include her own husband among the skeptics.

"Since there was no proof to show them, I had no choice but to let it drop."

"I needed to hear that six years ago. It's too late now. I have to proceed as though nothing has happened. Although I don't see how."

"Mama," Dara said impatiently.

Pete smiled. "I think we'd better discuss this another time. In the meantime, I'll help you all I can, Lesley."

"Thanks, Pete."

When Pete drove up in front of the building Darren had chosen for Philadelphia Raiments, Lesley stared in admiration. It was a modern new building, different from Taylor's usual establishments. The task of whipping it into a fashion business seemed to be nearer completion than she expected. Darren must have had the work started right after he'd bought Raiments. It irritated her that he had been so certain of her compliance, when she hadn't been so sure she'd return to Philadelphia herself.

"So what do you think?" Pete said cheerily.

"I'm impressed."

"Me too," Dara added.

"Let's go inside."

Pete cupped Lesley's elbow and took Dara's hand, guiding them into the building. Darren hadn't missed a beat, she concluded. The place was everything she could have asked for in a work place.

"Your office is over there." Pete pointed to a hand-carved, heavy wooden door to the right.

He opened it and waved for her and Dara to precede him inside. For the second time that day, Lesley was speechless. The area was a combination office and designer's dream work area. The first room was elegantly decorated in mauves, blues and creams. An archway to the right led into a studio with many windows down one wall. A drawing board, sewing machine, dress form and a cabinet to house the notions were placed directly underneath the windows, so that when she created her designs she would have the full benefit of the sunlight.

It was so much like her office in Los Angeles that it brought tears to her eyes.

"Are you all right, Lesley?" Pete asked.

"Yes, I'm just overwhelmed, that's all. I never thought that Darren would do something like this."

"My cousin is full of surprises."

Lesley stared at him, wondering what he meant by those words. What kind of surprises? Was she being para-noid? Pete couldn't possibly be the one who... He said that Danna believed in her innocence. Had they really believed in her the way Pete made it sound? Had she shortchanged their affection for her?

"I'll be lending you my expertise until things are set up and until you don't need me anymore. Let's get on with the rest of the tour."

TWENTY-ONE

"What we need to do is give a party to welcome you back to Philly and into our family, Les," Jordanna exclaimed excitedly as she, Darren, Ash and Lesley ate their lunch.

"A party," murmured Lesley thoughtfully. Jordanna grinned. "My specialty, as you'll recall." Lesley didn't know if that was such a good idea right now. There would be whispers, gossip and innuendo about her sudden reappearance, especially since she came back with a child and married to the man she ran away to Los Angeles to escape.

Darren noticed the uneasy look that came into Lesley's face and thought to cancel ideas of a party for now, but he felt that the party might be crucial to his plans. It might make those involved in the plot to steal Taylor's designs feel overconfident, safe, lulled into a sense of false security, just enough so that they might make a mistake. More than ever, he was convinced that his wife was innocent. He wished he'd believed it six and a half years ago and lent Lesley his support.

"I've been to quite a few of your parties, Jordanna," Ash said with a smile. "You going to have plenty of your single lady friends there, as usual?"

"Don't mock me, Ash. I hope one of those single ladies snags the elusive Mr. Price."

"Not a chance. I wouldn't think of depriving the other hundreds of thousands of women of my charm and availability."

"I forgot that arrogance was a primary word in your vocabulary."

"Now, children," Darren interrupted.

"I don't understand why your lovely sister can't stand the idea of me being a happily confirmed bachelor who loves every minute of it."

"There is no such animal," Jordanna shot back. "All it takes is the right woman and you'll change your tune."

"What do you think, Lesley?" Ash asked.

"I'm with Jordanna."

"It figures. Women."

"Give it up, Ash," Darren answered. "You'll never convince Danna that there isn't a good woman to tame every man." He looked to Jordanna and asked, "Are you going to invite Brett?"

Her expression softened. "He's Lesley's brother. Of course he'll get an invitation."

Lesley wondered. Surely Danna and her brother weren't… She smiled. When she thought about it, they would make a perfect couple.

Recognizing that look, Jordanna said, "Don't get any ideas, Les. I hardly know your brother."

"And from the sound of it you would like to know him better. How interesting," Ash teased. "Jordanna Taylor and Brett Wells. I love it."

Jordanna glared at Ash. He shot her an annoyingly bright smile.

Lesley was enjoying herself, until she thought of what she had to do. If there was going to be a party she would have to go see her family and break the ice. Anyway, Dara wanted to know her other set of grandparents, her other aunt and uncle. She couldn't deprive her of that.

Millie was at the apartment when Lesley, Dara, and Darren arrived that evening.

"Why didn't you tell us when you'd be arriving, Millie?" Darren asked. "We could have had someone meet you at the airport."

"I didn't want to put anyone out." Her eyes slid to Dara and she stooped down and reached out her arms for the little girl. Dara flew into them. "I've missed my angel," Millie cried, hugging her charge tight.

"I've missed you too, Millie," Dara proclaimed happily.

Lesley smiled and looked up at Darren. The warmth of her smile zapped him as it always did. He loved her so much and wanted to tell her so, but he'd wait. His admission would mean much more when he proved his love by finding the guilty party and vindicating her name and winning her trust.

After Millie had settled her belongings in her room, they sat down to a light dinner of crab and salad ordered in from Dinardo's. Darren put Dara to bed while Lesley and Millie went out on the terrace to talk.

"My goodness, what a view," Millie said in amazement, as she looked out over the city. "I didn't know you'd be living in a penthouse."

Lesley laughed. "We won't be for long. We'll be moving into our own house soon."

"Thank you, Jesus."

"Now Millie, don't tell me you won't like living in this luxurious place," Lesley teased.

"I suppose a body could get used to it if they had to, but a house with space for Dara to run around in is the best place for my angel."

"I agree with you and so does Darren."

"But?"

"What do you mean?"

"You're still unsure about this move, aren't you?"

"I can't seem to help it."

"It takes time to adjust to change, especially to having a husband. Believe me, it took me quite a while to get used to Morris, and I loved that man to distraction."

"I needed to talk to you, Millie. You help me keep my feet on the ground."

"I'm glad. If you need to talk about anything, I'm here. Don't forget that."

"I won't. You think you'll be up to keeping Dara for me tomorrow?"

"You'd better believe it." Millie smiled. "I'm more than just her nanny. I love that little girl as if she were the grandchild I never had."

"I'm going to see my family tomorrow."

"And you're anxious about it. I can see that."

"The way things stood between us when I left…"

"That little girl in there should help mend some fences. They can't help but fall in love with her. Didn't you say that's what happened with Darren's folks?"

"If my family acts even half as pleased as his did, I'll believe there's hope for us."

"Miss Wells is busy. What is your name, please?" Lesley walked past the secretary.

"Miss, you can't—"

Lesley closed the door on the woman's agitated face.

"You've become so important you need a bouncer, huh, Jazz?"

Eyes identical in color met.

"Lesley!" Jasmine Wells rose from her chair behind her desk and rushed to hug her sister.

"It's been a long time, Jazz."

Tears moistened the older woman's eyes. "What? Why? After all this time…"

"I'm back in Philadelphia to stay. Darren and I are married."

"Married at last to a Taylor. Mother and Daddy should enjoy that, especially Mother," she said with a secret smile. "So how have you been, little sister?"

Lesley kneaded her lip with her teeth. She always felt unsure of herself around her glamorous older sister. Jasmine must have sensed her uneasiness because she asked, "It's still there, isn't it?"

"What?"

"The barrier of resentment Mother and Daddy unwittingly erected between us when we were growing up. So many times I wanted to tear it down, but you always backed away from me, little sister. I never understood why. Can we talk about it now, get the fears and the animosity out in the open?"

Tears choked Lesley. "Oh, Jasmine."

They were in each other's arms seconds later.

The door opened. "Jasmine, I need you to—Lesley!"

It was Brett.

Jasmine eased out of her sister's embrace and wiped her eyes. "Yes. The prodigal sister has returned."

Brett walked over to his younger sister and opened his arms.

Lesley went into them. "I've missed you so much. You're the only one in the family who gave me the benefit of the doubt when I said I hadn't stolen those designs."

"You didn't take them, I'm sure about that," Brett said strongly.

"Unlike your big sister. Lesley, I'm sorry for doubting you."

"It's all right, Jasmine."

"No, it isn't. I thought you'd done it to show Mother and Daddy that you—oh, never mind."

"I can't really blame you for thinking that I'd do anything to get their attention. I certainly tried enough times in the past."

"Where have you been all this time?" Brett asked. "Mother and Dad hired a whole slew of investigators to find you. It was like you dropped off the face of the earth."

"I've been living in Los Angeles." She paused. "There's something else. You have a niece. She's six going on thirty. Her name is Dara."

"You don't have to tell me why you named her that."

"Now, Brett," Jasmine admonished. "You always knew our little sister was in love with Darren Taylor. It shouldn't surprise you that she would name her child after him. I know you've never been overly fond of him, but he's her husband now."

"Darren found me and we got married a few weeks ago," Lesley related, glossing over the details.

Brett's eyes widened. "But you said our niece was— That means you were pregnant when you left. God, Lesley. Why didn't you tell us? We could have helped you."

"I couldn't, Brett. Not after what happened with the designs and Mother and Daddy. I just couldn't. I wanted to, but I knew what they would say, and I didn't want to hear it."

"What are you going to do about the them? Our parents, I mean," Jasmine asked.

"I'll have to face them, there's no getting around it. It's important to Dara that she know her family. All of her family, that includes Mother and Daddy."

"Do you want us to smooth the way for you?"

"No, Brett, this is something I have to do for myself."

"You've changed, little sister," he said with admiration lacing his voice.

"Yes, I have. I'm tougher now. Where are Mother and Daddy? I called the house and Mrs. Lowell said they were out of town."

"They'll be back this evening. They went to New York to attend a fashion gala."

"Jasmine and I can be there and—"

"No, I want to meet them alone," she said strongly. "I'd appreciate it if you wouldn't say anything to them about my being back in town."

"You got it." He looked at Jasmine. "Jazz?"

She nodded her agreement.

"In a few weeks Darren's sister, Jordanna, is going to throw a party to welcome me into the family and help heal whatever you want to call it."

"Sounds like a good idea to me," Brett answered. "I've wanted to meet Jordanna Taylor in a relaxed setting for quite a while. She's a real knockout."

"For a Taylor," Jasmine added.

"As a beautiful woman. Period."

Judging from the look in her brother's eye, Lesley wondered if he wasn't already halfway in love with her sister-in-law. She thought how wonderful it would be if something happened between her brother and Darren's sister.

Lesley sat in the living room of her parents' home, drinking a cup of coffee while she waited for them to get there. The confrontation she'd put off for so long was about to be played out. She couldn't help feeling nervous. How was she going to handle it?

"Lesley!" her father exclaimed in shock and surprise as he and his wife entered the living room.

Her mother just stood staring at her. "Yes, it's me, Daddy. Mother."

"What are you doing here?" Merideth Wells demanded.

"There's something that needs clearing up between us." Lesley looked from one parent to the other.

Merideth began, "After what you did, I don't see—"

"Before you go off on one of your tangents, Mother, you're going to listen to me, really listen this time. Something you've never really done when it comes to me."

"Are we back on that I-love-my-other-children-more-than-you nonsense?" she said exasperatedly. "No, we're not, Mother, although you made me wonder enough times in the past if all the things you used to say about me were true."

"Now, look, Lesley—" her mother began.

"Merideth, I want to hear what our daughter has to say. Please, give her the courtesy of your full attention and respect."

"Curtis—"

"I mean it, Meri."

"All right," she sighed, reluctantly giving in.

"First of all, I didn't steal those designs, as I told you back then. And second, I never sent them to you."

"Your name was on the envelope, Lesley," Her mother reminded her.

"But I didn't send them to you."

"If you didn't, then who?"

"That's what I intend to find out. There's something else you should know. Darren Taylor and I are married and we—"

"You married him after all that's happened! I can't believe you!"

"I love Darren, Mother. I've always loved him. And we have a daughter. She's six years old."

Her mother and father exchanged glances, then turned to her.

"A daughter!" Curtis said, amazement filling his voice. "You mean we have a grandchild!"

Tears suddenly swam in her mother's eyes. "We have a granddaughter?"

"Yes, you do."

"You say she's six years old?" Curtis walked over to Lesley. "That means that you were pregnant when you disappeared. You knew it before the espionage episode, and you didn't tell us." He pulled her into his arms, something he hadn't done much even when Lesley was a child. She glanced over his shoulder at her mother, who turned away from her and walked over to the mantle.

"You'd rather fly off somewhere alone, not knowing anyone, than come to your family!"

"You didn't make me feel as though I were part of this family, Mother."

"You're saying it's all my fault you got involved with the Taylors!"

"It wasn't a matter of fault, Mother. I fell in love with Darren. It wasn't something I planned, it just happened, and now we're married and have a child."

"You think that makes up for the pain and embarrassment you caused this family."

"It's no use talking to you, Mother. You'd rather believe the worst about me no matter what, wouldn't you? What is it about me that makes you…"

"We've never understood you, Lesley."

"It's not we, Meri," Curtis interjected and looked to Lesley. "If anyone is to blame, it's me for neglecting our children. I was always so busy with work. I left the raising of you children to your mother. I wasn't there when you needed me. After you left Philadelphia, I realized that we hadn't given you a chance to defend yourself. For that, I'm ashamed. We looked for you. I flew to several places when bodies of young women fitting your description were found in their morgues."

Merideth's eyes widened in stunned disbelief. "Curtis, you never told me that!"

"I know, Meri. I didn't feel I could confide in you about it. You've always distanced yourself from Lesley for some reason. Even though I wasn't around much, I saw that."

"I might have been harder on her, but I still loved her." Merideth turned to Lesley.

Lesley walked over to her mother. "You never showed it. It was always Jasmine or Brett you rained all your loving attention on. You singled me out to complain about whatever it was I did wrong. You wanted a perfect daughter and I was a big disappointment to you."

"I'm sorry, I didn't realize you... I know it's coming a little late. Can't we try to—"

"I don't know, Mother. So much has happened between us."

"Please, just try, Lesley," her father pleaded.

"All right, Daddy. I want to bring Dara to visit you."

Merideth smiled. "Yes, please do. We want to see our only grandchild."

TWENTY-TWO

"So what do you think?"

"About?"

"Come on, Ash. I need your input."

"I think the party is a good idea, Darren. That way all the players in the game can be revealed."

"I thought you believed that Lesley was guilty."

"After meeting your lovely wife the evidence doesn't compute somehow. So I've had to reevaluate my opinion."

"The great Ashton Price concedes that he can make a mistake like the rest of us mere mortals."

"Darren! You know I go on gut instinct."

"Is it telling you my wife is innocent?"

"It's telling me that things aren't as they appear. There are a few more things I need to check out before I'm prepared to say without a doubt that Lesley Wells Taylor is not guilty." Ash shot Darren a sidelong glance. "You know something, don't you?"

"Let me know when you come up with anything concrete, Ash."

"That goes without saying. You're not going to tell me anything more, are you. Damn it, Darren. You know I don't like surprises."

"What I know in my gut, I can't prove."

"I gotcha. When I have something you'll know it."

"Thanks, Ash."

"No problem, man. So how are you enjoying married life?"

"It would be perfect if this thing about the designs wasn't hovering over us like a storm cloud." Darren's lips eased into a smile. "My daughter is really something special, Ash. Maybe you should give marriage and family a try?"

"You're beginning to sound like that matchmaking sister of yours. I'll stay happily single, thank you."

"There's got to be a special woman out there for you, Ash. I've found mine."

"Your surrender to domestic tranquility is—look, I'm outta here," he said over his shoulder as he headed for the door.

Darren shook his head and laughed.

Lesley returned to the penthouse late that evening.

"Where have you been?" Darren demanded. "I've been so worried, Lesley."

"I went to see my family."

"It took you all this time?

"No. I rode a taxi out to the river."

"Things go that badly between you?"

"Not really." Lesley let out a tired sigh. "They want to see Dara."

"I'll bet they're not too eager to see me. What else is new?" He frowned. "There's something you're not telling me, isn't there?"

"Give it a rest, Darren. I'm too tired to discuss it tonight."

"Well, when?"

"Tomorrow, all right?" She sighed.

Lesley headed for the stairs. Darren remained in the living room for a few minutes, thinking. Had she found out anything that could help exonerate her? Or had she found out something that might make her appear even guiltier?

Lesley lay awake, going over in her mind all that had happened with her visit with her family. They honestly thought she'd sent them the designs. How could they think she would do something so unethical when they were the ones who had taught her the meaning of honesty and loyalty! But then she'd strayed away from the fold and defiantly dated a person they actively disapproved of. What else could they think? She'd prove to them and everyone else how wrong they'd been if It was the last thing she ever did.

But where did she start? it had been over six years. She didn't think to ask her parents if they still had the envelope. That would be her first priority.

"You're awake," Darren said. 'Want to tell me what's bothering you, sweetheart?"

"Nothing is bothering me, Darren. Go back to sleep."

He eased to a sitting position and pulled her into his arms. "I can think of better ways to while away the night."

Lesley smiled, the tension of the moment beginning to slip away under his tender ministrations.

After making love to her, Darren fell asleep. Lesley watched him for long moment He was an exquisite lover, a caring husband, and a wonderful father. He'd made her head of her own company. He'd cried out that he loved her at the height of his passion, but not at any other time.

Would he ever say the words out of bed? Was it asking too much? He could be so tender and loving when they were with their daughter or making love to her as he did every night.

Lesley kissed Darren's forehead. He moaned and drew her closer to his body before drifting back to sleep.

"Oh, Darren, I love you so much."

Lesley called Jordanna to invite her to lunch. When she arrived, Millie took Dara to the park across the street. They had lunch on the terrace.

"How'd it go with your family?" Jordanna asked.

"I don't know. Oh, it went all right with Jasmine and Brett, but—"

"Brett," Jordanna said softly with a dreamy look on her face.

Lesley watched her. "Is there something between you and my brother, Danna?"

"No, not that I would mind if there was. Your brother is, in a word, fine."

A wry smile came to Lesley's lips. "Do you intend trying for double sister-in-lawhood?"

"I wish. I doubt if Brett knows I'm alive. There have been a few occasions when we were in each others' company, but nothing to consult Dr. Ruth about."

"Maybe things will change at the party and the two of you can get better acquainted."

"You think he could really be interested in me? Listen to me. I sound like some giddy teenager with her first crush."

"We've got to create a special gown for you to wear to the party that'll make him sit up and take notice."

"Will you, Les?"

"Of course. What are sisters-in-law and friends for?"

"About what happened six years ago…"

Lesley's smile faded. "I don't want to talk about that right now, Danna."

"You've talked it over with my brother?"

"Not all of it. He knows how I feel, though. And he doesn't believe me or love me the way he did before I left. I don't know if we'll ever be able to gain back what we lost. Somebody set me up and I have to know why. And I will find out who."

"Is that the reason you agreed to have the party? You're hoping to flush this person out? Ashton Price is the person you should leave something like that to. Why don't you talk to him about it?"

"Maybe I will."

"You never told me what happened with your parents."

"There isn't that much to tell. I'm taking Dara to see them tomorrow. Maybe my beautiful little daughter will help smooth the way for a better relationship between us."

Jordanna smiled. "She's a real charmer, all right. My guess is she'll have them eating out of tiny little hand in no time."

"I hope you're right."

Jordanna smiled conspiratorially. "Now about that dress you offered to create for me."

Lesley felt apprehensive about introducing Dara to her other grandparents. Her father seemed happy about the revelation. She wasn't so sure about her mother. She chose the prettiest dress Dara had for the occasion. Her child was eager to meet her mother's parents. Lesley hoped it went as well as it had with Darren's family. She wasn't worried about Jasmine or Brett; she was sure they would love their new niece.

It was time to stop speculating and get the show on the road, she thought as she drove through the gates of her parents' home in the car Darren had gotten her; she'd sold the one she had in Los Angeles. There were two cars parked in the drive, which probably meant that Jasmine and Brett were inside. At least she would have them to lend her moral support if she needed it.

"What are they like, Mama?" Dara asked.

"You'll have to wait and see, baby."

Lesley parked the car, then she and Dan started up the long walkway.

Jasmine came out to welcome them. She smiled at Dan. "I'm your Aunt Jasmine. You have to be my niece."

Dan smiled. "My name is Dara."

Jasmine held out her hand to the little girl and Dara took it. Jasmine looked to Lesley. "It'll be all right, little sister. You'll see."

They all walked into the living room. Brett got up and came to greet them.

I'm your uncle," he said, hunkering down to eye level with Dara. "You can call me Uncle Brett. You know, you're the only niece I have. That makes you very special to me."

Dan smiled and threw her small arms around Brett's neck and planted a wet kiss on his cheek.

Curtis walked toward them. A glimmer of moisture shone in his eyes as he shifted his gaze between his daughter and granddaughter. Lesley wondered what he was feeling. The look was almost sad. Did he have regrets, as he'd said?

"Do you know who I am?" he asked gently.

"You're my grandfather. My mama's daddy."

"Yes, I am."

Dara shifted her gaze to Merideth. "You must be my grandmother. You look just like my mama."

Merideth took her granddaughter's hand and led her over to the couch. "Sit next to me."

Dara reached out to touch her hair, then her face, seeming to be fascinated by the resemblance between her mother and grandmother. "I was worried that you wouldn't like me,' she said. "My mama gets sad when she talks about you with my daddy. Are you mad at her?"

The look in her mother's eyes brought tears to Lesley's.

The room was held in an awkward silence for a moment, then Curtis spoke. "No, we're not mad at your mother, we love her. We haven't always shown it or said it enough, but we do. Now we also have you to love. And I want you always to know that, Dara."

"Your grandfather is right," Merideth confirmed in a soft tone.

Lesley saw regret in her mother's eyes for their past relationship. Maybe Millie was right and they could become a closer knit family. It seemed that her little daughter was the bridge over troubled waters.

Jasmine signaled Lesley over to where she and Brett stood by the windows.

"I've never seen Mother so moved by anything other than her drawing board."

"Me either," Brett agreed. "I never considered her grandmother material. She was never a doting mother to any of us."

"Maybe there's hope for her after all. Dara has a way of wrapping everyone around her little finger."

"She certainly looks like her father," Brett remarked.

"And her Aunt Jordanna," Lesley tacked on.

Brett smiled. "You're right, she does."

"You'll be getting an invitation to the party she's giving. What you do after that is up to you," Lesley teased.

Curtis cleared his throat. "We're going sailing this weekend. Do you think it's possible we could take Dara with us, Lesley?"

"I'll have to ask Darren, but I don't see why not." Lesley looked at her mother.

"You will get back to us about it?" Merideth asked. "If it means that much to you."

"It does."

Lesley had a drink waiting for Darren when he got home.

"You do this too often I'll demand that you do it all the time, Mrs. Taylor." Darren smiled, sipping the brandy Lesley had poured for him. "I take it everything went all right with your parents."

"They want to take Dara sailing with them this weekend. Is it all right?"

"Yes, it'll be good for our daughter to get to know both sides of her family."

"I'm glad to hear you say that, considering your opinion of my parents."

"They made you unhappy when you were growing up. I won't stand by and let them do that to Dara."

"Oh, I don't think they will. They seem genuinely delighted to have a grandchild. I must admit that I didn't expect them to take to her so quickly."

"Has Uncle Stewart contacted you yet?"

"No." Lesley quirked her lips. "Considering how he feels about me, I'm not surprised. He'll probably wait until the last possible minute so he won't have to deal with me any more than he has to."

"If he says anything out of line—"

"I don't think he will. Vera is being helpful, which surprises me, considering her feelings for you. She still has a thing for you."

"Vera!"

"Why are you so shocked? You knew that she—you really didn't know, did you?"

Darren put his drink down. "There has never been— Pete said something once, but I didn't pay any attention to it. I told him he was wrong. Vera's never said or done anything to make me think she felt that way about me. Are you sure?"

"As sure as any woman can be where her man is concerned."

"She's been with Taylor's for a long time."

"As long as she continues to do her job—"

"If she starts giving you a rough time, I want to know about it. She's good, but she's not indispensable. If she does anything to hurt you, she's gone." His brows smoothed out and he drew Lesley into his arms. He shuddered, thinking about the many times he himself had hurt her and that he would have to make up for.

TWENTY-THREE

Lesley looked around the new Raiments building. Things were shaping up just as she wanted them to. They'd need to present their new spring line by the end of November. It gave them less than two months to get all the materials and people settled and the designs drawn. She'd already begun detailing the ones she'd completed so far.

And it was a month until this party that had ended up being a 'welcome home' ball. Lesley let out a sigh of satisfaction because the design for Jordanna's dress was completed and her own was partially finished. She and Jordanna had plans to borrow several of Taylor's seamstresses to work on them so they'd be ready in time for the ball.

She was adding finishing touches to her dress design when Pete walked in.

"Danna have your nose to the proverbial grindstone? She told me you were creating something spectacular for her to wow your brother."

After one last stroke, she held out her pad to him. "I've finished hers. You want to take a look? I don't think she'll mind too much."

"Very impressive, Mrs. Taylor. I know Taylor's appreciates talent. I'd say we should feel damned lucky to have you working for us."

"Pete."

"I'm sorry. That didn't come out right. It makes me sound like I resent you and don't feel appreciated myself, doesn't it?"

"Around the edges. Why should you feel that way? You have a high visibility position in the business. You have a knack for organization, Pete."

"I guess I've been around my father too long. He's always complaining because Uncle Darren didn't turn the headship of Taylor's over to him instead of Darren when he decided to retire. He's dissatisfied with his position, having to do as Darren says. He's always tried to make me feel angry about Darren's authority and position."

"And have you felt angry, Pete?"

"I'd be lying if I said it hadn't gotten next to me at one time or another."

Lesley began to wonder if Pete had felt strongly enough about it to—no, not Pete. But there was a doubt. She changed the subject and asked.

"What do you know about Niven Alexander, Pete?"

"Niven? She's a very smart lady, and attractive too."

Lesley quirked her lips. Was that interest she detected in his voice? Or was it more than that?

"Why do you want to know about her?"

"She works closely with my husband."

"Oh, I get it. You're jealous."

"I'm not jealous. I don't even know the woman, never even met her."

"I doubt if she's interested in Darren in the way you mean."

In the way you wished she felt about you, Pete? "What do you know about her?" Lesley asked. "She has several degrees, one in research. She's single and very mysterious about her past. I've tried drawing her out, but so far I haven't even gotten to first base."

"How long has she been working for Taylor's?"

"Ever since you left. It was my father who recommended her to Taylor's. He knew her when she worked for a fashion house in London."

"Where does she come from originally?"

"Chicago, I think. You really are curious about her, aren't you?"

"How's your love life, Pete?"

"I don't have one at the moment. The only other woman I ever cared about is already taken." His gaze lighted momentarily on her. She'd known that he cared for her, but all she could ever see was Darren. Surely Pete's feelings for her hadn't driven him to…

"Have lunch with me, boss lady?"

"Maybe another time, Pete. Give me a rain check, okay?"

After Pete had gone, Lesley thought about their conversation. Was it possible that Pete was the one? Or Vera? Or Stewart? Did this Niven Alexander figure into it in some way?

The next morning Lesley watched her daughter and husband eat breakfast and smiled, wondering what it would be like to have a son who also looked like them. She hadn't said anything to Darren, but she suspected that she was pregnant. She hoped he didn't notice that she hadn't been eating very much of her breakfast these past few mornings.

"You don't have any appointments this afternoon, do you?" Darren asked Lesley.

"No. Why? You have something planned?"

"I want to take my two ladies out to our house."

"Daddy said it has a big backyard."

"Yes, I think it's big enough for a certain little girl."

"Me?

Lesley laughed. "Yes, you."

"Daddy said I can have a dog, too."

"As long as he or she stays outside," Darren reminded her.

"Is Millie going to live there with us?" Dara asked.

"Of course, I am, angel," Millie answered as she started to pour Darren another cup of coffee.

"No more for me." Darren smiled at her. "We want you to come with us this afternoon, Millie. Have to keep my little girl happy." He wiped his mouth on a napkin and stood up. "I'd better be going. I have a few things to take care of before my meeting with Niven. She's eager to go over her report from Ireland with me. If the negotiations turn out as I planned, we should be revealing our new research find very soon." He kissed Lesley and Dan. "I'll pick you and Millie up after lunch, little sweetheart." He looked at Lesley. "Can you meet us at the house?"

"No problem."

"See you then," he said on his way out of the room.

Dara slid off her chair. "I want to play with the computer Daddy bought me."

"Be careful with it, Dara."

"Daddy showed me how to use it, Mama."

Lesley sighed, shaking her head. Her daughter was growing into a dynamo like her father.

"Have you told him yet?" Millie asked.

"No. The timing isn't right"

"He'll be happy about it, don't you think?"

"I don't know. He wanted to wait before we started enlarging our family."

"Most men say that if it were left up to them, the right time would never come."

"Oh, Millie, you're priceless."

"I hope so."

Lesley paced back and forth in the living room of the house Darren had built for her, waiting for her husband and daughter to arrive. It was well after the time for them to be there. She hoped there hadn't been an accident.

Just then, she heard a car drive up outside and looked out the window. Relief swept over her. They were here, safe and sound.

"I'm sorry we're late, sweetheart," Darren apologized. "The meeting with Niven ran over. We'll have to get you a cell phone so I can contact you in case there is an emergency. So what do you think?"

"It's exactly as I wanted it to be."

Millie cleared her throat "Dara and I are going to explore the backyard while you two talk," Millie said with a smile, taking Dara's hand and leading her through the dining room.

Lesley remained quiet for a few moments.

Darren gave her a sidelong glance. "You aren't upset that I was late, are you?"

"No. I understand that it couldn't be helped." She left the room and headed for the stairs.

Darren followed, studying her body language, and when she reached the top of the stairs, checked the expression on her rice. He wondered if she was saying that to placate him, and she really was upset. Why would she be upset about that? But what else could she be upset about?

A wistful expression came over Lesley's face when they walked past the nursery.

"You thinking what I am?" he asked.

"That if I had stayed this would have been Dara's room. "I used to think about it all the time after she was born. But it's a time we can't ever get back, Darren."

I know, but in the near future we'll put another baby in here. For now, I just want the three us to enjoy settling into family life."

Lesley sat down in the window seat of the master bedroom. She'd always wanted one back when she was growing up. Jasmine's bedroom had one, but hers didn't. It all seemed so long ago. She had her own house now, and her own child, with possibly another one on the way.

"Are you really happy about the house, Lesley?"

"Yes. And I'm beginning to feel more comfortable about being back in Philadelphia than I did when we first arrived."

"I'm glad. I wouldn't want you to feel that you made a mistake coming back here."

If that were the only area where they had a problem. She wished she could exonerate herself in his eyes.

He smiled. "I think we'd better round up the little one and head back to the apartment. The weather is starting to turn cold. Fall is definitely around the corner."

Over the next week Lesley began to notice that Darren was spending a lot of time at the office. He told her it was because of his research project, but she was beginning to wonder if it was because of his research colleague. She had yet to meet the mysterious Niven Alexander.

Deciding on impulse to invite Darren out to lunch one afternoon, Lesley left her office and drove to the Taylor building. She saw Joseph when she stopped at the security desk. Being in his company made her feel uncomfortable, bringing back memories of his part in her humiliation six years ago. It wasn't an easy task to put the episode in the past where it belonged. Straightening her spine, squaring her shoulders, she reminded herself she was now a Taylor.

Lesley stepped off the elevator on Darren's floor. Vera eyed her curiously, as though she were an alien from another planet Lesley knew that at some point she would have to make her feelings concerning Darren clear to Vera or there would be no way they could work together. Today was not the day.

"Is Darren in?" Lesley asked her.

"Yes, but he's in the conference room with…"

Lesley headed in that direction without waiting for Vera to finish what she was saying. "Don't bother announcing me, Vera, I'll just go on in."

Vera rose from her desk and started after her. "You can't go in there, he's—"

Lesley opened the door of the conference room and shut it in Vera's flustered face. Her own heated up when she saw Darren and Niven seated side by side at the conference table, his dark head close to her auburn one. Niven turned to him, smiling, as though sharing something intimate with him. Jealousy seared Lesley's insides.

Darren looked up from the papers spread before them and smiled at Niven. When they realized she was in the room, a look of surprise washed over Darren's face and one of confusion doused Niven's.

"Sweetheart? What are you doing here?" he asked. "Is something wrong?"

"No, I just wanted to invite my husband out to lunch, that's all."

Lesley could tell by the expression that flowered on the other woman's face that she had picked up on the tone in her voice.

Darren smiled. "This is Niven Alexander, Taylor's research expert. I mentioned her to you before. Right now we're in the middle of something, so I won't be able to have lunch with you. Another time, sweetheart. Okay?"

"It's not a big deal, I just thought…"

Niven looked anxiously at Darren. "I can finish this. Go ahead and have lunch with your wife."

His eyes shifted to Niven. "There are aspects to the formula we need to go over and test today." He turned to Lesley. "I'm sorry, sweetheart."

"No problem. I should have called first to make an appointment." She quickly turned and walked over to the door and left.

Niven glanced uneasily at Darren. "Darren, you really—"

"My wife has to get used to my schedule and know that I just might be busy when she comes by."

"But—"

"It's all right, Niven." He flipped over a page of the report. He had wanted to go with Lesley, but he seized the opportunity to set into motion the next step of his plan, to make it look as though all wasn't paradise between him and Lesley. It was bound to interest the guilty person or persons, possibly make them reveal themselves.

After speaking to Ashton Price and making an appointment with him, Lesley concluded that it was easier than trying to make one with her own husband. She wasn't likely to forget the way he'd acted when she had dropped in unexpectedly. Lesley called Jasmine to ask her to go with her to see Ash, and when she agreed, told her she'd be by to pick her up.

As Lesley drove to Wells of Fashion, she thought about what had happened with Darren at Taylor's. Had he really been that busy? Or was he more involved with Niven Alexander than he would admit, even to himself?

There were quite a few obstacles in the way of their happiness. She wondered if she should consider Niven Alexander one of them? What about Vera? She was still as crazy about Darren as she ever was. Then there was Pete and the feelings he once had for her. He had plenty of reasons to sabotage her relationship with Darren. His father was trying to stir up bad feelings between the cousins.

Stewart Taylor was certainly suspect. He resented her as well as Darren. He probably resented his own brother even more. Was his resentment strong enough to move him to sabotage the company, as well as his nephew's personal life?

Jasmine was out front waiting when Lesley drove up.

"You sure you need me to go with you?' she said as she climbed into the car.

"Very sure. There is something unsettling about Mr. Ashton Price."

"You think because I'm an ex-model I can handle his type better than you can, is that it?"

"Well?"

Jasmine smiled. "It's all right. You're probably right in this case. I've heard Mr. Price is quite the womanizer, it wouldn't hurt for him to be taken down a peg. It might help."

Lesley parked the car and she and Jasmine walked inside the building, then rode the elevator to Ashton's office. She had to admit that his suite of offices was very impressive.

The secretary showed them into his private office.

Ashton stood up and smiled as they walked in. "Have a seat, ladies."

"This is my sister, Jasmine Wells. I asked her to come with me." She turned to her sister. "This is Ashton Price, Jasmine."

Ash shot Jasmine a look of appreciation which she pretended to ignore, Lesley noticed.

"How may I help you, Lesley?"

"I want to find out who set me up, and I need your help."

"Do you have any suspects?"

"Yes." Then she listed them. "My sister has the envelope and the original designs that were sent to my parents at Wells of Fashion."

Jasmine handed it to Ash. When his fingers accidentally brushed hers as he took the envelope from her, he smiled at her.

Lesley observed that Jasmine swallowed hard after the encounter. Surely she wasn't attracted to Ashton Price.

He examined the envelope and its contents. "Your personalized stamp is on these, but anyone could have gotten hold of it and done that. Was there anything else in the envelope besides the designs?"

Lesley turned to Jasmine. "You were there when Mother and Daddy opened it, weren't you?"

"Yes. There was nothing else in it."

"No note?" asked Ashton.

"I said nothing, Mr. Price."

"I guess that's that," Lesley said. What do we do next?"

"At this point—" Ash began.

Jasmine interrupted, "You're a hot-shot detective, surely you—"

"I am an investigator, yes…but I'm no miracle worker, Miss Wells." He shifted his gaze back to Lesley. "Give me a few days, Lesley. If there is any evidence that'll clear you left after all this time, I promise you, I'll find it."

"Promises, Mr. Price? Talk is cheap," Jasmine shot back. "If you don't or can't, we can find someone who will. You probably think you're the best thing since sliced bread."

"You don't know what I think, Miss Wells." His jaw tightened in suppressed temper. He ignored Jasmine and looked at Lesley. "I'll get back to you."

"You were a little hard on him, weren't you?" Lesley remarked to her sister when they were in the car and on their way back to Wells.

"He deserved it, the arrogant macho man. I've dealt with his type before. They're all alike."

Lesley smiled. It seemed to her that Jasmine protested a little too much. Maybe—nah. She'd been around her matchmaking sister-in-law too much lately.

TWENTY-FOUR

"The records have all arrived, Mrs. Taylor," Vera said to Lesley as she directed the maintenance men to transport the records from the Los Angeles branch of Raiments.

Raiments was closer to becoming operational. To Lesley it was more than a little exciting, even frightening. She'd have the complete responsibility of Raiments. Though she'd always wanted that when she was in L.A., now that she had it, she wasn't sure how she felt, except that she wanted to make Philadelphia Raiments a vital cog in the fashion industry wheel one day.

Darren had a lot of confidence in her abilities in that area at least. Personally…now that was another story.

"I've had a special place cleared to put the immediately important papers, Vera." She walked into an adjoining room next to her office. "I want them within easy access if the need arises."

Vera shot Lesley one of those looks that said why-are you-worrying-about-thieves. Lesley knew the woman considered her an industrial thief, not good enough to be a Taylor, certainly not good enough to be married to Darren.

The woman was attractive enough in a cold, distant way. Although she was too serious by half, that wouldn't put Lesley off from dealing with her. Vera had to realize that Darren belonged to her now and she didn't stand a chance in the wind of getting him.

"I need to have a talk with you, Vera, as soon as we have everything situated."

She shrugged her shoulders and kept on organizing.

"Need any help?"

"Pete! Did we have a meeting I've forgotten about?"

"No, nothing like that. I thought you might need my help. There is so much to do before Philadelphia Raiments is ready to officially open."

"You're genuinely happy for me, aren't you, Pete?"

"Of course I am. Why would you doubt it? Oh, I see. It's my father, isn't it? I'm not my father, Lesley."

"I know you're not—it's just that…"

"I understand. Father has never liked you and now to have to work so closely with you… He would be the perfect liaison if it wasn't you he had to 'liaise' with."

"I don't understand why he hates me so much. My being a Wells doesn't seem like enough reason for his attitude. There has to be more to it than that."

"I agree. If there is, only he knows the answer, and he's not likely to tell either one of us."

"You're right." She returned her attention to Vera as the secretary ordered the men around. The woman was wasted in the position of secretary; upper management seemed more her speed, particularly with her educational background. At Taylor's being a woman wasn't a deterrent. So why hadn't Vera made a move in that direction? The reason she hadn't was because of her feelings for Darren. She lived for day-to-day contact with him.

Lesley decided it was time to talk to Jordanna about promoting Vera. With any luck, they'd transfer her to another branch of Taylor's. Hawaii or Chicago would be good.

"You have a strange look on your face. What's going on?" Pete asked.

"Nothing I can't take care of myself."

"I'm curious to know what you're hatching in that fertile brain of yours. But I can see you aren't going to share it with me. You, in other words, want me to butt out? Say no more, I'm outta here."

"I didn't mean to run you off."

"You didn't. I'm not offended, just curious. The way you were looking at Vera, I'd watch my back if I were she. I think you have plans for her. Ones I'm sure she won't like." He gazed thoughtfully at her. "You know about her feelings for Darren, don't you?"

"You're right, I do."

"You see her as a possible obstacle to your happiness. I can't blame you for wanting to do something about it. You really love my cousin a lot, don't you? You don't have to answer, it's written on your face." He looked at his watch. "I'm having a business lunch with Jordanna in half an hour. I think I'd better be on my way. Don't be too hard on Vera. None of us has a say in who we fall in love with."

"I'll remember that, Pete. There is someone out there for you."

Vera came back into Lesley's office seconds after Pete left.

"You wanted to talk to me, Mrs. Taylor?"

"It can wait. Now I want to see where everything is. You can go back to Taylor's and tell Darren I have all the files. And that we can discuss them when I get home tonight."

"I understand, Mrs. Taylor."

"I'm sure you do, Vera. Call me Lesley. Nadine Taylor comes to mind when you call me Mrs. Taylor. There's no need for you to be so formal with me. After all, you call my husband by his first name."

"Okay, if that's what you want."

Lesley watched her leave. Yes, sending her to another branch would be good for the Taylor marriage, the company, and in the long run, Vera herself. Now what to do about Niven Alexander? Maybe Pete could help there.

"Vera told me you had everything under control at Raiments, sweetheart. I'll be over there later in the week to see how things are progressing," Darren said, relaxing on the living room couch with a brandy. "Danna has a good idea. She thinks we should have an intimate dinner party with just your family and mine. A sort of mending fences kind of thing. What do you think? Millie could help you with it."

Lesley snuggled against him. "I think that we should have one. I agree that we need to unite our two families. It would make it so much easier for Dara, and us too. We can break the ice before that ball Jordanna wants to have at the Palace Hotel."

"I'm glad you think so. We're going to make this marriage work."

She couldn't help wondering about his reasons. Did he want it to work because he believed it had a chance? Or was it only to make their daughter happy?

"You're kind of quiet tonight," Darren said. "Is there anything wrong?"

"No, everything is fine."

Somehow Darren didn't quite believe her. Something was going on with her, but she refused to let him in on it. She was still a woman of secrets, despite their vow not to keep any from each other. Then he didn't have much time to talk. He was keeping his own secrets. Hopefully, not for long, though.

Lesley and Darren were deep in a discussion of how to proceed with Raiments the next morning.

"You know, Darren, you should promote Vera. She's qualified for a management position. I know there are openings in several of the other branches, according to Danna."

"There are, but why would you want to help Vera? She wasn't very nice to you six years ago. And as far as I can see, her attitude toward you hasn't changed. She's polite and respectful, but barely. Why would you want to do that?"

"I may not care for her personally, but she deserves recognition. Being your secretary is certainly not a challenging position for someone with her educational background."

"You're right. I don't know why I never thought of that. She's so efficient, but any good secretary can take over her job. I'll sound her out about it. You've changed, sweetheart."

"Is that good or bad?"

"Definitely good. How about having lunch with your husband?"

"Sorry, I have a working lunch planned with Pete. Your uncle is going to be there, too."

"I hope you don't get indigestion," he said with a laugh.

"Very funny."

"Maybe we can do it tomorrow."

"It's a date. One o'clock all right?"

"That should work."

Lesley was anxious about this meeting. If it were only Pete she wouldn't care, but Stewart Taylor was a different proposition. She glanced at her watch. He and Pete were late. Stewart was probably instructing him on how to act with her. Knowing Pete, he'd ignore it, but still...

"Sorry we're late, Lesley," Pete apologized as he and his father entered her office.

"It's all right." She outlined her plans for Raiments' grand opening.

"For such a small company, I think it's a little too ambitious," Stewart said coolly, yet in a subtly insulting tone.

"Father, I think—"

"It's my job to advise her about things like that. She hasn't any experience with such an undertaking."

"If we don't show our pride in our designs, no one else will, Stewart," Lesley argued the point.

"You think that because you've become a Taylor—"

"Father, this isn't—"

"I can answer for myself, Pete," Lesley spoke out. "You're right about it being your job to advise me, but the decision is ultimately mine, isn't it? Now, can we get on with the meeting?"

Stewart shot her a venomous look that should have disintegrated her on the spot.

"I'll have to report this to the board as an unwise expenditure of company funds."

"I've already sounded Jordanna out about it. She agrees with what I have in mind. I'm sure she can convince the other board members that it's not an unwise expenditure."

"We'll see," Stewart said indignantly. "I have influence with them also." He sat down and passed her a copy of his report about the materials she intended ordering.

Lesley frowned as Vera stormed into her office. After Stewart and Pete, she definitely wasn't in the mood for a confrontation with Vera about whatever was on her mind.

"You said call you Lesley and not Mrs. Taylor when all the time you wanted me to know the power you now wield with that title, didn't you?"

"Vera, I—"

"Don't bother lying about it. You couldn't stand seeing me in a job I love."

"Is it the job you love? Or is it my husband?"

"You're jealous. You know he doesn't love you, only the child you kept hidden from him all these years. Now that he has her, I'd watch out if l were you. I know you talked him into getting rid of me. Someone just might talk him into getting rid of you. I'd be happy to see that happen."

"Were you the one who tried to do that six years ago, Vera?"

She laughed. "You really expect me to tell you? I'm not going to tell you anything, one way or the other. I want you to wonder and worry. I want you to wonder every time you're away from your husband if he's with—I think you already know that he's attracted to Niven Alexander.

"I saw the look on your face when you came out of the conference room. I'll tell you one thing, Niven started right after you left Philadelphia. Darren may not be attracted to me, but he was and still is attracted to Niven. She was very comforting and supportive, and he spent a lot of time with her."

Lesley balled her hands into fists at her sides, wanting to punch a few of Vera's teeth out.

Vera saw that look and laughed. "Oh, I would love for you to try it."

"I won't give you the satisfaction. Where is Darren sending you? Timbuktu wouldn't be far enough as far as I'm concerned. For the record, you deserve the promotion, Vera. I may not want you working for my husband, but with your management training and designing knowledge you'll be an asset wherever you go."

"I'm being transferred to the Chicago branch of Taylor's. Darren intends to make it official at the Taylor ball."

"Then you accepted the position."

"Yes. What else could I do? Darren said he was proud of me and wanted to see me in a position I was qualified for, and that he had confidence in my abilities." She turned away from Lesley.

Lesley had seen the sheen of tears in the other woman's eyes and felt sorry for her. She knew what it felt like for the man you loved to have confidence in you in one way, but not love you in the way you wanted to be loved.

"I'll be leaving the day after the ball. I guess that makes you happy."

"I'm not happy to see someone else's misery, Vera. It's best that you leave, though. Darren us totally committed to me and our child."

"You made sure of that"

"Just like someone made sure I looked guilty six years ago. If you know anything—"

"I don't."

"And if you did, you wouldn't tell me, right?"

"I hope you and Darren make a go of your marriage, for Dara's sake. She is a wonderful little girl. I like her very much. She's so much like Darren. You won't have to deal with me for much longer. I've done all I'm expected to where you and Raiments are concerned. Darren wants me to work with Jordanna and Pete to learn more about the running of Taylor's since I'll be one of its new directors."

"There's someone for you out there, Vera."

"But not Darren Taylor, right?" She walked out of the office.

Lesley relaxed and put her feet up. One down and how many more to go? Because Vera was leaving didn't mean she hadn't had anything to do with framing her, but somehow she didn't think she was involved. But who was?

TWENTY-FIVE

"I think you'd better sit down," Millie suggested to Lesley.

"I'm fine, Millie. Stop fussing." She smiled, sure now that she was pregnant. She had to admit that she was getting more tired than usual these days. Her only problem now was how and when to tell her husband.

"You're beginning to have that glow some women get when they're expecting."

"I wonder if Darren has noticed."

"You should tell him," Millie admonished.

"I know, but I'm waiting until the right time. Right now, I'm into getting this house in shape in time for the dinner party. It's going to be interesting to see how the in-laws get along."

"They've been rivals for a long time, I take it?"

"Since before I was born. I'm not sure of the reason for the animosity, though. Being rivals doesn't necessarily mean they have to hate each other the way they seem to. There must be a particular reason. Hopefully, they can put that aside for the sake of their grandchild."

Millie smiled. "If anyone can bring them around, it'll be Dara. She's really looking forward to the party."

"I know, she mentioned having her two sets of grand parents together. She was very impressed with the yachting trip she went on with my parents, and the shopping spree Darren's mother treated her to."

"There's nothing like shopping to make us girls feel good. Dara is going to love going with you to shop for things for her new brother or sister. I have to admit that I'm looking forward to it too."

"You're happy about the move to Philadelphia, then?"

"It's a big change from L.A., that's for sure, but yes, I am. I'm with the people I love most in the world. I've found a church to get involved with and some friends my age."

"I'm glad. I want you to be happy with us, Millie. The movers should be bringing the rest of the furniture this afternoon. The pieces I saved from the house in L.A. should fit in my sitting room/office. You know, I'm surprised that Darren kept the house after I left."

"I'm not. That man loves you, Lesley. I know you don't believe he loves you the way he used to. You think his commitment is more for your daughter's sake, but I don't agree. He'll tell you what's in his heart when he feels more secure in the marriage. You both hurt each other, and that takes time to heal."

"What you're saying is that I should be more patient?"

"Exactly. If two young people were ever meant to be together, it's you and Darren Taylor."

"Have I told you lately how much I appreciate you?"

"You do it every day when you leave your darling little girl in my keeping. Seeing you both happy makes me happy." She glanced at her watch. "I'll have to go pick up the darling in question from school in another thirty minutes."

"You think she's really adjusting to her new school?"

"I think so. She's made two new friends already."

"I'm glad. I was worried about that at first. Moving to Philadelphia is such a big change for her. And she's had quite a few changes to get used to all at one time."

"Children are very resilient, more so than adults."

Lesley looked around her living room. This was her dream house, the place she hoped to enjoy future happiness with her child and the man she loved. She would fight to keep them. She'd find out who framed her. Who dared to turn her life into a living nightmare.

For now, she was concentrating on solidifying her relationship with her parents and Darren's. Hopefully, the dinner party would help.

"We need to talk about what we're going to serve at the party, Millie."

"Your sister-in-law's suggestion about going half and half is a good one. Let the caterers provide the main course and the drinks. We'll do the canapés. And I'll make the dessert."

"You really want to do all that work?"

"I'm looking forward to it. Dara wants me to show her how to bake."

"I'm going to sit in on those sessions myself and learn right along with her."

"You're the bomb, according to our daughter. I agree you're really something in that dress, Mrs. Taylor," Darren bent his head and whispered in Lesley's ear as she sat before the mirrored vanity in their bedroom brushing her hair.

"Thank you, kind sir." She knew she looked good in the simple, semi-fitted black sheath. The glass-beaded, single red rose at the shoulder made the dress exceptional. It was part of Raiments' evening gown collection the previous year.

"You're not nervous about this evening, are you?"

"I wouldn't be human if I weren't. This dinner is so important to Dara, and to us and the future of this family." She put the brush down and turned to Darren.

"It'll work out, sweetheart. Your parents and mine know how important it is to their relationship with their granddaughter. And they all love her as much as we do."

"I hope your uncle Stewart doesn't cause trouble."

"I know what you mean. I would love to have excluded him, but unfortunately, he's a part of my family. Maybe he'll behave this evening. If he doesn't…"

"Oh, I think he'll be civilized, at least on the surface anyway!"

"He'd better. I won't have him upsetting you or Dara."

Lesley smiled lovingly at him. Her husband was so protective of her and Dara, so caring. Could she turn that caring into a love that would surpass what they had before?

Darren saw the wistful expression on his wife's face. There would come a time when he could show her how much he loved her. When she stood up, he put his arms around her waist and held her close.

"It'll be all right, sweetheart."

Lesley closed her eyes, reveling in his warmth and the security of his touch.

The bedroom door opened and Dara walked in, dressed in a puff-sleeved blue confection of a dress with a tied satin bow on the wide-bibbed, antique white collar. The dress set off her caramel skin and black hair to perfection. Millie had dressed her long thick hair in an adorable profusion of Shirley Temple curls. Lesley thought her little girl looked like the angel Millie always called her.

"Is it time for all my grandparents to get here?" Dara asked anxiously.

Darren pulled Dara into the embrace. "Not yet, my little sweetheart."

"Millie's gonna be there, isn't she, Mama? She's my very special grandmother."

"Yes, she'll be there, baby."

Lesley went out to the kitchen to see if the caterers had everything set up. Millie removed her apron after placing her special pomegranate flan cake in the warming oven.

She sighed as she looked around. "This kitchen is a chef's dream."

Lesley gazed at the kitchen clock. "You have just enough time to change before everyone gets here."

"Change?"

"You're included on the guest list. Didn't Dara tell you that she wanted you to be at the party?"

"Yes, but—"

"We want you with us, Millie."

"I don't think I have anything appropriate to wear."

"Yes, you do. There's a dress for you on your bed. We hope you like it. I designed it especially for you as an appreciation gift. I was going to wait until your birthday, but I decided to give it to you now and design another one for that occasion later."

Tears came to Millie's eyes and she hugged Lesley. "You're the daughter of my heart, Lesley Taylor."

Dara stood looking out the front window, and then suddenly ran over to her father. "Grandfather and Grandmother Taylor are here and Uncle Stewart and Pete!" she chirped excitedly.

Darren glanced warmly at Lesley, his eyes conveying encouragement. Then together they all went to open the door.

Darren Senior handed Lesley a bouquet of roses, almost the same color as the one on her dress. Nadine kissed her cheek. Dara gazed up at her grandparents and gave them a toothy grin, making them her slaves for life. Stewart nodded politely as he entered the house, taking in the decor, grudgingly complimented Darren and Lesley on the house and handed them a housewarming gift.

Pete scooped Dara up in his arms. "How's my girl?"

"Fine," she giggled.

"Well, Miss Fine, I have something for you."

"You do?"

Pete reached inside his pocket and produced a flat black gift box.

Dara opened it. Inside there was a gold chain with a cherub charm attached.

"It's so pretty, Pete." She kissed his cheek. "I'm going to wear it always. Thank you."

"You're welcome, little cousin."

Lesley watched Pete. He just couldn't be the one who had framed her six years ago, could he? He was so wonderful with Dara. Surely…

A few minutes later Jordanna arrived with two gift-wrapped boxes.

"One for my favorite brother and sister-in-law and one for my very special niece."

"Can I open my present now?" Dara asked her mother.

"Yes, hurry up, I'm dying to see what it is too."

Dara tore the paper off, opened the box and gasped in delight.

"My doll is going to love these!" She held up a wardrobe case full of dresses and accessories for her doll.

"You're going to spoil her," Stewart remarked.

"I think she deserves to be spoiled, Uncle Stewart. We've been deprived of the first few years of her life."

Stewart shot Lesley a condemning look. "Whose fault is that, I wonder."

"Uncle Stewart!" Darren warned.

Lesley wanted to blurt out that it wasn't her fault, but she pretended not to be offended by Stewart's cruel, taunting words.

Millie entered the room and was introduced to the Taylors. She gave Stewart an admonishing look, having overheard what he had said. The older man had the grace to look away guiltily, which surprised both Darren and Lesley.

Lesley tensed when she heard the doorbell; her family had arrived.

Curtis and Merideth handed Darren their gift and quietly walked into the living room and seated themselves on the couch across from Darren Senior and Nadine.

Brett and Jasmine followed them into the living room. Brett handed Lesley the gift from him and Jasmine, then, smiling at Jordanna, took a seat next to her on the loveseat. Pete stood up and signaled Jasmine to fill the empty place beside him.

"It's good to see you again, Pete."

"You're beautiful as always, Jasmine."

There seemed to be only a friendly rapport between the two, Lesley observed. She smiled. Not the sparks and fire that blazed up between Jasmine and Ashton Price. She glanced at Brett. There definitely appeared to be something special developing between her brother and Jordanna.

Lesley noticed something else. That there was a certain intense hostility existing between just her parents and Stewart Taylor. What was it between the three of them? she wondered.

After dinner Dara was put to bed. And, of course, both sets of grandparents wanted to do the honors. That left Darren and Lesley to entertain his uncle. Millie stepped in to fill the void. For some reason she seemed to have a calming effect on Stewart, Lesley realized.

Jordanna commented on it to Lesley.

"Millie has certainly captured my uncle's attention."

"She has, hasn't she?" Lesley shook her head in wonder. "I knew she wasn't about to let him ruin our evening. So far everything has gone well. The initial uneasiness between my parents and yours seems to have mellowed away."

"You can thank our beautiful daughter for most of that," Darren said. "Both sets of grandparents dote on her, each making the special effort to make a little girl happy."

Lesley noticed how Brett monopolized most of Jordanna's attention during dinner and for most of the evening after that.

Merideth signaled Lesley over to the terrace doors.

"What is it, Mother?"

"I wanted to tell you that I'm proud of you."

Lesley shot her a skeptical look.

"I know I haven't always shown it. You reminded me so much of myself when you were growing up. I wanted you to be stronger than I was. Curtis made me see the flaw in my thinking. You see, my father considered me a disappointment when I was growing up. He'd thought I'd redeemed myself only after I showed a talent for designing.

"I wanted to instill in you the strength you'd need early on so you wouldn't have to go through what I did. I realize now that I went about it the wrong way. You had to learn and grow and make your own mistakes. Seeing Dara, getting to know her and observing how you are with her, has helped me see so many things I've failed to notice for so long. I just hope you can forgive me."

"We've never really talked, have we? Maybe in time we can—"

Curtis walked over to them. "I hope you can forgive me for neglecting you, by not being around when you really needed me. The business was so important, or so I thought.

It can never make up for human contact and caring. I know you and Darren won't make the same mistakes with Dara that your mother and I made with you."

"No, we won't. Daddy, why the tension between you and Stewart Taylor? It's thick enough to cut with a knife. What happened between you?"

Curtis and Merideth exchanged uncomfortable glances.

"I—we'd rather not talk about him." Curtis' expression turned harsh.

Her mother looked away. She was definitely uneasy talking about Stewart. Lesley wondered why they were being so evasive, but she didn't press the issue. Maybe in time they'd open up and tell her the truth about the hostility between them.

Lesley glanced at Stewart and saw the hard, bitter look he riveted on her mother. Why was he looking at her like that? Almost as though he wanted to kill her. She realized the tension didn't seem to involve Darren's parents. What could have possibly happened between her parents and Stewart Taylor?

When the evening was finally over and everyone had left, Lesley and Darren sat relaxing on the couch before the fireplace. The night had turned cool enough to light a fire and Darren had.

"How do you think it went?" Darren asked her.

"I think it went the way Jordanna expected it to. I'm glad we had the dinner party before we all assembled at the ball. I don't think we're going to have a problem with either of our parents in the future. Now, your uncle is another story."

"If Millie has her way, he won't be a problem either. That's the first time I've ever known my uncle to respond so quickly to anyone the way he has to Millie. We'd better make sure she comes to the ball. My uncle has been lonely since Aunt Grace died. I think if she had lived that maybe he wouldn't have turned out as he has, not been so complaintive and bitter. Millie reminds me of Aunt Grace in a lot of ways."

"You think—"

"Who knows. Anything is possible." He kissed Lesley.

She slipped her arms around his neck and kissed him back, stealing his breath.

"Is that an invitation, Mrs. Taylor?"

"Could be. I want you inside me, Mr. Taylor."

His eyes darkened with passion and he got to his feet and pulled her into his embrace.

"It's exactly where I want to be, sweetheart."

He swept her up in his arms and headed for the bedroom.

Darren undressed Lesley slowly, kissing every part of her as each piece of clothing came off. He noticed that her breasts seemed fuller, the nipples more prominent and much darker. His heart rate speeded up as his eyes slid lower to the silky dark vee of hair between her legs. He didn't think he'd ever get enough of looking at this woman.

Lesley removed Darren's jacket, and after unbuttoning his shirt, moved her fingers inside to caress his chest hair.

A groan escaped his lips when her finger flicked his nipple, and he bent his head to kiss her.

"I need you, Lesley," he groaned.

"I need you more." She undid the fastening on his pants and pushed them and his briefs down his hips, smiling with satisfaction when she heard them make contact with the floor.

Darren stepped out of them and slid his hands around to cup her buttocks, drawing her closer to his body. He felt her shudder when his aroused manhood throbbed against her femininity.

He carried her over to the bed and laid her down on it, then slid his body over hers and thrust his shaft deep inside her. They fitted together as though they were meant to do it for all time.

He tasted her lips with his tongue as his manhood delved into her dewy nether lips. The friction of their joining made them both go up in flames of ecstasy seconds later.

"No matter how often we make love, it gets better each time. How do you manage that, sweetheart?"

"It's because I love you, Darren."

"I never get tired of hearing you say those words."

He kissed her again and again, until they were once more adrift in the sea of love.

TWENTY-SIX

Lesley existed in an emotional haze of happiness all week. Things were going so well, almost too well, she thought. She felt like pinching herself to make sure it was all real.

Vera seemed to be the only fly in the ointment. She was being her usual less-than-pleasant self, but then that was nothing new. Soon she would be gone. As for Stewart, there was no change in his attitude toward her, but he wasn't being overly offensive. He was probably just biding his time.

Lesley was still concerned about Niven's relationship with Darren, but so far she had no reason to suspect that they were anything other than colleagues who worked together closely.

The phone rang. Lesley pushed the button marked CEO.

"This is Ashton Price, Lesley."

She couldn't keep the eagerness out of her voice and blurted, "Have you come up with anything?"

"I have, but it's not anything I can prove yet. And until I can talk to the person involved... He's the messenger who delivered the envelope to Wells. But right now he's on vacation and won't be back for another two weeks."

"It's the first solid thing that's come up, isn't it?"

"Yes, it is. We can only hope he remembers who gave him the envelope. According to the messenger service, someone from Taylor's specifically requested the special pick-up. If that doesn't pan out, don't get discouraged. We're going to clear you, Lesley."

"I'm so glad you agreed to help me, Ash."

"Me too."

Lesley had finished most of the designs for Philadelphia Raiments' winter line and the Christmas Specialty Review set for the middle of October. She would have to talk to Stewart Taylor about the Taylor models needed for a preliminary showing in a couple of weeks. Lesley dreaded that. She hoped he wouldn't give her a hard time.

"I've come to collect my rain check on lunch," Pete said from the doorway of Lesley's office. "And I won't take no for an answer, lady."

"You won't, huh? I'll go under one condition, that you'll let me take the Specialty sketches along. Maybe a fresh opinion is what I need."

"It's a deal. Although I don't know how much help I'll be."

"You have something on your mind, Pete?"

"Yeah, how to impress one Niven Alexander."

She gazed thoughtfully at Pete. He was the soul of grace and amiability. Almost too much so at times. She didn't know what to think about him. Was he really what he seemed?

When Lesley arrived back at Raiments after her lunch with Pete, she found Darren in her office, waiting for her with a frown creasing his forehead. She looked beyond him and saw the safe standing open. It was happening again!

He got up from his chair in front of her desk. "You're going to have to be more careful, Lesley." He angled his gaze in the direction of the open safe. "I found it like that when I got here."

Seeing it gaping open like that and hearing his words brought back in vivid detail that awful day six years ago.

Lesley had the feeling that Darren was silently condemning her—again.

Darren saw that look. It was one of deja vu. Was history repeating itself?

"I didn't leave the safe open, Darren."

"I'm not accusing you of anything. Just be more careful in the future. I wanted to take you to lunch, but your secretary said you'd already gone with Pete. I guess I have to follow my own advice and call first to see if you're free. You're just as busy as I am." He studied her for a moment. "You've been looking a little tired to me lately. I hope you're not overdoing."

"Don't worry, I'm not. I'll see you at dinner."

"Don't let the door hit you on your way out. Is that it?" "I didn't mean for it to sound like that."

"But it did. I have a meeting in another hour anyway."

"With Niven Alexander?"

"Yes, as a matter of fact. I'll see you at home."

Lesley stood looking out the window as her husband drove away. Then she glanced at the safe. Someone had been inside the safe. Supposedly, only she, Pete, Stewart and Jordanna knew the combination and, of course, Darren. Luckily she had taken all of the new designs with her when she left. Evidently someone was monitoring her comings and goings, but who?

She thought about her new secretary. Cherie Morgan seemed trustworthy and loyal. She'd been one of the junior secretaries at the main office of Taylor's for only three years. She couldn't have had anything to do with the theft six years ago.

Lesley felt completely confused. She'd been out to lunch with Pete, so he couldn't have been the one. Maybe Stewart… The only others left were Jordanna and Darren.

Lesley buzzed her secretary to come into her office. "Yes, Mrs. Taylor."

"Did anyone come to see me while I was out to lunch?"

"Miss Jordanna Taylor and her uncle, Mr. Stewart Taylor. I know they didn't have appointments, but they wanted to see you. When I told Mr. Taylor you'd gone out to lunch with his son, he stayed for a while, then left."

"Did he wait in the reception area or in my office?"

"In your office. I thought it would be all right. Did I do the right thing?"

"I'd rather that he waited out in reception from now on when I'm out of the office!"

"Miss Taylor too? She waited in your office for a while before leaving."

"Which one of them came in first?"

"I can't remember. I'm sorry."

"They the only ones who came to see me?"

"Yes, except your husband, of course. Is anything wrong?"

"My husband said the safe was open when he walked into my office."

"It was! I didn't—"

"I'm not accusing you, Cherie. I want you to keep track of the time and order of whoever comes into this office from now on. I'm sure I didn't leave the safe open, and you don't even know the combination, so it couldn't be you. That'll be all, just remember what I said. The designs for our spring line will be kept in there, so you see why the caution."

"Yes. I'll be careful."

Lesley watched her secretary leave the office. Pete had recommended her. Surely he wouldn't... She had to stop thinking like that, seeing shadows where there weren't any. She didn't have any proof against anyone. Maybe she was doing Pete a disservice, but right now she didn't know who she could trust. She wasn't even sure about her own family. Maybe Jordanna's idea to have the ball...

Jordanna.

Surely she hadn't been the one to open the safe? She shook her head to clear it. She was going Looney Tunes.

Maybe the ball would lure the guilty party out into the open. She hoped so. This not knowing was really getting to her.

She couldn't keep her condition a secret from Darren much longer. But after this afternoon and the look in his eyes... He hadn't accused her of anything. God, she wished she knew who had stolen those designs. That person was still wreaking havoc with her life. Maybe the ball would draw him or her out into the open.

"I want to go with you," Dara pouted as she watched her mother dress for her evening out.

"I'm sorry, baby, but you can't come with us. It's a party for grown-ups."

"Millie is going, too. Mrs. Spencer is nice, but—"

Lesley smiled at her Dara, understanding perfectly where she was coming from. She was so much like her father; stubborn and determined to have her own way.

"I know she's not Millie, baby, but you want Millie to have a good time, don't you?"

"Well, yes, but—"

"But you also want her here with you. Right?"

"Yeah."

Lesley kissed her cheek. "I can understand that."

"Are you ready yet, Mrs. Taylor?" Darren said from the doorway of the bedroom.

Lesley took in how handsome he looked in his tux as he walked in. She melted every time she looked at him. He was gorgeous, even if he was her husband.

"You're a hunk, Daddy. That's what my friend Ericca calls you."

"Thank your friend for me. How about a kiss?"

Dara launched herself into his arms.

"You and Mama working on getting me a brother or sister?"

"We're doing our best."

Lesley knew she should tell him now. Before she could, Darren spoke to Dara.

"Don't you want me all to yourself for a while, little sweetheart? We've got a lot to catch up on."

Lesley felt a stab of hurt for some reason and decided now wasn't the right time to tell him about the baby after all.

Dara squirmed out of her father's arms.

"I'm gonna go and help Millie get ready." And she dashed out of the room.

Darren reached out and pulled Lesley into his arms. "I didn't mean to make it seem like I was excluding you."

"It's all right."

"I can see that it isn't. It was a thoughtless remark. I'm sorry." He drew her closer. "You look ravishing this evening, Mrs. Taylor. I'm tempted to skip the ball and have our own private party at home."

"How would it look if the honored guests didn't show up for their own ball? We'd be scandalized."

"Since you're already dressed, I guess I'll have to wait to have the kind of party I have in mind."

Darren observed how beautiful his wife looked in her floor-length, gold and cream silk gown. The strapless, heart-shaped bodice made her breasts look more voluptuous. The slim skirt was slitted from just above the knee to the floor. His wife was one hell of a designer.

"Do you like my dress?"

"Oh, I more than like it, although I'd much rather see you without it, but that can come later. If Jordanna's gown is as spectacular as yours, your brother doesn't stand a chance of resisting her."

"You wouldn't mind if my brother and your sister got together?"

"Not as long as it's what they both want!" Darren sensed his wife's anxiety. Maybe tonight would go a long way toward banishing the cloud she'd been living under for so long. He realized that he was just as anxious as she was.

Darren walked over to the closet and took out the brown velvet, cream-silk lined cape and wrapped it around Lesley's shoulders. The cape gave the illusion of fur.

"I'm going to have to keep a close eye on you, sweetheart. I'm a very jealous man."

"And I'm a jealous woman, so be warned." "Is there a hidden meaning in there some place?" "Maybe."

Darren decided to let the remark go. He knew she was referring to Niven Alexander. He wasn't so sure that Niven didn't have anything to do with framing Lesley. If Ash was right, she could very well have been a part of it. Niven's father and his Uncle Stewart were friends. But that didn't make her guilty of anything, just suspicious as hell.

The Palace Hotel, known as the leader in a style that closely followed European standards in cuisine and luxury living, loomed before Darren and company as he eased his car into the Parkway side lane that led to the ballroom.

"What a hotel!" Millie gasped at the imposing cylinder made of marble and glass.

"The whole northside bank is the ballroom," Darren told her.

"I can't believe I'm actually going to a ball. I feel like I imagine Cinderella must have."

"I don't think you'll turn into a pumpkin by the end of the evening," Lesley teased.

"Neither do I. For all we know there may be an elderly Prince Charming in there waiting for me. I still believe that fairy tales can turn into the real thing."

The ambience of luxury and exclusivity revealed itself when a richly-dressed valet parking attendant approached their Mercedes.

As they stepped out of the car to head for the ballroom, another car drove up. Ashton Price uncoiled his tall frame from the candy apple red Porsche.

Lesley had to admit that he was fine. He was also charming, witty and mysterious. She could see why women went for him, even though he wasn't her type. She glanced at her husband. He was definitely her type.

Ash walked over to them and said to Darren, "You seem to be flanked by lovely females this evening. Surely you can part with one." He flashed Millie a dazzling smile and held out his arm. "I'm at your service, Miss...?"

"Mrs. James, but you can call me Millie. I'll be the envy of every single lady at the ball tonight." She wrapped her arm around his and glanced at Lesley and winked. "Is he a Prince Charming or what?" Then she let Ash escort her inside.

Millie was elegant in her peach and pearl-beaded gown, Lesley thought, smiling with pride as she gazed at her creation. The dress had a detachable tier skirt so that Millie could wear it long, as she had chosen to tonight, or shorten it to after five length for less formal occasions.

Lesley remembered that she and Jasmine had celebrated their debutante balls here. The huge room was more luxurious now, she observed from her position at the top of the staircase. As they descended the elegant marble staircase after checking their wraps with the attendant, Lesley saw a few of the people she'd known and been friends with six years ago. Eyes seemed to follow their progress into the room.

"Relax, sweetheart," Darren whispered in her ear when he noticed the anxious look on her face. "You're trembling. Are you sure you're feeling all right?"

"Just a few butterflies." That wasn't all, but she would handle it.

Darren and Ashton guided Lesley and Millie to the dining area. Vera sat at a table with a drink in her hand. Lesley could feel her glaring eyes burning holes through her. The woman had a chance to make a name for herself and start a new life, yet she hated Lesley for giving her that opportunity. There was nothing for her here. Being an office wife was all she'd ever be, because Darren was committed to his wife and child. She'd have seen that eventually. And maybe by then it would be too late.

Lesley saw Stewart and Niven standing on the terrace talking, and wondered from their intense expressions what they were discussing.

Darren followed her line of vision. Judging from her expression he was sure that Lesley had learned of the connection between his uncle and Niven.

They reached the table reserved for both their families. No sooner had they sat down than Pete walked in and made his way to the table.

"Uncle Darren and Aunt Nadine are going to be a little late."

Darren's brow creased anxiously. "There's nothing wrong, is there, Pete?"

"Not exactly. Uncle Darren and my father had a little disagreement earlier and decided not to come together."

"What kind of disagreement?"

"They wouldn't enlighten me. You'll have to find out when they get here. I see my father has stolen my date. If you all will excuse me," he said, heading in their direction.

Lesley watched him make his way to Niven. A few words passed between father and son, then Stewart headed toward the family table. He nodded, gave a polite greeting, took his seat and silently stared at Lesley, making her feel as though he could see right through her.

She knew he was doing it on purpose to unnerve her. Why did he hate her so much? She couldn't understand it. His expression changed and became more hostile, if that were possible, when her parents entered the ballroom.

As usual, her mother looked beautiful and her father suavely handsome. For the first time Lesley noticed grey hair at her father's temples and a tiny network of wrinkles around her mother's eyes. Like most children, she'd never thought of her parents as ever getting old. Lesley now saw them not as her parents, but as people like everyone else, people capable of making mistakes and having a history that didn't include their children.

She observed her brother and sister, noting the changing expression on Ash's face when he caught a glimpse of Jasmine. The scarlet gown her sister wore looked like one of their mother's creations. It set off Jasmine's long, statuesque figure to perfection, and she could see the effect it was having on Ash, even though he was trying hard to appear unaffected.

Brett appeared to be looking for someone. Lesley realized it was Jordanna when a big smile spread across his face when she arrived with her parents.

The look Stewart shot Darren Senior alluded to an old hostility between the brothers. Lesley knew that Stewart resented the fact that his brother had been made president of Taylor's. And since Stewart was the older brother, she couldn't help wondering why he hadn't been given the position, even though Darren Senior had the more amenable personality. Whatever had happened between them earlier was evidently still simmering beneath the surface.

Darren noticed throughout the meal that there was an intimidating silence around the table, as though the many nuances swirling in the air were reaching the boiling point.

To what end he wasn't certain, but the evening should prove interesting and, he hoped, helpful in clearing his wife.

Stewart asked Millie to dance. The man was definitely drawn to her, Lesley realized. She didn't know if she approved, but then she was biased when it came to Stewart Taylor. She turned her attention to Ash and Jasmine.

"Would you care to dance, Ms. Wells?" Ash asked Jasmine.

Jasmine looked as though she wanted to refuse, but knew that politeness required that she accept. Lesley couldn't help being amused at her sister's expression when she nodded her agreement and rose to her feet, allowing Ash to escort her onto the dance floor.

Jordanna laughed. "It seems that our friend Ash is quite taken with Jasmine, doesn't it, Darren?"

He shook his head. "You never let up on the guy, do you?"

"I think he's finally met his match. What do you think, Les?"

"I'm reserving judgment. But I have to admit that they do spark off each other, and they don't have to say anything for that to happen."

"Dance with me, Jordanna," Brett said.

She smiled and let him lead her away.

"It seems that we're the only ones not dancing, sweetheart."

"Maybe later, Darren. That lobster from dinner needs time to settle in my stomach."

"You've never had a problem with it before." Concern crinkled his forehead. "Are you sure you're feeling all right?"

Just as she started to answer, a wave of nausea hit her and she rose abruptly from her chair.

"I think I'll go out on the terrace for some air."

Darren frowned and followed her. He didn't like the way she looked.

"What's wrong, sweetheart?"

"Would you get me a ginger ale? I feel queasy."

"Queasy? You haven't been eating much lately," he said thoughtfully. "And you've looked so tired, too." Suspicion beetled his brows. He gazed at the fullness of the bodice of her dress.

Lesley realized she'd waited too late to tell him about the baby when she saw the moment he guessed the truth.

"You're pregnant, aren't you? Why didn't tell me?"

"I was going to, but there never seemed to be a right time. And I knew you wanted to wait before we enlarged our family."

"It comes down to trust. You've never really trusted me, have you? I let you down before. And I insisted that we get married and come back here. Lesley, I…"

She didn't mean for this to happen. The look in his eyes said how much her omission and lack of faith had hurt him. It spoke of betrayal, and it wrenched her heart.

At that moment Darren despaired of their relationship working out. His lack of trust six years ago was still haunting their lives. Even if they found out who framed her, the damage was already done. He wondered if they could restore their love.

"I'll get you that ginger ale." He turned to leave.

"Darren."

He ignored her and walked back inside.

"Trouble in paradise, Mrs. Taylor?" Vera inquired from the doorway, then stepped out to join Lesley on the terrace. "Is this a situation you can't tailor?" She laughed at her play on the Taylor name. "You can't tailor every situation to suit yourself, can you?" She saluted Lesley with her drink.

"I'm sorry you resent me for what I did. There is nothing for you here, and there never can be, Vera. Can't you see that? You were wasting your talent and abilities working as Darren's secretary."

"Not to mention usurping your position as his wife— or so you thought."

"I was never worried about that where you're concerned because I knew Darren wasn't even aware of your feelings for him."

"You're not so sure about Niven Alexander, though, are you?"

"They're only colleagues."

"Are you sure that's all there is between them?"

"I think you've said enough, Vera," Darren said as he stepped out onto the terrace with Lesley's glass of ginger ale in his hand.

"You're the boss." Vera glared at Lesley. "And don't you forget that if you're ever tempted to, Mrs. Taylor. He's his own man." Weaving slightly, Vera swept past Darren and back inside the ballroom.

Darren handed Lesley the glass of ginger ale. After a few moments he asked, "Feeling better now?"

"Yes."

"When is our baby due?"

"May. I was going to tell you sooner, but—"

"I'm sorry for blazing up at you like that."

"I understand."

"How do you feel about being pregnant so soon after our marriage?

"I don't mind. I was worried that you would."

"I missed seeing you carrying Dara, missed being there to watch the progress of our child's growth inside you. I curse myself for making you run away from me."

"It wasn't all your fault. The person or persons who set me up helped."

"Let's leave it for later. Do you feel up to dancing with the father of your child?"

Lesley smiled and answered. "Yes."

As they danced Darren noticed how closely Ash was holding Jasmine and saw the look of desire on his face when he gazed into her eyes. Jordanna was right about something going on between those two. Ash definitely had that besotted look on his face. He had a feeling that his friend's carefree bachelor days were numbered.

Darren and Lesley returned to their table. He asked Millie to dance.

Lesley saw her mother pass through the terrace door and decided to ask her about the hostility between her and Stewart Taylor. Just as she was about to step out on the terrace she heard Stewart and her mother talking. What they were saying stopped her cold.

"She's the exact image of you at that age, Merideth. She should have been our child. Seeing her brings to life how I felt after your betrayal."

"I never betrayed you, Stewart. I fell in love with Curtis."

"You're lying," he spit. "You loved me, I know you did."

"Why are you doing this, Stewart? It's ancient history now. You married my best friend, Grace. Was it out of revenge? Or did you really love her?"

"I cared for her, and yes, I even loved her, but no, I never felt the passion for her that I felt for you. I don't think I ever will for any other woman."

"I'm sorry for hurting you, Stewart. I tried to tell you that, but you wouldn't listen."

"Why should I have listened? I know what you and your father did."

"What are you talking about?" she demanded.

"You know that your father convinced mine to pass me over for the presidency of Taylor's."

"I don't believe that my father did—"

"Oh, he did it all right, just like he handpicked Curtis Wells for his precious daughter. I heard our fathers plotting to make it happen one night in the study." Stewart laughed at the look on Merideth's face. "I believe you really didn't know."

"You're wrong. Curtis loved me."

He continued as if she hadn't spoken. "Your father despised mine."

"I don't see how that—"

He cut across her. "Taylor's was in financial trouble and your father used it to his advantage. When he found out I was seeing you and was serious about wanting to marry you, he pressed that advantage. My father went along with it, of course. They hadn't counted on my refusing to give you up, so they decided to punish me."

"All these years you've blamed me for what my father and yours did to you, haven't you?"

Lesley couldn't listen to any more and had turned to go back to the table when she saw her father heading toward her.

"What's wrong, Lesley?" he asked.

Just as she opened her mouth to answer him, her mother and Stewart entered the room. Her father's expression turned harder than stone. Stewart shot him a mocking smile and walked away. Curtis started to go after him, but Lesley put a restraining hand on his arm.

"Let him go, Daddy. I think he and mother resolved some old unanswered questions," she said, looking at her mother's taut face.

Merideth glanced at her daughter. "You heard, didn't you?"

"Yes, I did. I'm beginning to see why there's so much hostility between the Wells and Taylor families. It's because of Stewart and his hatred for both of you, isn't it? He blames you and Daddy for everything. And he also resents Darren's father for accepting the position he feels should have been his.

"He saw a way to get his revenge through me and Darren. To him, seeing us together and so in love was like seeing history repeat itself. He couldn't hurt you and he couldn't hurt his brother so he used me and Darren as his licking stick."

Darren came to Lesley's side.

Merideth gasped and looked at her daughter. "Oh, God. You really were innocent. Stewart framed you."

"If I had decided to bring charges against Wells of Fashion, it would have marred your reputation and cast doubt on your credibility. I think he was counting on that happening," Darren said to Curtis and Merideth.

"My father just told me what he and Uncle Stewart argued about. He tried to convince him not to come to the ball and lost his temper and told him why."

"Stewart has been carrying all that bitterness and hatred around all this time about us, then," Curtis said in a stunned voice.

"According to my father," Darren went on, "it was Stewart who kept the two families at odds all these years. He recommended Niven after Lesley left town because he wanted me to forget about her and take up with Niven. It ruined his plans when I didn't get interested in her and still continued to love Lesley." He said to Lesley, "I want you to know that I never really stopped loving you. I tried to convince myself that I had for a while, but it didn't work."

Curtis and Merideth excused themselves and left Darren and Lesley alone.

"You didn't actually believe I was repressing my guilt, then?"

"Oh, I did at first, or so I tried to tell myself. When we were on the plane, I replayed in my mind that fateful day in my office, and thought about all that had happened since. I realized the truth and knew I had to help you find the guilty party."

"I thought all this time that you— You really do love me! And didn't just marry me for Dara's sake? Or—"

"I married you because I love you and always have and always will."

"Oh, Darren. What are you going to do about your uncle?"

"Dad asked me not to do anything. He never realized how Uncle Stewart felt or why he resented him so much until tonight. To find out grandfather had passed over Stewart just to punish him really bothered Dad."

"You think he should get away with what he did to us?"

"I don't think he's gotten away with anything. Uncle Stewart has made his own life miserable by dwelling on the past. He hasn't had a life since Aunt Grace died. He's practically alienated his own son, and his hatred has kept him from having any kind of relationship with my father."

"What do you think will happen now?"

"I don't know. The point of this ball was to unite our two families. Uncle Stewart tried to sabotage it, but managed to accomplish just the opposite of what he intended. All the hostility is out in the open now."

"I'm glad. I've been so suspicious of everybody—Pete, Jordanna, Vera and Niven and—"

"Even me."

"Darren, I—"

"It's all right, sweetheart. I can't blame you after the way I hurt you."

"You did hurt me, but I loved you anyway. I'm glad you came to Los Angeles to find me."

"You weren't at the time."

"No, I wasn't." She laughed.

"You fought me tooth and nail, as I remember."

"I know."

"I hope you can forgive me for—"

Lesley put a finger across his lips. "I do. That's all behind us now. I'm back where I belong—with you."

"I hope you remember that. And please don't run away from me again." He pulled her into his arms. "You're my life, woman."

"As you are mine." She kissed him.

EPILOGUE

"The part of the evening I've waited for," Darren said, leading his wife into their bedroom.

"I liked the announcement you made about our expanding family."

"You did?" He grinned. "Me too. I want everyone to know how proud I am of my family."

The door opened. "Daddy."

"What are you doing up, little sweetheart."

"I was waiting for you and Mama and Millie to come home."

Lesley looked to Darren and he smiled, then nodded his approval for what she intended.

"We have something to tell you."

"You do?"

"Your father and I are going to give you that brother or sister you wanted in May."

She squealed. "Now I can tell all my friends."

"Is that the only reason you wanted one?" Lesley asked.

"No, I want to hold him and love him."

"You sure it's going to be a boy?"

"Yes. Millie said she told you I was going to be a girl. I'm gonna ask her right now what she thinks." Dara ran from the room.

"Do you think it's a boy?" Lesley asked Darren.

"I don't care whether it's a boy or a girl as long as it's healthy."

Darren drew Lesley into his arms and kissed her, then slipped his hand around to the back of her dress to lower the zipper.

"You've already planted your seed, Mr. Taylor."

"There's no law that says I can't continued to stay in practice, is there?"

"No. But even if there were, I'd have to sneak and let you practice on me."

"I love you, sweetheart?"

"And I love you." She stepped out of her dress, revealing her underwear.

"You knew what you were doing, didn't you? You know how a garter belt and stockings turn me on."

"Yes, I do. You want to help me out of them?"

"It would be my pleasure, ma'am."

ABOUT THE AUTHOR

Working in the editorial department of the L.A. *Herald Examiner*, **Beverly Clark** was given her first exposure to professional writing. From there she wrote fillers for the newspaper and magazines such as *Red Book, Good Housekeeping,* and *McCall's.* She also wrote 120 romantic short stories with Sterling/McFadden Magazines. Clark joined the RWA, a national writer's organization that helps writers, published and unpublished, reach their writing goals. In order to gain more knowledge, she attended creative writing classes and other related courses at Antelope Valley College, and classes and seminars at L.T.U. This talented writer, who once managed a second-hand bookstore, The Book Nook, for two years, has since completed eight full-length books. She is now currently working part-time for Walden Books. She also helps a group called Friends of the Libraries, encouraging children and adults to read and enjoy books. Her goal is to have several of her works adapted into movie and television scripts. She lives in the High Desert Community of Lancaster. Her hobbies are reading and sewing. She is a widow.

January

A Lover's Legacy
Veronica Parker
1-58571-167-5
$9.95

Love Lasts Forever
Dominiqua Douglas
1-58571-187-X
$9.95

Under the Cherry Moon
Christal Jordan-Mims
1-58571-169-1
$12.95

February

Second Chances at Love
Cheris Hodges
1-58571-188-8
$9.95

Enchanted Desire
Wanda Y. Thomas
1-58571-176-4
$9.95

Caught Up
Deatri King Bey
1-58571-178-0
$12.95

March

I'm Gonna Make You
  Love Me
Gwyneth Bolton
1-58571-181-0
$9.95

Through the Fire
Seressia Glass
1-58571-173-X
$9.95

Notes When Summer
  Ends
Beverly Lauderdale
1-58571-180-2
$12.95

April

Sin and Surrender
J.M. Jeffries
1-58571-189-6
$9.95

Unearthing Passions
Elaine Sims
1-58571-184-5
$9.95

Between Tears
Pamela Ridley
1-58571-179-9
$12.95

May

Misty Blue
Dyanne Davis
1-58571-186-1
$9.95

Ironic
Pamela Leigh Starr
1-58571-168-3
$9.95

Cricket's Serenade
Carolita Blythe
1-58571-183-7
$12.95

June

Cupid
Barbara Keaton
1-58571-174-8
$9.95

Havana Sunrise
Kymberly Hunt
1-58571-182-9
$9.95

July

Love Me Carefully
A.C. Arthur
1-58571-177-2
$9.95

No Ordinary Love
Angela Weaver
1-58571-198-5
$9.95

Rehoboth Road
Anita Ballard-Jones
1-58571-196-9
$12.95

August

Scent of Rain
Annetta P. Lee
158571-199-3
$9.95

Love in High Gear
Charlotte Roy
158571-185-3
$9.95

Rise of the Phoenix
Kenneth Whetstone
1-58571-197-7
$12.95

September

The Business of Love
Cheris Hodges
1-58571-193-4
$9.95

Rock Star
Rosyln Hardy Holcomb
1-58571-200-0
$9.95

A Dead Man Speaks
Lisa Jones Johnson
1-58571-203-5
$12.95

October

Rivers of the Soul-Part 1
Leslie Esdaile
1-58571-223-X
$9.95

A Dangerous Woman
J.M. Jeffries
1-58571-195-0
$9.95

Sinful Intentions
Crystal Rhodes
1-58571-201-9
$12.95

November

Only You
Crystal Hubbard
1-58571-208-6
$9.95

Ebony Eyes
Kei Swanson
1-58571-194-2
$9.95

Still Waters Run Deep –
Part 2
Leslie Esdaile
1-58571-224-8
$9.95

December

Let's Get It On
Dyanne Davis
1-58571-210-8
$9.95

Nights Over Egypt
Barbara Keaton
1-58571-192-6
$9.95

A Pefect Place to Pray
I.L. Goodwin
1-58571-202-7
$12.95

Other Genesis Press, Inc. Titles

Other Genesis Press, Inc. Titles (continued)

Other Genesis Press, Inc. Titles (continued)

Falling	Natalie Dunbar	$9.95
Fate	Pamela Leigh Starr	$8.95
Finding Isabella	A.J. Garrotto	$8.95
Forbidden Quest	Dar Tomlinson	$10.95
Forever Love	Wanda Y. Thomas	$8.95
From the Ashes	Kathleen Suzanne	$8.95
	Jeanne Sumerix	
Gentle Yearning	Roshelle Alers	$10.95
Glory of Love	Sinclair LeBeau	$10.95
Go Gentle into that Good Night	Malcom Boyd	$12.95
Goldengroove	Mary Beth Craft	$16.95
Groove, Bang, and Jive	Steve Cannon	$8.99
Hand in Glove	Andrea Jackson	$9.95
Hard to Love	Kimberley White	$9.95
Hart & Soul	Angie Daniels	$8.95
Heartbeat	Stephanie Bedwell-Grime	$8.95
Hearts Remember	M. Loui Quezada	$8.95
Hidden Memories	Robin Allen	$10.95
Higher Ground	Leah Latimer	$19.95
Hitler, the War, and the Pope	Ronald Rychlak	$26.95
How to Write a Romance	Kathryn Falk	$18.95
I Married a Reclining Chair	Lisa M. Fuhs	$8.95
Indigo After Dark Vol. I	Nia Dixon/Angelique	$10.95
Indigo After Dark Vol. II	Dolores Bundy/	$10.95
	Cole Riley	
Indigo After Dark Vol. III	Montana Blue/	$10.95
	Coco Morena	
Indigo After Dark Vol. IV	Cassandra Colt/	$14.95
	Diana Richeaux	
Indigo After Dark Vol. V	Delilah Dawson	$14.95
Icie	Pamela Leigh Starr	$8.95
I'll Be Your Shelter	Giselle Carmichael	$8.95

Other Genesis Press, Inc. Titles (continued)

I'll Paint a Sun	A.J. Garrotto	$9.95
Illusions	Pamela Leigh Starr	$8.95
Indiscretions	Donna Hill	$8.95
Intentional Mistakes	Michele Sudler	$9.95
Interlude	Donna Hill	$8.95
Intimate Intentions	Angie Daniels	$8.95
Jolie's Surrender	Edwina Martin-Arnold	$8.95
Kiss or Keep	Debra Phillips	$8.95
Lace	Giselle Carmichael	$9.95
Last Train to Memphis	Elsa Cook	$12.95
Lasting Valor	Ken Olsen	$24.95
Let Us Prey	Hunter Lundy	$25.95
Life Is Never As It Seems	J.J. Michael	$12.95
Lighter Shade of Brown	Vicki Andrews	$8.95
Love Always	Mildred E. Riley	$10.95
Love Doesn't Come Easy	Charlyne Dickerson	$8.95
Love Unveiled	Gloria Greene	$10.95
Love's Deception	Charlene Berry	$10.95
Love's Destiny	M. Loui Quezada	$8.95
Mae's Promise	Melody Walcott	$8.95
Magnolia Sunset	Giselle Carmichael	$8.95
Matters of Life and Death	Lesego Malepe, Ph.D.	$15.95
Meant to Be	Jeanne Sumerix	$8.95
Midnight Clear	Leslie Esdaile	$10.95
(Anthology)	Gwynne Forster	
	Carmen Green	
	Monica Jackson	
Midnight Magic	Gwynne Forster	$8.95
Midnight Peril	Vicki Andrews	$10.95
Misconceptions	Pamela Leigh Starr	$9.95
Montgomery's Children	Richard Perry	$14.95
My Buffalo Soldier	Barbara B. K. Reeves	$8.95

Other Genesis Press, Inc. Titles (continued)

Naked Soul	Gwynne Forster	$8.95
Next to Last Chance	Louisa Dixon	$24.95
No Apologies	Seressia Glass	$8.95
No Commitment Required	Seressia Glass	$8.95
No Regrets	Mildred E. Riley	$8.95
Nowhere to Run	Gay G. Gunn	$10.95
O Bed! O Breakfast!	Rob Kuehnle	$14.95
Object of His Desire	A. C. Arthur	$8.95
Office Policy	A. C. Arthur	$9.95
Once in a Blue Moon	Dorianne Cole	$9.95
One Day at a Time	Bella McFarland	$8.95
Outside Chance	Louisa Dixon	$24.95
Passion	T.T. Henderson	$10.95
Passion's Blood	Cherif Fortin	$22.95
Passion's Journey	Wanda Y. Thomas	$8.95
Past Promises	Jahmel West	$8.95
Path of Fire	T.T. Henderson	$8.95
Path of Thorns	Annetta P. Lee	$9.95
Peace Be Still	Colette Haywood	$12.95
Picture Perfect	Reon Carter	$8.95
Playing for Keeps	Stephanie Salinas	$8.95
Pride & Joi	Gay G. Gunn	$15.95
Pride & Joi	Gay G. Gunn	$8.95
Promises to Keep	Alicia Wiggins	$8.95
Quiet Storm	Donna Hill	$10.95
Reckless Surrender	Rochelle Alers	$6.95
Red Polka Dot in a World of Plaid	Varian Johnson	$12.95
Reluctant Captive	Joyce Jackson	$8.95
Rendezvous with Fate	Jeanne Sumerix	$8.95
Revelations	Cheris F. Hodges	$8.95
Rivers of the Soul	Leslie Esdaile	$8.95

Other Genesis Press, Inc. Titles (continued)

Other Genesis Press, Inc. Titles (continued)

The Little Pretender	Barbara Cartland	$10.95
The Love We Had	Natalie Dunbar	$8.95
The Man Who Could Fly	Bob & Milana Beamon	$18.95
The Missing Link	Charlyne Dickerson	$8.95
The Price of Love	Sinclair LeBeau	$8.95
The Smoking Life	Ilene Barth	$29.95
The Words of the Pitcher	Kei Swanson	$8.95
Three Wishes	Seressia Glass	$8.95
Ties That Bind	Kathleen Suzanne	$8.95
Tiger Woods	Libby Hughes	$5.95
Time is of the Essence	Angie Daniels	$9.95
Timeless Devotion	Bella McFarland	$9.95
Tomorrow's Promise	Leslie Esdaile	$8.95
Truly Inseparable	Wanda Y. Thomas	$8.95
Unbreak My Heart	Dar Tomlinson	$8.95
Uncommon Prayer	Kenneth Swanson	$9.95
Unconditional	A.C. Arthur	$9.95
Unconditional Love	Alicia Wiggins	$8.95
Until Death Do Us Part	Susan Paul	$8.95
Vows of Passion	Bella McFarland	$9.95
Wedding Gown	Dyanne Davis	$8.95
What's Under Benjamin's Bed	Sandra Schaffer	$8.95
When Dreams Float	Dorothy Elizabeth Love	$8.95
Whispers in the Night	Dorothy Elizabeth Love	$8.95
Whispers in the Sand	LaFlorya Gauthier	$10.95
Wild Ravens	Altonya Washington	$9.95
Yesterday Is Gone	Beverly Clark	$10.95
Yesterday's Dreams, Tomorrow's Promises	Reon Laudat	$8.95
Your Precious Love	Sinclair LeBeau	$8.95

Order Form

Mail to: Genesis Press, Inc.
P.O. Box 101
Columbus, MS 39703

Name _____
Address _____
City/State _____ Zip _____
Telephone _____

Ship to (if different from above)
Name _____
Address _____
City/State _____ Zip _____
Telephone _____

Credit Card Information
Credit Card # _____ ☐ Visa ☐ Mastercard
Expiration Date (mm/yy) _____ ☐ AmEx ☐ Discover

Qty.	Author	Title	Price	Total

Use this order form, or call 1-888-INDIGO-1	Total for books	
	Shipping and handling: $5 first two books, $1 each additional book	
	Total S & H	
	Total amount enclosed	
	Mississippi residents add 7% sales tax	